THE SPEAK OF SILENCE

J. HALE JR.

www.thespeakofsilence.com

www.silencesometimesspeaks.com

Cover and Interior Design by JuLee Brand for Kevin Anderson & Associates

Images by Shutterstock

The Speak of Silence /J. Hale Jr. – 1st ed.

Paperback ISBN: 978-1721723058

Hardcover ISBN: 978-0-692-14360-5

To my darling,

for her unwavering faith

and support of this journey.

CONTENTS

He was as typical a writer as one would expect, spending much of his time pacing the floor or staring at a screen or shaking off carpal tunnel. He lived a solemn life in a one-room apartment in the Marina District. While many of the writing elite of his day found strength in numbers in New York City, Marty Bornstein preferred the 180-degree views of the Bay, the ever-present coolness of coastal fog, and the clashing cultures that gave San Francisco its spirited heartbeat.

Over the past twelve years, Mr. Bornstein had accomplished rather little compared to you and me; no family to speak of, no car, no steady work, not many belongings, and his only real friend was a small, dirty white schnauzer he'd named Frank after his grandfather. But, though not elevated in any social or literary sense, the novels that Marty methodically churned out in that time period stymied even his demanding editor. His rise was led by his first, *The Red Sweater*, which sold feverishly after being spied in the hands of a Hollywood starlet.

From *The Red Sweater* to *Poison Locker*, his eighteenth, our little introvert in his little apartment in his dirty city with its beautiful view and its wet fog became one of our nation's most prolific writers of romance. But was he proud of it? Hardly. Never once did he settle down to a day of book signing. Never once did he allow the publicist to even include his picture in the back pages of his books. Never once did he grant an interview or participate in a promotional event of any kind. In fact, after *The Red Sweater*, he was all but written off as a one-hit wonder, because never again did he use his given name, but rather went by the pen name of "Rex"—for he thought that name embodied all of the manliness he might acquire in his next life.

Marty was as drab and boring as a person could be, yet his mind churned out the most colorful, sensual, and exhilarating of stories. Were it not for Frank and his need for an occasional walk and Marty's need for an occasional visit to the grocery, one might never have seen the man, for all of his writing, correspondence, and otherwise was generally done via computer. And since he really had no family—and hermit-like life generally doesn't produce many friends—it might strike you as quite strange that our friend Marty, who was as unknown as unknown can be, was the unlucky recipient of the malice of a common thief just then out of retirement. For it was during a damp and quiet evening in the Marina District in the rather bare apartment of this rather boring man that our story really begins to unfold—a story that would change the life of one for the better, but adversely affect countless others; a story that would prove ignorance to be a most prolific and silent killer.

CHAPTER 1

WEEKLY CHINESE

"Frank! Stop barking. *Halt die Klappe!* You're driving me crazy. You're driving the *neighbors* crazy. You're driving *yourself* crazy!"

Franklin spoke neither English nor German, nor did he react to the growing agitation in his owner's voice; instead, he kept barking.

"Franklin, for the love..."

Finally, the command was loud enough to somewhat shock the poor little dog into silence, or so Marty thought. Frank stopped barking. Whatever had spooked him was now at the apartment door. Not wanting to leave his keyboard, Martin kept hammering the keys. There was no knock, no doorbell, no sound. Marty kept typing. Though not necessarily working under any deadline, the words, the thoughts, and the story were stampeding through his mind, and it was all he could do to corral them with the sound of his furious typing.

The sun had just set, though one might not have known if not for the light gray sky suddenly becoming dark gray and heading swiftly to black. The noise of the city actually grew louder now in Marty's world, as the streets in the Marina became alive with workers returning home, an occasional child pleading for fast food rather than leftovers, and neighborhood dogs in high gear at the beginning of their evening walks.

"Frank. Can't go tonight, *Junge*. I've got to work," Marty explained, assuming Frank's alarm was an announcement that it was time for his evening walk. But Frank had already given up on the walk and was now at Marty's feet, at full attention, facing the front door.

Abruptly, the typing then stopped above, which was probably about the only event that could have broken Frank's radar lock on the front door. The stampede had either been corralled or had broken through the fence and was now gone, but no matter. Writing time was now over. It was now time to focus on Chinese.

Marty's chair swiveled eagerly at the sound of soft knocking at the door. As he had done every Tuesday for the last nine years, he had ordered Chinese—one order of chicken fried rice, one order of lo mein, one order of orange peel chicken, three fortune cookies (one for him and two for Frank), two packets of soy sauce, and a set of chopsticks. As one can probably deduce, Marty was not in the best physical shape. Years of sitting, coupled with a loathing to spend much time outdoors, resulted in his very generous build. This was in addition to the fact that he was about to turn 64, and, as many of us know too well, age is generally no friend to one's metabolism. But on Tuesday evenings, he moved quite anxiously at the sound of the knocking, much like those impulsive dogs of Pavlov's.

Now his dog Frank, began to bark again, emphatically. No familiar smell wafted under the door. There had been no buzzer from the street. No cute voice of Mr. Ma's daughter, Val, calling for "Mr. B."

And yet none of these oddities kept Marty from opening the door, which he did with a grand smile. But Marty did not open the door to Val or to his heavenly Chinese order. Quite the contrary; he opened to a man, and to the sharp blow of the man's maple slugger to his stout face.

The force of the blow shattered Marty's glasses and knocked him, unconscious, to the floor. Frank took the second cut, which left the poor little dog dead, flattened on the floor like a Barbie version of a bearskin rug. With both foes subdued, the batter slid into the apartment and slowly eased the door shut with his boot. Eerie silence filled the apartment, the kind of silence that matched its somber décor.

Three miles away and two hours earlier, Stevin McDonald had walked away from two crying kids, an irate wife, an impatient landlord, and a mountain of other problems that might seem insurmountable to most—the kind of problems that drive people to do things they should not, or things they had previously given up and vowed never to do again, like a little assault and a lot of larceny. For Stevin, now two years clean after serving four years for a second strike, not much else mattered but getting what he felt he was due.

Four years in prison had taught Stevin hard lessons—lessons he thought he would never forget—yet his circumstances seemed combined to fade the memory of those lessons in a haze of injustice. No amount of effort could gain him ground. While he was remarried, he could not find steady work or seem to craft a life like most around him, which caused him consuming envy. Today was the day he just had to get out.

Out on the street, Stevin's racing thoughts had caused his pace toward Duboce to crescendo. His countenance grew dark. He did not look right; he did not look left. Once at Duboce, he leaned against a new-looking sign that held the bus schedules, waiting, thinking, rationalizing. The more time that ticked by, the deeper his resolve to take became. Then he could take it no more. It was time to feed the swelling rage.

Turning at the stop, he looked across the sleepy park at a group of neighborhood kids taking a little batting practice while hopefully waiting for others to show so they could start up their daily game. He started walking, much slower and more methodically like a hunting lion, never taking his eyes off the boys. Closer now, fly balls landed and rolled by him. On he marched, over the mound and directly to home plate.

By now, those who were shagging balls were on edge, as a very uneasy fellow was walking right into their game.

"Nick, hold up," cried one from the field, to stop the pitching.

All of the boys now stood and watched, dumbfounded at what was happening. Without a word and hardly a motion, Stevin walked to the batter and took a firm hold of the bat. No words were necessary between man and boy; Stevin's eyes told all and more. The batter quickly released the bat and took two wobbly steps backward. Now, with bat in hand, there were no more troubles for Stevin—just pure amperage: no more worries, no more constant nagging and noise...oh, that noise! Power again surged in his veins, a current that he would struggle to unplug. He walked mightily back through the silent and still ballplayers and across the park, the wooden bat resting comfortably on his shoulders as Maximus might rest his sword, then he climbed on a northbound bus.

On the bus, he sat where all rebels, ruffians, and the raucous generally sit: in the back, dead center. Like old men from the South sit with canes, both of his hands were on the butt of the bat, which stood on end between his widely spread feet. He didn't bother to look out the window as the bus slumbered along. But at exactly the eleventh stop, he stood up, walked to the front, and stepped out onto the corner of Divisadero and Bay.

He admired the fine houses, the small shops, and the monotonous middle-class people around him going about their day as they did the day before and the day before that. As a man who clearly came from much humbler circumstances, and who was standing on a street corner holding a bat, he began to feel awkwardly conspicuous, and quickly sought refuge in an out-of-the-way place where fewer of those middle-class people might notice him.

What am I doing here? What am I about to do? Stevin reasoned with himself. *I can't screw it up again!*

And then he paused, and in his ruminations, came to a sense of sinister clarity. There simply was nothing to screw up! In reality, he had nothing. The kids were really his wife's from a previous marriage. He had no steady job. He'd never truly loved Alexes like she deserved, but he had married her hoping it would keep him rigidly centered on the straight and narrow, a kind of selfish convenience.

How hard would it be to just walk away from it all? he wondered to himself. "Wait! I just did!" he exclaimed, and then began to chuckle.

Just as this black light flickered in his mind and its dark influence took hold of his soul, his eye caught a glimpse of a slender Asian girl across the street. She seemed a little out of place too. He watched her. The black light burned steady and strong now, fueled by the focus of his eyes. The girl's short steps and straight, jet-black hair bounced while keeping time with her delicate footsteps. He crossed the street behind her, trying to keep the bat concealed alongside his leg.

Where is she going? he wondered. *Why is she here?*

He gained on her, moving to within ten feet, and then he understood. The familiar vinegar smell from the plastic bag in her hand that held small containers with sharp square corners left little to question.

"Excuse me," Stevin blurted, surprising himself by doing so.

The young girl paused, turned, and immediately noticed the bat at his side.

"That smells great. Is your restaurant close? I'm starving!" he said, quite sincerely.

Val said nothing, knowing all too well that this sore thumb in the Marina District was either intent on robbing her, or, hopped up on years of porn, raping her. Judging by the bat hanging loosely at his side, her mind settled on 'robbing'.

She quickly turned back around and, while hastening to her every-Tuesday-at-6:30 p.m. delivery, said, "Just 'round the corner on Beach."

"Wait!" he pleaded.

It was too late; she was well on her way, trying to get safely to her destination while at the same time trying to stay close to other people on the street.

"Damn it!" he shouted. "Damn it!"

Stevin stood there, stewing for reasons most would never think twice about.

"That little Asian—" he said, stopping short of cussing in public.

His grip on the bat tightened. She was still in sight, and now, with eyes fastened securely on that black hair, he started to tear down the street after her, still keeping the bat concealed at his side as best he could.

Though she never looked back, something inside Val told her he was coming, and was close. Her pace quickened. She got to Marty's street door and turned to look back up the street. Her instinct was right. The man and his bat were not far now.

She reached for the buzzer, hoping to escape behind the safety of the locked door. The buzzer held the names of the 42 inhabitants of the complex, and though she had rung the same bell for the last three years since taking over this weekly delivery from her mother, she recklessly and in haste pushed the button of Mrs. Carmichael. Luckily for her, Mrs. Carmichael happened to be hurriedly passing her front door at exactly that moment on the way to the bathroom, and, not wanting to stop and get the details of the visitor for fear of soiling herself, she simply pushed the buzzer.

Stevin was now steps away. He could see the panic in her eyes, and he could see that she was about to slip from his reach. His wicked stare made her blood run cold, and her world was now moving through a malaise of slow motion. Why she didn't just walk out in the middle of traffic and make a spectacle of herself, one will never know.

In the door she sprung, Marty's tightly packed dinner sliding across the floor. With all quickness and strength, she moved to get the door closed behind her, but to her horror found the butt end of a bat now wedged in the doorjamb. She screamed, but paralyzing terror all but silenced her shrill cry for help. Now Stevin was upon her, and rationality and sanity were no longer conducting his runaway train. The door shut. They were alone.

In rage, Stevin attacked—first a blow to the sternum with the slugger, which knocked the wind out of her, and then, coiling for a shot to deep center, he struck with all of his might at the base of her neck and collarbone. Val crumbled like a lifeless string puppet as the blow blasted her head against the stair rail, causing blood to steadily trickle onto her forehead and over her eyes.

The attack and fallout were no louder and sounded no different from within the apartment house than the front door closing. On this occasion, the door seemed to simply close twice, and no one thought a thing of it. Perhaps the age of the building's inhabitants and their fading faculties played into the lack of alarm.

Now, Stevin stood over his victim, trying to figure out what the hell had just happened and what the hell he was doing.

"I was just hungry, damn it!" he said to the lifeless girl at his feet. "I was just hungry!"

She lay there nearly dead. Her white dress, now disheveled, revealed her slender legs, panties, and flat stomach. Standing there, Stevin realized how beautiful she actually was. A dark thought crossed his mind. He kept staring at her.

What if? Stevin thought to himself. But he knew too well that where his mind was going was altogether too risky and just plain wrong.

He had to hide her quickly. Getting caught for assault again would mean decades in prison, and if she died here, he would surely die there. He surveyed the apartment house. Behind him, a single flight of stairs rose to the first set of apartments. In the lobby next to him was an elevator and a small coat closet. He quickly opened the closet and found it fairly well-packed with very dated coats, a dead giveaway that the apartments housed older people. Stevin eyed the sturdy wooden suit hangers. He looked at the hangers, looked at his victim, and looked at the hangers again. Finally, he sparked a brilliantly stupid idea.

"Ah, shit..." he mumbled, quietly admitting to himself that it was, in fact, a stupid idea. But under the circumstances, he had no option, other than walking her down the street to some unknown depository.

Bending down on one knee, he slid his arms under her—one under her knees and the other behind her shoulder blades. She was very light, maybe a hundred pounds. Easily lifting her, he walked her to the closet and dropped her legs to the ground. They now stood together as if slow dancing at prom, her head on his shoulder. He could tell that she was still alive by the slow beat of her heart, but her limp body signaled grave injuries. Reaching into the closet, he grabbed a hanger and slid it into the back of her dress. Now, letting go of her, he held the hanger with both hands. His stupid idea, it appeared, was actually going to work. He moved into the closet and simply hung her up. Her head and arms drooped limply, while her legs were mostly covered by her dress. After moving a few heavy coats against her, the senior citizens would certainly never discover such tomfoolery—at least not for a while. With her out of sight, that left only Marty's dinner to be reckoned with. He picked up the bag from the floor and tore the receipt from the top, which detailed the order as well as giving an address: *2200 Francisco, # 9*. On the receipt was also handwritten the name *Mister B*.

Although famished, Stevin had more sinister pursuits in mind as he stood there feeling much like a fox in a henhouse. Wanting to get out of sight quickly, he placed the bag of aromatic food under Val's feet in the closet, picked up his wooden peacemaker, and began ascending the crackling stairs to Apartment 9, where an unsuspecting writer and his dog would face a beast and his bat.

CHAPTER 2

READ IT TO ME

Inside the apartment, with the occupants out of commission, Stevin made short work of rifling through the place. Had no one answered the door when he'd knocked, he probably would have concluded that it was vacant, or perhaps inhabited by a squatting meth addict. The apartment was so sparse that he couldn't even find anything to eat, let alone any valuables to loot and plunder. This agitated him. He began to wish he could turn back the clock. Risking what would certainly be a life sentence—and perhaps the death penalty if Little Miss Delivery Girl didn't make it—did not remotely justify the spoils in this bare apartment.

"I killed some girl for this?" he mumbled. "What a damn waste!"

He found himself slamming drawers and doors, and pretty much destroying anything he could get his hands on. The small apartment had only two bedrooms and, by the looks of it, offered one bedroom for the poor bastard with a caved-in face and one for the dog. Stevin contemplated every room, opened every drawer, and even found himself digging through the trash. Nothing! There was nothing to steal except maybe the computer, nothing to do, and certainly nothing to eat. After twenty minutes of furiously working through the apartment, he abruptly stopped, remembering that there was food downstairs.

Contemplating some unknown risk, he waved his hands about and rationalized to himself: *If someone sees me, I could just say I was visiting somebody, or even delivering the food. No! No! It's too risky.* However, at long last, he decided to roll the dice.

He walked over to the front door and gently eased it open. There was no one in the hall, and not a sound in the entire house. He slipped out and quietly descended the stairs. At the first step, he could smell the food. The only noises seemed to be his stomach growling and the drone of cars on the street below. Now, in the entry, he opened the closet door and beheld, quite amazed, a large pair of brown eyes staring right back at him. Still on the hanger, his poor victim had come to.

Stevin stared right back, speechless. Both of them were mortified with the anticipation of what this particular moment might bring, like two gunslingers on a dusty street—she obviously fearing for her life, and he seeing nothing but her on a witness stand with outstretched finger exclaiming, "*Him!*" But before she could muster enough energy to fire any sort of distress signal, Stevin's 'shoot first, ask questions later' instinct beat her to the draw. Almost without thinking, he cocked and unloaded a tremendous right to her left temple. Her limp body shook violently among the coats and then came to rest again. Stevin leaned in. He did not detect any sounds of breathing as he quickly surveyed the lobby for any sign of others. With his back to the closet so as to keep an eye on the front door, he slowly bent down and found the plastic bag of food, but he did not notice the blood pooling on the floor. Now, with dinner in hand, he again closed the closet and made his way back upstairs to eat.

Once upstairs, our dumb thief and potential murderer (or proven murderer, in the case of poor little Frank) wasted no time in gathering a fork, plate, and napkin and tearing into the food. He went for the orange peel chicken first, after spreading some rice on his plate. His mouth was salivating unbearably as he raised the first bite. Just as he did, though, he was rudely interrupted by a weak voice from behind the sofa.

"Who are you? What do you want?" the voice asked.

Instead of surprise, Stevin felt impatience. *Does anyone else want to interrupt my attempt to eat?* he thought to himself.

Putting the fork down, he stood and strolled over to Marty, who was now leaning on one hand, trying to get his bearings. Glaring over the couch, Stevin could see the old man's bloody face and frail body, but he decided to speak from behind the couch and out of sight.

"Listen, old man. I'm going to finish your dinner. Then I'm going to walk out of here with your computer, since that is the only thing of any damn value in this dump, and we're going to go about our merry ways and not think another thing of it," Stevin insisted.

The old man didn't answer. Stevin again glanced over the couch and saw Marty staring at his trusted little friend, who had clearly died a most vicious death. Stevin didn't quite know what to say, so he waited a few awkward minutes for Marty to speak again.

Seeing Franklin, Marty knew that he had to keep composed, and that his freedom would greatly depend on his ability to outthink his opponent. Pondering a moment, he replied, "I have a few dollars cash and an old Rolex you can take, but you can't take my computer."

"Ha!" Stevin responded, incensed at the demand made of him.

"It's of no value to you. But to me it is of great value, because it holds my entire livelihood. I'm a writer."

"A writer?" Stevin asked rhetorically. "Like what? Sports column, kids' books, self-help, or something? I know it's got nothing to do with fashion or interior design, since you live in an empty box."

"Romance," Marty replied.

There was a long silence, followed by bellowing laughter from Stevin. "Romance! *Romance!* You're shitting me, right? Romance?"

Marty could barely see; his head was basically caved in and now he had to carry on a conversation with his clearly unstable and ignorant captor. "It doesn't matter," he responded. "Let me just give you the cash and watch, and you can go. I haven't seen you. You can just leave and, like you said, we'll go our merry ways."

Stevin was starting to have fun. "Not a chance, old man!" he exclaimed. "Not until you read it to me first."

"Read what?" came the exhausted response.

"What you're writing right now. I just can't imagine you—a tired, lonely old man—up here in this box writing romance novels. No way! Before I leave, you have to read it to me," Stevin demanded quite genuinely.

Marty was on the verge of tears. He was exhausted and needed medical help. Hoping that his words might free him of this psychotic tyrant, he mustered enough energy to slide over to his desk, pull himself into the chair, and 'wake' his computer.

"I can't see to read. I have no glasses," Marty said calmly.

"Old people have glasses lying around all over the place," Stevin said, flustered. "There are some in the bathroom. They are, like, the one damn thing I found in this whole place!"

Stevin slipped from behind the couch, through the kitchen, and into the bathroom. Marty knew he had a few moments before Stevin would return. Reaching across his desk, he picked up the receiver of the phone and quickly dialed 911. Just as he was putting the phone to his ear, he heard Stevin returning. Marty couldn't bring himself to hang up, so he simply laid the phone on the desk and haphazardly covered it with papers.

When Stevin returned with the extra pair of glasses, he tossed them on the desk just as the faint sound of the 911 operator could be heard answering the call: "911. What is your emergency?"

Marty acted as if he couldn't hear anything. To pick it up would surely mean another beatdown. To let it go might mean the same thing. He froze.

The awkwardness was quickly bombarded when Stevin landed a blow to the phone with his bat, like a muscleman at a carnival demonstrating the bell-and-hammer game. Shards of the phone blasted thoughout the apartment. Marty was still frozen, convinced that his head was about to become something like one of the watermelons in a Gallagher routine. He slowly opened his eyes. He first saw the bat, the tip still lying on the table. His eyes followed the bat to a pair of coarse hands, up his attacker's arms, and then to his face. Now eye-to-eye, Marty saw only fiendish, apathetic darkness. The silence of that second in time whispered death to a dying man.

"Try a stunt like that again, old man, and I'll pound you into so many pieces the cops will think someone put you through a wood chipper and tried to paint the walls! Now, read!" Stevin demanded without so much as blinking.

Marty slowly wheeled closer to the monitor, put on his glasses, and began to read the last written page from his work in progress titled simply *Noel*. Reading was a difficult task in his condition. His voice was weak, his lips quivered and strained, and the chore of holding his head up became increasingly excruciating. However, all of these physical ailments combined to kindle heat in his fiery prose.

> Snow began to fall like wild, wet feathers floating eagerly to Earth. From her room, she could see the twinkling lights of the moored boats in the distance. Their soft swaying reminded her of their chance meeting at the Miami Yacht Club a month prior. But here in the great north, the warm sun played but a brief cameo during the day, leaving the cold to drive them indoors, which is just where they wanted to be driven. The tormenting tension, the yearning, the fever, made each waiting second all but unbearable.

"I can't believe people buy this shit!" Stevin interrupted. "Do people really buy this shit?"

Marty glanced up over his glasses, not saying a word, and then returned to the screen and continued:

> Her heavy breath billowed over her warm lips onto the frigid window pane. She thought of what she might say during the first awkward moments when he arrived. Perhaps there would be no words. Silence sometimes speaks.

As the last 'S' rolled off Marty's tongue, in tow was his last breath. Abruptly he choked, froze, and then with panicked eyes fell face-first onto his keyboard.

At first Stevin thought the old man was still nursing the ill effects of his injuries, so he waited a moment before prodding.

"Hey, old man?" he said matter-of-factly. "Old man..."

Stevin pushed Marty's limp shoulder with his bat. No response. Stevin took a step back in disbelief. In an instant the old man, who had seemed to be overcoming the daze of head trauma, was now...dead?

Stevin poked again. Nothing. He stepped forward and gently put his finger on Marty's neck, then stepped back again in shock. Marty was dead. The lonesome romance novelist who lived a solitary life in a sparse apartment in a big city had passed in an instant, but not before penning his grandest achievement and arranging his unfortunate freedom.

Stevin's mind was reeling. He hadn't planned on murder. What began as simply a walk for fresh air had snowballed into something he wasn't ready for. He decided it was time to put this runaway train in reverse and get out. His mind flashed to all of the evidence around him: the fingerprints on nearly every inch of the apartment, the murder weapon in his hand, the witnesses who probably saw an out-of-place man running down the street with a bat. How could he undo what was done? Was there time? Would he just leave through the front door? What about the girl in the closet? How would he get home if he couldn't catch a bus? Worst of all, what would he tell his wife?

Stevin was now panicked. He peered discreetly through the

drapes at the window behind the desk. Darkness had fallen and only a few local stragglers remained on the street. He shuffled silently over to the front door and eased it open to check the hall and stairs. No sound nor soul, though he could hear the faint twitter of TV sets throughout the building, its occupants 45 minutes deep into *Murder, She Wrote.* He wondered if he could, in fact, simply slip out the front door. As he stood there in a bit of a daze planning his escape, the buzzer from below tore through the silence and startled Stevin so severely that he impulsively slammed the door shut. The buzzer sounded again. Someone on the street wanted entrance. Stevin raced back to the window. There below, in front of the building, was now parked an SFPD squad car.

"Shit! Shit! Shit!" he stammered, then let out a long sigh.

He knew he was only on the second floor and could probably make a jump, or he could try to get to the roof and weigh his options there. But wait! Was there another option for this bold, brazen bully? Why not let them in?

Stevin moved quickly. He had to, in order for his suicidal plan to work. The first order of business was to lose the bat. He thought about throwing it out the window or hiding it under the bed. Instead, he decided to simply place it in the closet, speculating that it would be perceived as a weapon the old man might have kept for protection.

Finishing his preparations, he stepped into the hall, closed the door behind him using the sleeve of his jacket, and quickly descended the stairs into the lobby. Taking a deep breath, he opened the front door.

"Good evening, officer. Didn't anybody let you in?" he said innocently.

"Not until you came along," came the response.

"Well, happy to be of service," Stevin said, easing out farther on his thin branch. "Is there a problem?"

"Just here to make sure everything is okay," the officer said, looking perplexed at the furry bulge in Stevin's jacket.

Stevin looked down, laughed, and then explained: "Oh, we were just headed out for a walk, but he's so doggone tired that I decided he had better ride in here."

The officer chuckled. "Well, at least you'll get some exercise!" he said as he moved toward the stairs.

"Yeah. Sometimes that's just how it is," Stevin replied, holding the front door open.

"You heard any commotion or seen any problems here tonight?" the officer casually inquired.

"Been quiet, as far as I know. Most people here are pretty old and keep to themselves," Stevin said.

"You know a Mr. Bornstein?"

"You mean Mr. B.? Sure. He's all the way at the top. Number 53," Stevin answered.

"Thank you. Have a nice walk. I'm sure we'll be gone by the time you two get back," the officer said, now halfway up the stairs.

Stevin calmly walked out onto the sidewalk. He could see into the squad car. The dim blue light from the computer screen lit the silhouette of another officer, who glanced up just in time to see Stevin's face as he turned up the street in the opposite direction of the parked car. At the first corner, Stevin calmly turned left. Out of sight of the police, he sprinted across the street, deposited Franklin in a city garbage can, and slipped away into the night.

CHAPTER 3

OFFICER DOWN

"911. What is your emergency?"

Across town at the police station, Mary Kay Gonzales waited for a response, and then waited some more. She could make out some shuffling, maybe some breathing, then a tremendous crack followed by emptiness.

"Hello? Hello? This is 911 Emergency. Can you hear me?" she inquired anxiously.

The line was dead. No one had said a word. Looking at the computer screen, she read: *M. Bornstein, 2200 Francisco, Apt. 9.*

Do I send somebody or let it go? she reasoned with herself. Her mind contemplated the infinite scenarios that could be at work...a misdial, a child calling accidentally, a choking victim, a fallen victim, a robbery, a rape. Not knowing exactly quite what to do, she decided to punt to the SFPD.

"SFPD dispatch. This is Michelle."

"Michelle, this is Mary Kay at the call center. Just had a hang-up or disconnection up in the Marina District. I didn't speak with anyone, but I thought I would let you know. There was a loud crash at the end of the call. Not sure what to make of it."

"Okay. Maybe I'll see if someone is in the area and can check it out. What's the address?" Michelle asked.

"M. Bornstein. 2200 Francisco, Apt. 9," Miriam said.

"M. Bornstein. 2200 Francisco, Apt. 9," Michelle confirmed.

"Correct. Thank you."

"Thank you."

Michelle Miceli had been with the SFPD for thirteen years, most of them as a dispatcher. Father Miceli had been a career beat cop, and after basically growing up on the force, it was a natural decision for his daughter to be involved in some aspect of law enforcement.

After hearing from Mary Kay, Michelle glanced at her computer to see who was in the area. Being a fairly quiet night in the city, she figured it probably wouldn't hurt to have someone stop by and check into it. Units are rarely ever dispatched in that area, so it would be nice to fly the flag a little and show some presence.

With a simple click, she had her boys on the line—two experienced guys she called out of Ghirardelli's gift shop: Cesmat, who loved stopping by for a little chocolate that he would take home to his five kids—assuming it made it that far—and Bradley, who despised the place and rarely got out of the car. Though tourism is probably San Francisco's largest trade, Bradley couldn't stand the hordes of them on the trollies, at the Pier, on the bridges, and especially here, snaking into the courtyard in line for chocolate and ice cream.

The call pulled Cesmat out of line, which he was pretty riled about. He had been enjoying the large, nearly exposed breasts of the young girl in front of him, who couldn't help but bounce and dance while gossiping with her friend. As he stood there trying not to stare, he yearned for them to break loose with each hop and turn. They were so perfectly shaped and beautiful. He could see them in his mind's eye, free from their strained captor, captivating and smooth, peeking from behind the drape of long, silky hair. If only! Don't think him a scoundrel, though. He's as true to his wife as he is to his oath as an officer of the law, but he is just a man. Cannot a man admire the majesty of the hills on a clear day?

After snapping from his daze to answer the call, Cesmat walked back to the squad car to find Bradley asleep, at which he rolled his eyes. This he did, just as his large body crashed into the driver's seat and his hand accidentally hit the siren button. So startled awake was Bradley that he immediately opened his door and exited the car like it was a runaway barreling down Powell just before going airborne at Sutter. His beloved tourists on the sidewalk instinctively froze as he rolled in front of them, assuming that if a policeman was on the ground in evasive action, their lives must be gravely at risk.

"What are you doing?" Cesmat mustered, holding back the tears.

Bradley scurried back into his seat, shut his door, and muttered, "Drive! And turn the damn siren off!"

Francisco was a few short blocks east, and they arrived without incident. The street was nearly vacant; most residents had finished what they needed to accomplish before seeking refuge for the night. They pulled up in front of 2200, which seemed as quiet as a convent. Cesmat stepped out, adjusted his pants, and began searching for a piece of chocolate, which of course he never found because he was abruptly called to duty. Bradley stayed in the car and ran a background check on one Martin Bornstein.

At the door, Cesmat found the name Bornstein on the call box and pushed the buzzer, expecting an answer. None came. He tried knocking. Nothing. He turned back to Bradley and shrugged his shoulders just as the front door was opened by a kind young man embarking on a walk with his tired dog. After exchanging pleasantries, Cesmat made his way to the top of the building to apartment number 53 and gently knocked. He waited a moment and then heard some rustling behind the door. The door cracked open and he could see an older woman dressed head to toe, right down to her pink slippers, in crocheted clothing.

"Excuse me, ma'am. Is there a Martin Bornstein here?"

"No, officer. Mr. Bornstein lives a couple floors down, in number nine. He's a pretty quiet fellow. We really only see him when he's walking his dog. Is there a problem?"

Officer Cesmat paused a moment. The gears of his mind began spinning wildly. He snapped out of his easygoing posture and immediately radioed Bradley.

"Bradley! Bradley!" he shouted. "Did you see a tall white male exit the building after I entered?"

"Yep. Came out, looked at me oddly, and then walked up the street," Bradley replied.

"Go find him...*now!*"

Turning back to the now-anxious woman, Cesmat charged. "Ma'am... number nine, you said? Get back inside and lock your door."

Crashing down the stairs, he inadvertently caused the old building to rattle so loudly that it was as if the big one of 1906 had hit again, or the building had come under mortar attack. He could hear people talking in raised voices at nearly every door that he passed; some were even screaming. He felt a little bad about being so loud, but he had an eerie feeling that he needed to get to number nine as quickly as possible.

He got to the second floor and drew his weapon, a standard-issue .40-caliber Beretta. At the door, he gently checked the knob to see if it was unlocked. No luck. After a short burst of brisk knocking, he announced his arrival. "SFPD. Open your door!"

His hands were wet and sweat accumulated on his brows. His gut was churning. Years on the force had given him a keen sense for foul play. "SFPD. Open your door now!" he reiterated.

With no answer, he stepped back and put his size-thirteen, Christmas-present-from-the-wife boot against the door. Not a trim man, Cesmat was as immovable as a brick wall, and easily made short work of a closed, locked door.

"Bradley. Request backup and get up here to number nine ASAP. I'm going in."

The radio cackled back, "No sign of the perp! Be right there."

Cesmat approached the doorway and ducked his head right, then left. He could see the place was in shambles. Then, across the room, he saw Marty doubled over on the table.

"Sir. Are you okay?" He shouted. Now louder: "Sir, are you okay?"

There was no answer. No gentle voice. No playful bark of an innocent pup. Just unnatural silence. No movement. No breathing.

Gun drawn, he took his first step into the apartment just as Bradley buzzed from below, being locked out. Marty apparently was a tad hard of hearing, because the buzzer was turned to the max volume. And, being only a foot from Cesmat's head, it was as a discharging cannon to an already on-edge cop, especially one with his gun drawn. Luckily, Cesmat did not have his finger on the trigger, or he may have killed the neighbor through the wall. He simply turned pale white and froze for an instant, the abrupt constriction causing a sizable report from his rear exhaust. (But we won't make too big a mention of that. He wouldn't want you to know.)

"Holy...mother...gahh!" Cesmat shouted as he ducked back out of the apartment. Peering down the stairs, he could see Bradley's shadow through the glass and hear the door nearly coming off its hinges as Bradley tried to shake it open. Cesmat glanced at the speaker on the wall and noticed a red button. Pushing it let Bradley through like Cigar out of the gates at Del Mar at the ringing of the bells.

"Whatta you got?" Bradley mumbled, barely able to breathe.

"Man down across the room, on the desk. I'll move to him. You go right."

They split and cleared the apartment of any remaining danger. Cesmat, approaching Marty, could see his heavily battered face, and gently reached down to take his pulse. Nothing.

They could hear the cavalry in the street below—sirens, revving V8s, and screeching tires. Others in the building were now in the hall.

Betty Pratt from next door came wandering through the front door. "Is...is everything...?" She shrieked, seeing the officers standing over Marty. "Oh...oh...oh...Mr. B!"

"For goodness' sake, Bradley. Secure the area!" Cesmat fumed.

Bradley whisked Ms. Pratt into the hall and began crowd control. With so many curious eyes on him, he decided on a quick group interrogation. "There has been an incident in Mr. *Burnsteener's* apartment. Did anybody see any strangers, or hear anything unusual in the last couple of hours?" he inquired, to which most of the replies were a simple "What?", since most couldn't hear him though were clearly within earshot of his announcement. Ms. Pratt was able to say that she did hear a loud noise about thirty minutes before and some loud talking, but she thought it was the TV. Frustrated, Bradley swung the apartment door shut and hustled downstairs to open the front door for the other officers.

Cesmat radioed for an ambulance and then quickly scoured the apartment for clues, knowing that once the detectives showed up, he and Bradley may as well be back in line at Ghirardelli. Doing so, he quickly came to the same realization and frustration that Stevin did: there just wasn't much there—a computer that was still on, a phone dashed to pieces, a bat in the closet, and a few other odds and ends. Really, the only clue was a now-cold order of Chinese takeout sitting on the table. He picked up the empty bag and investigated the receipt, which detailed the order, named the restaurant (China Ease), and gave the phone number. He quickly took out his notepad and wrote down the information just as he heard a host of voices behind him enter the apartment.

"Officer Cesmat," one voice called.

Cesmat surfaced from the kitchen. "Yes," he reluctantly replied, knowing what was coming next.

"I'm Detective Hibl and this is Detective Howe," the man said, pointing to his partner. Of course, Cesmat knew the detectives. Apparently, they wanted to be asses today.

"What do you got?"

"Yes, Detectives. We worked on the Holmboe homicide together last year," Cesmat responded, playing along.

"Uh...not much. White male, looks to be in his late sixties or early seventies, dead by the computer; Chinese takeout; and a suspect who went out the front door."

"Out the front door?" Howe inquired suspiciously.

"I thought he was a resident. Seemed nice enough. He was going for a walk with his dog as I was coming in. He opened the door for me. Bradley looked for him, but he didn't find him."

"All right. We'll expect a full report in the morning. We'll take it from here," Hibl said with a smirk.

Cesmat made one last casual pass through the apartment, hoping to find any kind of lead. He knew he could recognize the intruder if he found him again. He knew he couldn't be too invasive—Forensics had already arrived and were dusting the place. The bat in the closet caught his eye again. He took a closer look. 29-incher...a kid's bat. It seemed so out of place in such an empty apartment of an older man. Without much else to see, he walked into the hall. The inhabitants of the building had been dispersed by backup, and Bradley was trading notes with the detectives.

"Bradley. Let's roll," Cesmat said as he started down the stairs. Bradley fell in behind him. Just before they hit the ground floor, a frantic Asian woman raced in the door.

"Where Val? Where Val? Where Val?"

Mrs. Ma's voice reverberated in crescendo through the apartment house. Officers in the apartment stopped all investigation, and neighbors froze in their apartments as if the murderer had returned looking for them. Ms. Carmichael in 27 soiled herself. Passersby on the street stopped in a moment of wonder. For a split second, time itself paused in intrigue. Cesmat and Bradley stood frozen, looking at the woman, not knowing exactly what she was saying or, even more, why she was so panicked.

"Ma'am. Calm down, please. There has been an incident here with one of the residents," Bradley explained. "Did you know somebody here?"

Val's mom continued, "Where Val? Where Val?"

Finally understanding that she was looking for someone named Val, Bradley asked, "Who is Val?"

"She delivah Chinese Mista B. Where Mr. B?" Mrs. Ma asked, becoming more frantic.

"Delivered the food to Mister B," Cesmat mumbled to himself.

The gears in his head churned and then, remembering the Chinese food containers in the trash can upstairs, it hit him. "Val is your daughter, ma'am?"

To which the old lady nodded in grief.

"Bradley. The guy who left was alone, right? He had only a little dog. The apartment upstairs is vacant except for Mister Bornstein. Let's assume the girl was here at the same time. She's not in the apartment. She's not further up the stairs, which leaves...only the lobby?"

At the word "lobby," both officers instinctively surveyed the room, spinning like a couple of radar dishes that simultaneously locked on the closet door. Cesmat eased his hand onto his gun.

"Bradley. Take her outside, please," Cesmat said, pointing to the distraught mother.

As Bradley escorted Val's mom to the door, Cesmat stalked closer to the closet door, looking over every square inch. Something caught his eye in the crack at the bottom, but it was too dark to make out. He pulled his flashlight and shined the light on the edge of a growing pool of blood, now visible under the door. The hair on his neck rose and instinctively he pulled his gun. He reached for the door handle but caught himself, knowing he would not want to foul up a good source of potential prints.

Bradley returned and, seeing Cesmat on high alert, pulled his gun. "What is it?" he whispered.

"Don't know, but there is blood under the door. Get someone from Forensics down here now!"

Bradley, also on high alert, danced up the stairs like Li Mu Bai in the bamboos. Just as he got to the apartment door, someone from Forensics happened to be walking by, so he reached in, grabbed his arm, and pulled him into the hall, then rapped on the door and signaled for the others to follow.

"What?" another officer yelped.

Bradley put his finger to his lips to signal silence and gestured with his gun for him and the others to follow. With five officers in tow, the two descended to the lobby. Cesmat instructed the forensics officer, Officer Jeppson, to delicately check the handle for any prints. The other officers, who were lined up the stairs, drew their guns like a cancan line of Bolivian police, waiting for Butch and Sundance to spring from the door. Jeppson eased up to the door and noticed the blood. Ever so gently he dusted the handle then scurried back behind the officers, leaving Cesmat open to moved in. Grabbing the handle, Cesmat swung the door open, ready to unleash a volley of lead. However, he found only coats hanging in the coat closet, which set off a flurry of razzing from the detectives on the stairs, who were not aware of the blood.

"Hey, Cesmat. Did you think you had the boogey man cornered?" came one jab.

"Yeah. Maybe he turned into a mothball. Check the pockets!" came another.

"Wait!" Cesmat snarled.

His eye caught a shimmer of glossy black near one of the hanger hooks, then he dropped to one knee and shined the light at the bottom of the coats. All the officers were looking, and all could see Val's limp little feet dangling among the heavy coats. Cesmat cautiously slid the coats apart to reveal the body of Mrs. Ma's daughter.

"She's alive!" Cesmat yelled, as he could hear her faint breathing. "Get the medics!"

Bradley holstered his weapon and the two officers gently unhooked the girl and laid her on the floor. By then, the forensics team had switched from canvassing the apartment to gathering in the lobby—taking samples here, dusting there, and generally being a nuisance to Cesmat and Bradley, who were tending to the girl. More sirens could be heard, louder now and closer, and it wasn't long before Mrs. Ma again came blasting through the front door, only to witness her daughter's bloody scene.

"Val! Val! Val!" she cried and fell limp on the floor next to her daughter.

"Not a good day for Asian ladies, apparently," Bradley blurted, hoping no one had actually heard him, and luckily no one did.

While Cesmat and Bradley continued tending to the girl and her mother, the forensics shuffle ground abruptly to a halt.

"Does anyone know where Anderson is? I need the camera," someone said, only to find no response.

"Must still be upstairs," came a voice from the crowd.

Detective Howe was at the top of the stairs and made his way back to the apartment. "Anderson, you in here? They need the camer—"

Stepping in, he could see Anderson slumped over in the chair by the computer.

"Anderson! Are you okay?" he yelled, which startled Hibl and the other officers below.

Rushing over to Officer Anderson, Detective Howe reached down and touched the man's shoulder, but found no life. He took his pulse. Nothing. Fearing that the killer was still close, he drew his weapon and went screaming into the hall. "Officer down! Officer down! Officer down!"

Such words distill as a tempest battle cry to the dutiful officers left behind. The hounds were now pulling at the leash and were about to be let loose.

Guns drawn, but with no apparent target, all officers scrambled for cover. Cesmat and Bradley blew out the front door and into the quiet street.

"You stay here. I'll go around back," Cesmat ordered.

The officers inside became desperate and undertook a systematic commando search of the entire apartment house. Actually, it was more like a military raid of the governor's compound in a coup, and more troops were eagerly on their way. The poor, sleepy inhabitants of 2200 Francisco opened their doors to frantic policemen who acted more like armed thugs than cops, bursting into apartments with guns drawn. There was no time for questions, no time for explanations. One of the hounds needed to pick up the scent of the fox responsible for two and maybe three deaths, and so far, all they had were noses full of Bengay, day-old soup, and musty clothes. Within minutes, they had searched every nook and granny. Cesmat had circled the building twice and found nothing. News choppers had begun to hover outside, spilling their spotlight onto the building entrance where the bloodhounds now congregated.

"Cesmat. You got anything?" Hibl questioned cautiously, already knowing the answer.

"Nothing."

"Fan out! Two blocks in every direction. Bring anyone on the street back here," Howe commanded. "Hibl! Stay here with me! We'll watch over the EMTs while they evac the ladies in the lobby."

"What the hell is going on here?" Hibl said frantically as they watched the other officers engage the neighborhood streets like a shockwave from an atom bomb. There was innocence in

Hibl's voice, like a child asking his father why mommy was in the hospital.

"I don't know," Howe responded. "Somehow, someone or something was still in that room."

CHAPTER 4

DARKNESS RULES

"Where the hell have you been? You look like crap!" Alexes complained.

Stevin marched by her without a word and made his way to the back room of their small apartment. There was no question that he was a wanted man. He was free now, but for how long? His mind raced over every detail of the past three hours—the boys in the park, the people on the street as he chased the Asian girl, the policeman at the door. How many clues did he leave behind? How long would it take until someone was knocking at his door? Stevin started to panic. His mind raced. He started to talk through it. "Okay. Yes, I attacked the girl and the man. But I didn't kill anyone. There is just no way he could have died from a bat to his face! Okay. He was old. But he was fine! He was reading that stupid trashy love smut. I wonder if the girl died, too. She was alive. I wonder if they found her. There has to be cops all over that place now."

He paced in a trance and then abruptly snapped to attention, like back in the VCR days when a tape was rewinding at 300 miles per hour and then *bam*, it stopped at the beginning.

"The news...the damn news has got to be there. The TV!"

He threw open the door and stormed into the family room, where they had a small TV.

"Are you okay?" Alexes asked cautiously, backing away from Stevin.

Stevin, realizing that by acting too psychotic he might arouse suspicion, calmly switched to cool mode. "Yes. I'm fine, babe. Just want to watch TV."

Flipping through the channels, he found his story...literally his story. But knowing that Alexes was looking over his shoulder, he channel-surfed for a bit to shake her interest, and then landed back in the Marina District.

At first, he thought he was mistaken. They were reporting on a fallen officer. But the street, the house, even the front door looked familiar. His mind failed to connect what he knew with what he was seeing, like a needle searching over and over for a groove on a scratched record but never finding it. He watched intently, taking in every detail. Then, suddenly, the screen showed a picture of a famous romance novelist believed to be an additional victim at the scene. The weight that had settled on him suddenly became crushing. His mind froze in disbelief, as if he was instantly slipping into the emptiness of a nervous breakdown. The night's scene played out again and again. The words "fallen officer" echoed in his mind a thousand times, and the realization settled upon him that his pursuers were now not only driven by duty but by rage and revenge. And yet, in all of his confusion—amongst all of the unanswerable, monumental questions—there came to him a fleeting thought, a shaft of clarity from a dark light, which his mind rambled after to escape its perpetual twirling: "...the officer was found dead in an apartment shortly after other officers found a third victim in the lobby closet," the TV blurted, popping Stevin back into gear. "Reports are coming in that the officer was alone at the time and was overcome by an unknown assailant as he was investigating the contents of the occupant's desk."

With this report, Stevin began to see order among the chaos of the puzzle pieces, as if after a million tries the pieces finally started to fit. He began to calmly and methodically piece the puzzle together, and though he could squint and see the image, there were still several pieces on the floor and under the couch that he would have to round up in order to fully appreciate the devilish masterpiece he was working on.

"The desk. The desk," he kept whispering as he tried to sort it all out. "The old man died at the desk. The cop died at the desk."

"What?" Alexes asked as she overheard him speaking, silently hoping her man was done focusing on the TV and was finally going to focus on her.

Stevin didn't hear a word and kept going over and over the pieces of his puzzle. The old man, the cop, and the desk—three pieces that now fit.

What was on the desk? he asked himself. He closed his eyes and thought back to the sparse apartment. He tried to imagine himself listening to the old man reading his book again—that horrible garbage that seemed only suitable as a sleep aid rather than an aphrodisiac—and envisioned the items on the desk.

A computer, of course; the phone that I blasted into pieces; maybe some pens; pictures? Not sure.

His mind pulled back from the minute details, and he began to realize that he could be the only one in the world aware that something rather than someone might be the culprit. He reasoned that he certainly did not kill the officer, since he was probably on his way back home when the officer died; and chances are that Old Man Bornwhatever couldn't have died from the slugger; which, to any reasonable person who could rule out aliens or pathogens, leaves only the Mac.

The dark light led him further into obscurity and Stevin's mind stumbled and staggered no longer, rushing now toward a place where men with aspirations to rule, conquer, and dominate go. The mind of our cheap thief and assailant metamorphosed, grew, and hardened. And in his madness, he began to see a path to insurmountable wealth, power, and destruction: the kind of addictive evil developed and distributed by the most notorious fiends in world history. And, in an instant, he knew what he must do and how he must do it.

"Here's some ice cream for you," Alexes said, setting a bowl in front of Stevin. "Let's watch the *Real Housewives* together."

Stevin turned and looked at her, only to see what felt like a perfect stranger—as if, by talking to him, she had broken the rules ascribed to the discourse between peasants and royalty. He said nothing, stood, and walked back out the front door in his second awkward exit of the day.

Alexes was so shaken that she began to cry. Her assessment of Stevin's actions and attitude produced only the result of insecurity and confusion, and she couldn't help but think that she was the cause. Setting her ice cream on the table next to his, she sat back on the couch and tried to fight off the rising swell of emotions by focusing on the TV, which was still tuned in to the night's top story. After watching for a while, she became enthralled at the details of the story and began to forget about her plight with Stevin. The sad details of the girl in the closet, the dead officer, and the novelist all seemed so impossible, as if she were listening to her friend read her something out of the fourth chapter of a cheap novel. She watched intently as they showed the building and scene in the Marina District, just a few miles north of them. She wondered what it would be like to be there, and what the other occupants were thinking as the reporters showed scared old people dazed in the confusion of the moment. Then she saw something that rocked her to the core: A sketch of the man the police believed to be their number-one person of interest. The man was clearly her husband.

Minutes passed as she sat there, stupefied. Her first inclination was to track Stevin down and beat him with a bat, a thought that just dripped with irony. Leaning back in her chair, she began to reason it out. If she didn't call the police, she could confront him and forever have leverage on him, which might be used to actually get him on the straight and narrow. However, that would make her an accomplice of sorts, and there would be no justice for those who died. If she did call the police, Stevin would be forever gone, along with her marriage, and she would have to start over...again.

She picked up the phone and dialed 9, 1, and then hung up. Her hand was shaking terribly. She tried again: 9, 1, 1. The line rang, then was quickly answered.

"911. What is your emergency?" came the response.

Alexes could not muster a sound from her twisted throat.

"911. What is your emergency? Hello?" the operator persisted.

Alexes finally managed an "Um..."

"Are you okay, ma'am? What is your emergency?"

"Um...I'm calling... I'm calling about the incident on TV," Alexes uttered.

"Which incident, ma'am? The one about the fallen officer?" Mary Kay replied.

"Yes."

"Do you have information about the incident, ma'am?"

"I...I...I think the man you are looking for is my...my..."

"Yes. Is who?" Mary Kay coaxed.

"My husband," Alexes finally stammered, feeling somewhat relieved, as might people who die and find that, though they have passed away, they are in a better place.

"What is your name, ma'am?"

"Alexes McDonald."

"Is your husband there with you now?" Mary Kay asked as she began furiously typing.

"No."

"Do you know where he is?"

Pausing for a moment, Alexes realized that she in fact didn't know where he was, so she replied, "No."

"Are you at 96 Walter, #3?"

Alexes' mind was still running scenarios as to where Stevin might be. En route to Mexico was at the top of the list, followed closely by in the deep recesses of the Sierra Nevadas. Running was more his sport than suicide.

"Ma'am! Are you still at 96 Walter, #3?" Mary Kay boomed. She was now standing at her desk, growing impatient.

"Yes. Yes," Alexes responded.

"Okay. I have an officer on the way. Please lock the front door and stay put. Is there anyone else there with you?"

"My two children."

"Okay. What is your husband's name?"

"Stevin. Stevin McDonald," Alexes answered hesitantly. His name escaped her longingly, as she still questioned whether or not to let it go. It moved away from her lips like a loved one on a steamer, forever slipping away across the horizon.

At dispatch, Mary Kay wasted no time in shotgunning Stevin's name across the radio.

Unfortunately for him, living in the information age, his bio, history, and old mugshot were now at the fingertips of every law enforcement officer for a hundred miles. It wouldn't be long until his face would be seen on every news station and in every airport, bus station, train station, and cruise terminal. This meant by morning, he would have to lay lower than low in order to move. For now, though, his waning freedom allowed him a certain measure of recklessness, which he was about to test to the fullest.

Unlike most criminals, who tend to scatter when the heat is on, Stevin's dark confidence was growing in his ability to elude and dodge, which is why he was on his way back to 2200 Francisco, into the very hornet's nest. His target: Marty Bornstein's computer. Something in that computer held the key to the mystery of instantaneous death. It could be the only explanation. However, he would first need to visit the SFFD in order to disperse the hornets.

Making his way on foot from his small apartment on Walter, Stevin worked his way north on Divisidero until he got to Grove, where he found just what he was looking for: a fire station. He needed to work fast in order to accomplish his plan and get back to *Borgenstinner's* place before the scene changed too much. Surveying the block, he spotted a lone pay phone not too far off, which was a stroke of luck.

Jetting across the street as discreetly as one can be in the middle of the night, he stood at the pay phone and thought through what he would say and what he would do once the doors went up. However, his cunning was abruptly interrupted by the sharp blast of a truck horn and all hell breaking loose down the street at the station. Turns out his timing was impeccable, and in fact a false alarm was not going to be necessary. He bolted back down the street and into the small alley adjacent to the station. He needed to time this perfectly. He waited as the firefighters donned their gear and the last of them scrambled onto the truck. Leaving the building, the truck made a right turn and pulled away as the door began to close. Just before it shut, Stevin slid underneath and was in. Laying there on the floor against the door, he wondered if there might be more firefighters in the firehouse. *If so,* he reasoned with himself, *they could be sleeping or even getting ready to trail the truck to the alarm.* He decided to find out if he was alone, figuring that was better than being surprised while rifling lockers. Tucking his right arm underneath his body the best he could, he started screaming for help as if a lion was dragging him by his foot into the bush for lunch. He glanced around as he yelled and could see nothing. He paused for a split second to see if he could hear anything. *Nothing*. He stopped for a moment, and then came the sound of footsteps from above. He began screaming again, now knowing that he was going to have to confront somebody, but not knowing exactly what he would do.

"What happened?" came a shout, as an older man ran into the truck bay.

"My arm is being crushed by the door!" Stevin shouted.

Having no time to reason as to why someone might be in such a predicament, the firefighter immediately spun to run back to the door button but slipped on the smooth floor. Stevin saw this as his opportunity and pounced. Jumping to his feet, he caught the man just as he had collected himself and was on one knee. With his hands firmly together like the head of a mighty medieval mace, Stevin clobbered the back of the firefighter's head as if it were a baseball sitting on a tee. The man went down hard with no sound, face bouncing awkwardly on the floor. Stevin stood over him waiting for signs of life—some movement, groan, or whimper. Nothing. Confident that he had immobilized his foe, he decided to see if there were any other people in the firehouse.

"He's hurt bad! Somebody help!" Stevin cried and then anxiously waited.

No response came, but though he had the whole place to himself, he was still driven to accomplish his plan, which meant he had to get what he needed and get back up to Francisco Street in a hurry.

He quickly surveyed the small firehouse and soon found what he had come for: a coat, a hat, some pants and boots and, as a bonus, a flare that was randomly sitting on a workbench. Wrapping them together in one of the large backpacks he found, he shut off the lights and exited into the street for his long walk north. Stevin was in decent shape, but thirty blocks is thirty blocks and not easy with a backpack—not to mention he was going to have to evade the hounds of Hell along the way.

Until now, Stevin was an opportunist with tidbits of a plan. He went here and went there in an effort to achieve a goal, but found himself playing defense more than offense—or, in other words, reacting to situations rather than influencing them. As he walked, he thought about how to be more calculated and cunning—characteristics that until now had evaded him even in thought but were now somehow percolating in his mind. The dark light was growing and Stevin's stride down the strange path was becoming more concise and rigid. While in this thought and nearing his destination, he was brought to by an approaching helicopter circling over the rooftops. He snapped back to reality and ducked in the shadows as it flew over. He was now entering the inner sanctum at two blocks out. Checking to make sure the street was clear, he made his way forward, feeling a little like Dr. Graham stepping off the Field of Dreams and knowing there was no going back. If he were even seen by an officer, it was ripcord time—time to retreat and run until the language turned Latin.

He decided on a flank attack, which wasn't a difficult decision seeing as the front door was cop, news, and neighbor central. He worked his way through the neighborhood. The hounds had settled a little after not finding much in their initial sweep, so this actually made it quite easy to get close to the crime scene. Besides, who looks for a criminal at the crime scene two hours after the crime anyway? Stevin got to within 80 or so yards of the building. He thought about making a run for the fire escape, but decided it was too risky. He looked up. Above him was another fire escape. He scouted his attack angle and could see the lit apartment where he just was hours ago. The hive was full of busy bees...nothing a little smoke couldn't clear out.

He went to work. Climbing to the top of the building, he made three quick rooftop jumps and was within twelve feet of 2200 Francisco. The twelve feet, though, was formidable. Unfortunately for our jumper, the building he was on was about six feet lower than the roof of his destination, something he couldn't see when he calculated his assault. In his disappointment, he reasoned that he would someday hire guys to do this minimum wage crime work. Not willing to make the jump or go back, he had no choice but to go down. If he went down on the inside, he would have to exit at the front of the building, directly adjacent to the media circus; but descending on the fire escape left him precariously exposed. So, contrary to his normal modus operandi, he sat down against an HVAC unit and thought it through, his hand resting on the backpack that he had taken off and set down beside him. His hand tapped up and down on the bag, making a scuffling sound as he thought. He didn't have much time and needed a way to get down one fire escape and up another. His hand kept tapping at the bag. The dark light gradually lit his mind. He had an idea. While not as glamorous as opening the door for a cop with a dead dog in one's jacket, this caper was sure to feature much less risk.

Ripping open the backpack, Stevin began to get dressed. He had not anticipated using the gear this early in his plan, but he was grateful to have it. The helicopter was still circling; there were police and people all over the streets. This would at least give him a sense of belonging.

Fully clothed and fully authentic in firefighter gear, he began to climb down the fire escape. But after only a few rungs, he was halted by a voice at close range.

"Hey! What are you doing up there?" a police officer inquired from below.

Stevin had already worked out his story in his mind, so the answer rolled off his lips as if he had acted out the scene a hundred times. "Someone called in a gas leak. I just checked the furnace on the roof."

"This entire block is on lockdown. How come we weren't advised of this? What company are you with?" the officer continued suspiciously.

"Station 21, down on Grove. The Presidio guys are busy with a jumper on the Bridge, so they had us come up," Stevin responded, intentionally disregarding the question about notification.

Letting down his guard, the officer continued, "Find anything?"

"Nothing here, but I want to check the one next door," Stevin said, emboldened by how easily the officer accepted him.

"You're just accessing the roof, right? Let me call it in first," came the response.

Before Stevin could extemporaneously come up with a way to dissuade the officer, the officer grabbed his mic and called it in. "Sergeant Renner, this is Officer Hackett."

"Go ahead, Hackett."

"I'm out back in the alley. SFFD is on site checking gas leaks and wants to check subject building. Please advise."

There was a long pause. Then a response. "SFFD? Here? Now? Let me check into this and let you know. I was not aware of SFFD being onsite."

Overhearing the response, Stevin nervously continued his descent. This was not in the script.

Renner continued, "Hackett, have him check in with Cesmat up front before he..."

There was a slight pause. Stevin was almost down now.

"Hackett, hold."

Renner held the mic on as another officer resumed talking with him out front. Both Officer Hackett and Stevin could hear.

"Sergeant, somebody just called in a 240 near the home of our man of interest. The description matches."

"Okay. Get Hibl and Howe down there to check it out on their way to his house."

"Hackett, let him go, but stand by and observe."

"Affirmative," Hackett responded.

Stevin dropped to the ground and adjusted his helmet low over his eyes.

"You're good to go. I'll stay here and watch," Hackett instructed.

"Okay. Shouldn't take but a minute," Stevin said as he walked toward the other fire escape.

Getting to the escape was one thing. But now laden with heavy clothing, he couldn't jump high enough to grab the ladder. He turned back to the officer. "Hey, can you give me a hand?" he asked boldly, keeping his face as hidden as possible.

"Sure. No problem."

With a single jump, the officer had the ladder pulled, and Stevin was on his way up with his gear...his plan and his anonymity intact.

As he climbed past Unit 9, he slowed his ascent. He could see a number of people inside, 'scurrying about with papers, cameras, and other instruments. Many others were going in and out of the apartment, presumably from the command center out front. A sly smirk came over Stevin's mouth as he sighted the computer, still on the desk.

Viewing the scene gave him an uncomfortable feeling, though. It wasn't but a few hours earlier when he'd innocently gotten off a bus and watched a pretty Asian girl bounce down the street. Now he was San Francisco's number one most wanted and was planning to blow up a building.

Continuing upward, he pondered his decisions, his life, his future, wondering if he could get this runaway train in reverse...or at least in neutral.

The sound of tapping broke him from his trance. As he looked to his side, he beheld the fragile finger of Matilda Kerr tapping at her window. It caught him by such surprise that it took a moment for him to comprehend that the little old lady wanted to talk to him. He stopped climbing and helped her open the window.

"Are you assholes about done? You stay here any longer and I'm going to send my rent check to the police department!" she exploded. Snickering could be heard from the street below.

Taken aback that such language could emanate from such a frail person, Stevin gathered his wits and rolled with it. "Sorry, ma'am. I'm with the San Francisco Fire Department, and I am investigating a gas leak," he replied, using his best customer-service skills. Though he really would rather have just punched the old lady, he restrained himself for fear of exposing his identity. "Have you smelled any gas, by chance?" he asked, basically lobbing a softball at Barry Bonds to send into the parking lot.

"Gas? Yes! In fact, I was just on the can. Wanna come inside and smell for yourself?" she snapped.

Stevin calculated that this time, she spoke softly enough so that she could not be heard below.

Looking down at the officer in the alley, he hollered, "A lady up here smelled gas. I'm going in."

"Going in?" the old lady said as her voice cracked. Her countenance resembled that of a poor poker player who was all in with a pair of twos.

Stevin climbed through the window and with a slight hop, caught Matilda square in the jaw with a wicked right. She was much frailer than he'd anticipated, because the blow lifted her off the ground and sent her headlong into her front door and then to the floor in a heap, as if he had blasted a blowup doll that then deflated.

Inside, the apartment was the exact opposite of the one a few floors down. There was hardly room to move. Furniture, boxes, plants, and clothes cluttered the ground. Walls were overladen with pictures, sconces, and drying flowers. But not there to plunder or loot, Stevin quickly made his way to the stove, tripping several times in the heavy boots.

Using a butter knife, he was able to pry it up, get his fingers underneath, and lift it out of the cabinet. Once settled, he grabbed the gas hose and ripped it off. The hose immediately began to whistle and he could smell the pungent gas. He raced into the other room. Removing the flare from his backpack, he lit it and looked for a place to set it down, trying to conceal the illuminating light. Not finding anything suitable—not that it really mattered—he threw it down on what appeared to be a pile of soiled clothes topped with cigarette butts and ran toward the window. Now it was time to get out and get down as fast as possible. He climbed out onto the escape and started down.

"Find anything?" the officer shouted.

"I thought I smelled something, but I think it was coming more from the bathroom than anywhere else," Stevin joked as calmly as possible, knowing that he had just armed a bomb with a short fuse and was still within the blast radius.

Suppressing the urge to run for his life, Stevin methodically worked his way down. In his mind, he rationalized that at least he had on gear that might protect him. Just as he passed Unit 9 and was near the bottom, it blew.

The explosion was monstrously more violent than Stevin had anticipated—like how movies depict the annihilation of a planet or star with an initial crack, a pause where time seems to stop, and then a deafening *whoosh*. The blast blew the entire roof off the old building and severely damaged the top floors of its immediate neighbors. Buildings that were not so proximate suffered broken glass and severe peppering from flying debris. Out front, debris rained down on the circus like the confetti finale of a Vegas show, which scattered the crowd like cockroaches. Stevin was still on the escape and collapsed against the building, trying his hardest to fit his entire body under the fire helmet for protection. Down below, Officer Hackett ducked behind a dumpster and disappeared in a pile of trash bags left loose on the ground.

The thunderous noise of the explosion echoed across the city, which was followed by a brief moment of silence, and then screaming and terror from all directions. Panic is never a good thing, especially when it overcomes the aged and the media. Surely there would be fantastical stories to tell for all of the survivors. Matilda Kerr, as well as several others in the building, would have to recount the episode on the other side.

With the building fully burning above, Stevin did not have much time to get back into Mr. B's apartment, get the computer, and get out. He hustled back up the escape a few feet. Wiping the dust from the window, he could see that everyone inside was hastily clearing out.

Wasting no time, he smashed the glass with his elbow and climbed in.

Being in the apartment again within hours of his first visit, and under the nose of half of San Francisco's finest, was a monumental feat—an achievement reserved for those with the greatest of sinister calculation, or those who draft the path cleared by stupidity and just plain dumb luck. In the case of Stevin, it could certainly be argued both ways. The old apartment had not changed much, even after so many forensic visitors; it was still as bare as Mother Hubbard's cupboard. Nonetheless, he was in, and wasted no time grabbing the computer. After unplugging all of the cables, he shoved it into the backpack, which he was grateful to have.

Making his way back to the window and sensing that he was alone, our bold thief-now-mass-killer decided to see if his old friend, the maple slugger, was still in the closet. He figured, *Why not pick up some evidence and dispose of other evidence all in one fell swoop?* Joking to himself, he reasoned, *Hell, I should just take out the trash too, while I'm at it!*

He opened the door to the closet to find the bat exactly where he had left it. It didn't quite fit in the backpack, so when Stevin put the backpack on, it gave him a kind of firefighter-ninja look as it stuck out over his head like the handle of a Samurai sword. This would provoke some hilarity as he exited the window, because the bat handle caught on the center window frame and shattered the upper portion of the window pane just as he was climbing out. Luckily for him, the brim of his helmet kept a lot of the falling glass from falling right down the back of his shirt. Unluckily, however, the glass shower at street level drew any and all eyes in his direction, like the ones from the police officer emerging from his shelter below.

However, yet again, Stevin's costume served to save him from too much suspicion. There must be something in the human psyche that refuses to trigger alarms when seeing a firefighter exiting the window of a burning building, even though that firefighter is exiting from a highly guarded crime scene with a bat.

Seeing the officer below watching him emerge again on the fire escape, Stevin figured he had better say something to keep his momentum rolling, but the only thing that came to mind was to exclaim, "This one is clear!"

On any other day, that may have seemed odd to those who obviously knew that the apartment was clear because cops were crawling though it like ants in a honey box, but today, after an explosion, those words seemed to soothe the shocked and bewildered.

Stevin made his way to the street, where he was met by the officer.

"Are you okay?" the officer said, shaking. "What the hell happened up there?"

"I don't know," Stevin replied. "The old lady said she smelled gas. I went in and didn't find anything. I guess I missed it somehow," he continued as he cautiously eased the bat from the backpack.

Officer Hackett was oblivious to his movements. The trap was set and in an instant, before another question could be posed, the slugger was again cocked and unleashed in fury.

Stevin caught the officer straight across the cheekbone and left ear. Cocked again as the officer staggered back, Stevin readied himself for another homer, but paused as he could see it was not necessary. The officer collapsed on the ground in a ball of lifelessness. Though certainly not dead, Hackett would unfortunately be feeling that shot for months to come.

Sirens could be heard in the distance, along with the drumming of helicopter blades that seemed to come from every direction as their chopping echoed in the alley. The top of 2200 Francisco was an inferno, as was the top of its neighbor, which fueled an ominous glow against the gathering fog. With just about every possible law enforcement agency, firefighter, and SWAT team surely descending upon him as riled Valkyries, Stevin knew he needed cover fast.

He surveyed the immediate area until the light of a nearby apartment caught his eye; he figured with a burning building in the area, a firefighter on the run wouldn't alarm anyone, so he ran in plain sight straight at the light.

The lobby of this building gave off a different vibe than that of 2200 Francisco. Instead of a closet with heavy wool coats, the lobby sheltered bikes and baby strollers, which made Stevin uneasy. His greatest fear, at least at this point in his sinister career, was to involve or harm children. This meant he would have to tread lightly and take a slightly different tack than barging through doors and blasting innocent people. He paused for a moment and remembered that he needed a mouse and keyboard in order to investigate the contents of the Mac. Again, the firefighter uniform would prove indispensable. He decided he would have to pretend the CPU held critical information about the explosion and he needed help to quickly access the information. It was a very weak proposition, and he knew it, but in the moment seemed plausible enough.

He knocked on the first door. Doing so brought back awkward memories of the summer he spent going door to door selling magazine subscriptions, something he really didn't want to remember and certainly never wanted to relive. Luckily, no one answered, or they would have caught him very off guard as he ruminated of days long past. He continued on, and, after several attempts down the hall, someone finally answered.

"Yes?" the female voice inquired from behind the slightly open door.

"I'm sorry to bother you this late, but there has been a horrendous explosion across the street. The first engine to respond was able to get some evidence out of the building that we think might hold clues as to what happened. The only problem is that we don't have a mouse and keyboard for a Mac computer. We've been going door-to-door to try and find someone with a Mac. Do you by chance have a Mac?" Stevin inquired, feeling very embarrassed for his ridiculously contrived ruse.

To his astonishment, however, the reply came back, "Yes. Come in and I'll get you hooked up."

As the door opened, Stevin's painted-on smile went flat. This time, however, it was not the memory of agonizing summer sales that caused his rigor mortis. This was much, much worse. Never in his life could he have prepared for what he saw, and for a moment his devious plan—in fact, all of his evil designs and propensities and darkness—seemed to flee from the glorious light he beheld. Stevin was in love. And not your everyday 'that chick is hot' kind of love, either. This was Keymaster meets Gatekeeper kind of nitro...despite her men's pajamas, retainer, and hair in a high pony.

CHAPTER 5

IT'S JUST HIM

Alexes' hand quivered at the cold touch of the door handle. She knew on the other side was a force that would change her life forever, yet she sensed that change might not be terrible, just difficult—and she wasn't in the frame of mind for difficulty. She opened the door to meet Hibl and Howe.

"Alexes McDonald?" Hibl inquired.

"Yes."

"May we come in?"

She opened the door wider and let the two detectives in. She continued to stand there as if in a trance. Doing so also let grief and fear enter the apartment.

"Please, have a seat," she offered, snapping out of her trance.

The officers sat down and took a moment to survey the room. It was a modest home with the apparent touch of a woman, yet humble at its roots. Finding nothing of interest, they began to question her.

"Is there anyone else in the house?" Hibl asked.

"Just my daughters, who are asleep."

"Okay," Hibl continued. "Why do you think your husband, Stevin, is someone we're looking for?"

"Well..." Alexes hesitated. This might be her last chance to back out of this growing nightmare. She could just come up with some lame reason and hope that they left her alone—and Stevin alone—or she could blow the top off the whole thing because she knew, deep down in her heart, that it was him. Pausing for a moment, on the fence, she answered. "The son of bitch did it. I just know it. We got in a fight this morning and when he came back, he was different—more crazy. He hardly even spoke to me, and he was enthralled with the news report of the horrible murders. And... the artist's sketch is him. It's just him.

"Do you know where he is now?" Howe blurted, smelling blood.

"No," Alexes replied. "He left about an hour and a half ago. I have no idea. The way he left seemed like he would never be coming back."

"Do you mind if we look around a little?" Hibl asked calmly.

The officers stood and proceeded to wander through the apartment, gently looking through trash cans, closets, and couch cushions, all the while being careful not to wake the girls. It was late and there was little to go on, but dead officers are a great inspiration to those left behind. When they had finished in Alexes' bedroom, they made their way to the front door. Just as they were about to leave, Hibl happened to glance down and notice a man's jacket on the floor under a chair.

"Hold up," he blurted.

He gently picked up the jacket and examined it on the table. He spread the front panels to investigate the inside pockets. Nothing... except a few strands of what looked like pet fur.

Hibl's mind began to crank with what fuel was left inside.

"Hey. Didn't Cesmat and Bradley say they saw a man leave Bornstein's building with a dog?"

"Yes. And I remember seeing a food and water bowl in the kitchen there," Howe responded, starting to understand where Hibl was going.

"Mrs. McDonald?" Hibl called to Alexes.

"Yes," she replied, walking into the room.

"Do you have any pets?" Hibl inquired.

"No."

"Do you know if Mr. McDonald has been around any pets?"

"Oh, definitely not. He doesn't like dogs or cats at all."

Hibl looked at Howe with a sly eye. Without another word exchanged between them, the two went to work. Howe peeled off and called the precinct to promote Stevin as a person of interest and have a forensics team dispatched to Alexes' apartment, while Hibl had a frank talk with Alexes about finding another place to live for a few days.

A few blocks north, two other officers were also still on the job, following up on the pummeled firefighter.

"Listen. I know this is something the detectives have already looked into," Cesmat rationalized, "but I just want to talk to the guy really quick before we punch out tonight."

"Fine. You go in. I'll stay in the car and cover you," Bradley mumbled, now barely awake.

Cesmat made his way to the door. It was almost 2 a.m. and he hesitated before knocking, knowing that he might not get a warm greeting. Something was urging him to knock, though; there was something inside he needed to know, so he rapped at the door. After a minute or so, a very tired firefighter came to the door wrapped in only a towel.

Cesmat couldn't help himself, even at this early hour. "Am I interrupting something intimate?" he joked.

The firefighter wasn't amused and said nothing, only motioning with his hand for Cesmat to get to the point.

"I'd like to talk to the guy who was attacked earlier. Is he here?"

"Last I heard, he was at Mount Zion getting some tests. He took a fair shot in the head," the man answered.

"Do you know what happened?"

"We found him unconscious on the floor when we got back from a call. The medics came and got him, and he called a few hours later and told us what had happened. He said some guy was stuck under the truck door when we left on a call earlier, and that when he tried to help the man, he was attacked. Said he didn't remember anything else. I'm sure your guys have already got his statement at the hospital. Hell, a couple of guys were here earlier. Don't you guys communicate?" the half-naked man stammered, becoming agitated.

"Anything else out of the ordinary here?" Cesmat continued, undeterred.

"Not really. Can't find a couple of things, but I'm sure they are around somewhere," the firefighter said, hoping it would be enough to end the conversation.

"Like what things?

"Just a jacket and a backpack, I think. Not sure. One of the guys upstairs said he was missing some stuff."

"Okay. Thanks. If you come up with anything else, please give me a call. I'd appreciate it. We lost a guy tonight and no one is going to rest until we find the bastard who did it," Cesmat said as he handed the man his contact information.

Cesmat began to piece the scene together as he walked back to the car. Talking to himself, he reasoned, "Okay. Let's assume that the guy stuck under the door was the same guy we're looking for, that same sly son of a bitch who let me in the apartment building. Why would he be here? Does he have some vendetta against the SFFD?" The pieces of the puzzle just weren't coming together.

Back at the car, Cesmat opened the door to find a very awake and exited Bradley wrapping up a call.

"We've got another man down at the scene!"

"Who?" Cesmat exploded.

"Hackett. He was attacked in the back alley just after the explosion. He's still alive, but took a hard shot to his head," Bradley explained.

"Hackett?" Cesmat inquired excitedly.

"And Hibl and Howe have a strong suspicion that a guy named Stevin McDonald is the guy we're looking for," Bradley continued.

The gears began to turn for Cesmat. He paused and thought for a moment. Bradley looked on as if waiting for a grenade to explode that took five seconds longer than it should have. Just as he was about to pick it up again, Cesmat blew. "He went back! He went back! But for what? Why was he there? What was he doing?"

"Who went back?" Bradley said, perplexed.

"The bastard went back. He was right under our noses. He came here, got some firefighting gear, and went back. But why?" Cesmat rambled as he climbed into the driver's seat.

Bradley was starting to catch on and the pieces were coming together, but, unfortunately, not quickly enough. After a very eventful day, it was time for the officers to retire for the night. Much-needed sleep would not come easy, though, their minds harrowed by the memory of their fallen comrades and the knowledge that much of this could have been avoided if they had just maybe questioned the guy at the door for a second longer. Seriously! Even old dogs find some fumes in the tank if it means they get to go outside. What dog goes to sleep when faced with the opportunity to go on a walk? A dead one does, apparently. The remorse of 20/20 hindsight rested heavily on the officers' shoulders, an unfortunate and lasting gift of ignorance and one they were fighting madly to give back.

The great city was now calm—the sirens off, the choppers stowed, the news dispersed, the force at rest. The only movement was the caution tape flicking in the silent wind around 2200 Francisco—well, that and Stevin, who was making all sorts of riotous noises across the street, the details of which we will leave to the adult imagination. However, if you are really interested, you might find something very close in one of those romance novels by the famous author—now, what was his name? Oh, yes...Rex.

CHAPTER 6

THE AH-HA MOMENT

Morning dawned in the city, and to the delight of many, brought no fog, just sunshine—the type of sunshine most find when they wake in San Diego or Scottsdale. Life had moved on through the night, and although the dramatic events of the previous evening were real and lasting, morning seemed to have downgraded the fear and threat to DEFCON 2. Surprisingly, the neighbors of 2200 Francisco, who were still shaking from the explosion, found themselves easing back into their normal routines. And to many who might have suspected otherwise, even the uniformed cops of the SFPD found themselves more focused on their normal routines now that the case was in the hands of hungry detectives.

Across the street, Stevin began to awake from a very peaceful night's sleep and release of much anxiety and frustration. Opening his eyes, he found himself staring directly into the eyes of a small, white schnauzer sitting on the floor. Initial confusion turned instantly into panic, and he could do nothing but lie perfectly still until his racing hard drive could query a viable solution in his mind's database. His first thought was that he had somehow passed out, dreamed the last day's events, and was now coming to in Martin Bornstein's apartment, with Franklin standing guard. Next, his mind ran to the supernatural, and he thought maybe it was Franklin who had come back to haunt him because he'd flattened him with a bat and tossed him like a soggy sandwich wrapper in a trash can. This thought troubled Stevin deeply because at that very moment he suspected this might happen to him every morning, like a sinister Groundhog Day. His mind kept spinning while the dog kept staring, not making even a twitch of movement. The dog's eyes captured Stevin's and seemed to hold him prisoner, like an animal who is overcome with fear just before being caught. It was a classic school kid staring contest, and Stevin was beginning to sweat. Not having much more patience, the dog finally exclaimed his victory by letting out a miniscule peep of a bark, no louder than if someone were to step on one of his chew toys. With that, there was movement behind Stevin, who was still frozen, trying to work through the showdown.

"Bubbles! Bubbles! Come here, girl," a groggy voice called out.

This sent Stevin scrambling to his feet on top of the bed, for he dared not approach the fiend on the floor, and couldn't muster the strength to turn and face the devil behind him. Stevin's eyes followed the dog as it ran around the bed and jumped into the arms of the stranger next to him—who, though still a bit groggy, was awake enough to find Stevin's actions very odd, wondering what on Earth he was doing standing over her on top of the bed wearing nothing but wide-eyed panic.

"Are you okay, Captain?" Taylor asked. The sound of her voice pierced his delusion, which allowed his hard drive to finally find the file. He knew where he was, but he was still a bit stymied by the presence of yet another white schnauzer. (Let it be known that our heartless and reckless killer was overpowered and consumed by a twelve-pound miniature schnauzer named Bubbles.)

"Um...yeah. Sure. I'm okay. I was having a bad dream," Stevin replied as he laid back down and quickly covered up.

Confusion turned to disgust as Bubbles heartily licked Taylor's outstretched lips, repeatedly, to the point that Stevin couldn't help but think that he had kissed those lips too and therefore indirectly had basically sucked on a dog's tongue. Stevin could think of nothing other than finding his clothes and getting out. But then he remembered why he had come in the first place: the Mac.

"Hey, babe, where's your Mac gear?" Stevin said, trying to be cool and forget about his sorry loss to Bubbles.

"It's all in the kitchen. Are you going to see what might have caused the explosion? I want to help."

With that, Taylor slid out of bed and walked to the closet. Stevin watched her like a kid staring in the window of a toy store. To hell with Bubbles and dog spit; his heart was melting. Her high pony had been demoed by the night's activities, and her long blond hair now cascaded over her shoulders and shoulder blades. She walked with small steps, almost scooting, and Stevin could see through her toned legs, thighs, and beyond.

"I should have been an effing firefighter a long time ago," Stevin mumbled to himself, still on radar lock with a smoking missile ready to fire.

At last, his dream ended when Taylor turned and smiled and closed the bathroom door.

Stevin jumped to his feet and got dressed. He knew he couldn't stay long, though he wanted to stay forever. He was all dressed and in the kitchen, hooking up Bornstein's Mac, when Taylor emerged.

"Find anything?" she inquired.

"Not yet. I'm not good with these things. Can you help me find a file?" Stevin asked sheepishly.

"I guess you just know how to charge into buildings and put out fires, huh?" Taylor said, chuckling.

Stevin thought to himself, *More like blow up buildings and start fires,* but then managed to blurt out "You got it, babe," while firing off his fingers like six-shooters and donning a big cheesy smile. When Taylor turned to face the screen, Stevin's eyes got big and he wondered to himself why he was acting so strangely. He felt choked up and awkward, like a freshman trombone player trying to game up the homecoming queen. Never mind he was married. But that reality was far behind him, and he started to wonder if he could actually figure out a way to be with Taylor.

"Okay. What do you want me to do?" Taylor asked, hands ready at the keyboard.

"Um..." Stevin hadn't gotten that far in his mind and he fumbled a little.

"I guess go to where you might write a letter or a book. Let's see if we can find some files to look at. Maybe there are clues there that will help our ongoing investigation of the incident," Stevin replied, trying to speak official-like and sound tough.

"Okay. Let's see. The last file accessed was called *Noel.* Must be about Christmas," Taylor concluded.

"All right. Open that one," Stevin said, not knowing exactly what he was looking for. However, something inside told him he was close. It was the only explanation, and the only material thing that linked the old man's death with the cop's.

"Wow, this is a big file. Over two hundred pages!" Taylor exclaimed, looking at Stevin.

Stevin played dumb, but he knew exactly what it was. The thought of its origins made him quiver, because he knew it would keep him from coming back tomorrow and forever.

Taylor began to read at the beginning:

> Noel stared at her voluptuous body in the mirror. Her fingertips danced on her smooth tummy in small circles. Her hair fell carelessly over her breasts. She admired how her skin flowed in a perfect arc from her ribs to her hips, and how her new breasts complimented her womanly shape. She looked deeply into her own eyes as one would into the eyes of a lover, becoming entranced. Her hands lay flat, now moving over her chest and thighs—rubbing, warming, massaging.

"Oh, I like this!" Taylor exclaimed with girlish pep and a growing grin.

Stevin, standing behind her, rolled his eyes and shook his head, having heard this thick language before. Though, coming from Taylor's lips, it seemed much more bearable—not to mention it was a little erotic. Taylor continued:

> Her fingers moved through her small, square tuft of hair and up over her lab...

"Okay, beautiful, this is official business here," Stevin interrupted. "You'll have to wait for the release of the novel to catch the rest."

"But it was just getting to the good part!" Taylor protested.

Big time! Stevin thought to himself, realizing that he actually kind of enjoyed this romance stuff.

"Gosh, if this is the first paragraph, I can't imagine what comes next!"

"Let's move to the very end and see if we can find anything," Stevin suggested, while trying to reconcile this prose with the nature of the man who wrote it.

Taylor scrolled slowly down to the end of the document, hoping to catch bits and pieces as the lines rolled by. "Come on. Get to the end," Stevin said, growing impatient but trying to be gentle.

Taylor glanced back at him in defeat and then kept moving down. All she was able to catch was something about mistakes on one page and something about a bus ride on another. She finally reached the last two paragraphs. "Do you want me to read the end, Captain?" Taylor asked innocently.

Stevin paused. He looked at Taylor with a blank expression. Something inside of him was prompting him to stop, as if an alarm was going off. But he couldn't muster the strength to heed the warning. His moral compass had moved far past center, and such inner premonitions were easily bullied by doubt and rationalization. Taylor waited for his response with a smile, her beautiful and pure eyes gazing into his.

"Wait...what?" Stevin stammered, coming to.

"Do you want me to read the end?" Taylor asked again.

"Yes, yes," Stevin answered, thinking nothing of the warning but only of escaping his awkward delay.

Taylor turned slowly, her eyes holding his until the last moment, and continued to read:

> Snow began to fall like wild, wet feathers floating eagerly to earth. From her room, she could see the twinkling lights of the moored boats in the distance. Their soft swaying reminded her of their chance meeting in the Miami Yacht Club a month prior. But here in the great north, the warm sun played but a brief cameo during the day, leaving the cold to drive them indoors, which is just where they wanted to be driven.
>
> The tormenting tension, the yearning, the fever made each waiting second all but unbearable. Her heavy breath billowed over her warm lips onto the frigid windowpane. She thought of what she might say during the first awkward moments when he arrived. Perhaps there would be no words. Silence sometimes speaks.

"Well, I guess there wasn't much there," Stevin said with a bit of frustration in his tone.

He turned and began to pace across the living room, his mind trying to reconcile the hope of finding something on the Mac with the reality that the one thing linking Bornstein and the cop resulted in absolutely nothing but a mouthful of romantic waste. He felt deflated, like all the gas in his getaway car had run out and now he was reduced to walking until the police caught up with him. His pace across the floor slowed and he contemplated his next move. What he really wanted was a clean break, the ability to smart-bomb the last 30 hours and start anew with Taylor.

"*Chhhh*...aaaahhh..."

An awkward noise stopped him in his tracks and fouled his thought. It was a low, dull choking sound behind him. It took a moment for him to process what it was. In an instant, he knew. Spinning around, he ran across the room to Taylor, barely catching her as she reeled out of her chair. She looked at him with complete despair—her pure eyes now wide, full of panic. There was no breath, no movement, no life as she slipped away in his arms. Taylor was dead, and Stevin could do nothing to stop it.

Stevin fell to the floor. He couldn't breathe. He couldn't think. He couldn't scream out in rage. He gritted his teeth and clung to Taylor, as if sliding off the deck of the *Titanic* into the icy surge below. His psyche began to turn on him. *You bastard! You did this! You knew it killed two others and now it's killed her. You deserve this!*

His mind unwound all around him. He was delusional. But...there was, lurking in the back, a monster of consciousness and clarity. The *ah-ha!*—the last piece of the puzzle. The realization that words can kill. Silence does in fact speak, and it speaks death: death to its creator, death to the law, and death to the innocent and pure.

Stevin lay in a heap on the floor. He couldn't move. Tears gushed from his eyes and saliva dripped from his mouth. He knew now what power he held and that it had cost him a new love, a light... his last light, and his soul. Why had he taken this risk? Why was he so stupid to test it on someone he cared so much for? He yearned to roll back time to undo it all, but all was lost. There was no power lifting him up, supporting him in his actions; just darkness pulling him down. He faced a treacherous fate and knew that if any lifting was to be done, he would have to do it himself.

Stevin closed his eyes for a moment until the sound of tiny hooves gathered behind him. He couldn't place in his mind what it could be. He froze, wide-eyed, as the sound stopped at the side of his head and then, without hesitation, something began licking his face. It was Bubbles—little Bubbles—who had come to lick his tears, and though just a wee pup with presumably little understanding, mourn the loss of her fallen owner. This act of unconditional kindness twisted Stevin's despair deeper in his heart, and caught him so crossways that he could do nothing but weep. For Stevin knew that he was not the victor today, but rather the object of revenge. Rex had reached back across the gulf of death and snatched away Stevin's most prized possession. Without warning, without alarm, and in a matter of seconds, Taylor was taken from him. Ironically, though, Franklin was not so sinister, for he sent an emissary of love—truly man's best friend, despite man's dark immorality. Perhaps when the great scroll is rolled back, we shall find that Taylor's death was not revenge, but rather compassion, pulling someone out of the game just before a very bad play.

Stevin took Bubbles in his arms and the three lay as one on the floor while Stevin sobbed.

CHAPTER 7

THE GRAND TESTS

"Hibl, Howe. Get your asses in here!" Chief Brenning exploded.

Hibl and Howe scrambled from their desks and beelined to the Chief's office. Actually, it was Captain Moore's office, but the Chief had made it his temporary abode after promising the people of San Francisco that he would spend more time in division offices at the "field level." Having him there was the last thing anyone wanted.

"Why are you here?" the Chief said with a stern voice.

The detectives were speechless.

"Have you found McDonald? Is he here? Did someone fail to tell me that you apprehended him?"

Still silence from the detectives.

"*Well?*" the Chief boomed.

"Well, Chief," Hibl reluctantly explained, "the trail has gone cold. We've got no leads, so we came here to go through the facts."

Now the Chief was silent, and awkward—very awkward silence

filled the room. Brenning appeared more a beet than human before the aftershock hit. "Get your asses out of here...now! And don't come back until you have his head on a platter."

Cesmat happened to hear the latter end of the Chief's inspiring speech, and watched as Hibl and Howe gathered a few files and exited the precinct. "One of these days the solution to a case like this is going to fall in my lap, and I'm going to rub it in those clowns' faces," he said under his breath. Cesmat had always wanted to be elevated to detective, but circumstance and age had worked against him his whole career. At first, he was too young, and now it seemed he might be too old. Grinding out his days in a black and white appeared to be his lot in life.

"Bradley," Cesmat called to his partner, who was cautiously admiring a few ladies of the night who had just been brought in. "Bradley!" he called again, this time elevating his voice so that all could hear. "Are you done shopping?"

The heavy laughter around him finally caught Bradley's attention. "What? Yes, I'm ready," he responded, not really hearing what Cesmat had said.

"You're ready? Ready to order?" Cesmat continued, with all now laughing hysterically. Bradley looked on, confused. "Come on. Let's go," Cesmat said, putting his hand on Bradley's shoulder.

The officers left the precinct and climbed into their patrol car.

"Just for fun, let's do a flyby of 2200 Francisco," Cesmat suggested. "There is something about that place I just can't let go of."

Bradley made a left and cruised north. The sun was out in full splendor, which meant so was most of the city's population—

mothers dressed in sandals and sunglasses walking young children, businesspeople extending their lunch hours at sunny café tables, and out-of-luck killers looking to dispose of bodies.

As much as Stevin loved Taylor, he knew that he would have to let her go. And by *go*, we need to understand *dispose of her body*. Perhaps he could use her apartment for a time, until someone missed her, but maybe that would be too risky. The prudent thing would be to run and hide as far away as possible, until at least the story was out of the headlines and his trail was iced over. However, armed with verbal death, Stevin felt empowered, emboldened, and resilient. And why wouldn't he? Here he was, hanging out in a nice apartment right across the street, while watching clean-up crews, forensics, and news people clamor around like ants at the onset of rain.

There was only one problem, though...at least for the moment. Taylor had to vacate the premises. Stevin ran through several scenarios of how to accomplish this; none felt comfortable. Despite his forced effort to "stop and think," it just wasn't coming to him. He gazed out the window, letting the gears churn in his mind. Then it hit him. He could see the end result—just not so much how to accomplish it. He decided that since Taylor was collateral loss from 2200 Francisco, that should be her resting place, among the ruins of the old building.

Then something caught his eye: a fire truck had just pulled up to the building. Watching closely, he could see three or four firemen step out, but they weren't in coats and boots, but rather wearing standard uniforms and holding clipboards. His plan started to gel. It would be a stretch, but it could work. Now he just needed to piece together his firefighter gear, which was strewn around the apartment. The inspectors were about to have someone join their company.

Scooting across the street, Stevin focused more on his access point than worrying about being caught. He needed to get in an apartment, find some clothes, and commandeer a wheelchair, which he knew might be a long shot. He was back in the alley now. Rubble still covered the ground and he was nearing the police tape. Luckily, nobody was around, so he was able to slide under the tape and immediately be in his element. A firefighter outside the tape would seem odd, but one inside conforms to all notions of normal.

He clambered up the fire escape he had come down just a day prior. He felt strangely at home, but he didn't want to take too much time or have to go too high in the building. Pulling a wheelchair down a fire escape was going to be odd enough, let alone if it turned out he had to do it for three or four stories.

The first apartment window he came to was mostly blocked by what once may have been a healthy potted garden. Now it looked like a garden of sprouting broken bricks. Through the window he could see the kitchen, and beyond that a couch, but nothing that might pique his interest. The next one was much the same, so he bounded up to the next level. Then he saw what he was looking for: a ramp. A ramp for wheels. A ramp for a *wheelchair*. Using his elbow, he popped the window and was in with nearly no disturbance. Through the front door, he could hear the other firefighter inspectors in the lobby stairwell. The apartment was laid out much the same as Mr. B's, so, being very familiar with the floor plan, Stevin walked directly to the hall closet and opened the door. There, in gleaming beauty, was a wheelchair folded behind a thick band of hanging clothes—which, as it turned out, was the other thing he was there for. He paused and smiled. He felt so lucky that he honestly believed himself to be invincible—

that his crusade was unstoppable and would yield unimaginable benefits. However, his godly daydream was interrupted by a rattle at the door.

“This one is still locked,” he heard outside.

“Didn’t we have all of the units unlocked?” the voice questioned.

Again Stevin felt emboldened. Could his luck be truly so magical that even doors were randomly locked? Either way, he felt he needed to hurry, not wanting to intentionally test his invincibility. He pulled the chair out of the closet and filled the seat with several samples of polyester, wool, and crocheted items.

That should do it, he thought as he headed back to the window.

“I wish I had a nickel for every time I was crawling in or out of a window at this place,” he said, snickering.

There was more rattling at the door as it was being unlocked. Stevin grabbed the lump of clothes and tossed them overboard. From the alley below, it would have looked like someone was being moved out in a hurry, maybe after being caught in an affair. Then came the finale: the wheelchair spinning, flying, then crashing to earth. Not only did it hit hard, but it landed on its back handles, which had the effect of catapulting it against an empty dumpster. The sound reverberated through the alley as if Thor himself had pummeled a massive kettle drum.

“Shit!” is all Stevin could think to say as he felt his luck train beginning to leak oil.

As he took his first step on the escape, he heard a voice say, “What was that?”

He hurried down the ladder and into the alley, quickly stashing the chair behind the dumpster; the clothes still lay scattered in the street. Not knowing what else to do, and feeling eyes on him, he calmly reached down and grabbed a large chunk of concrete and brick, then turned and looked back to the window above. Seeing four heads peering out the window, he yelled up, "Just cleaning up."

The firefighters seemed to buy it, as they smiled. One of them yelled down, "What company you with?"

Stevin smiled and froze, not knowing what he should say. All he could think to mutter was the infantry division his grandfather had served in during World War II. "The Ninety-Ninth," he yelled back with his fingers crossed. Then he added, "Ladder Division," inserting *ladder* in the place of *infantry*.

The men above nodded with a little confusion on their faces, then began to talk amongst themselves. Stevin continued cleaning, this time focusing on gathering the clothes.

With the men still talking in the window above, he ducked behind the dumpster and took off the firefighter clothes, slammed them on the wheelchair seat under the other clothes, got behind it and pushed hastily for the tape. A pedestrian with a wheelchair inside the tape would seem odd, but one outside conforms to all notions of normal. Just as the tape slid off his back came another shout from above.

"What company again?"

Stevin looked back with a baffled face, as if to say, *You talking to me?*

The man paused and was very confused. One minute there was

a firefighter cleaning up the alley; now there was a man with a wheelchair. "Uh, sorry," the man sputtered. "Did you see a firefighter down there?"

"Yeah. He just walked inside the building," Stevin replied, as he turned to begin gently pushing the chair in the opposite direction.

Thinking he was in the clear, his mind drifted as he walked. He thought of his grandfather and remembered the many summers he'd spent in South Dakota with his grandparents. His grandfather was an honorable man—chiseled into one by hardship and war. Stevin remembered always heading straight to the garage freezer when he arrived at the house. Having lived through the Great Depression and the War, his grandfather always overstocked the freezer with ice cream, fearing somehow it would run out again at the store. Ever since boyhood, Stevin had loved ice cream. It was magic to his taste buds—and to his memories.

Then something ominous snapped him back to his unfortunate reality, and he began to walk very slowly. He was now directly across the street from Taylor's apartment-house entrance—fifty feet from freedom, and on the verge of life in prison—as a black-and-white slid up the street. He knew the chances of escaping this time were very slim. He knew the police were looking for him and knew what he looked like. With nothing to lose, he had only one option, and it was piled in the chair below him. Hoping that they weren't looking too far up the street, he quickly grabbed the random clothing he had pulled out of the closet, threw them on, and plopped down on top of the firefighter gear, with the helmet squarely in his back and the boots under his right leg. He was just able to get the scarf over his head as the car slowly stopped in front of him.

"Hey, Cesmat. Look at this. This is sad. That old guy looks like his spine is bent like a pretzel," Bradley muttered.

"Yeah. When I'm that old and crooked, I hope they just roll me straight down Van Ness and into the Bay. Don't want to be no beggar on the street," Cesmat replied.

Stevin could feel the weight of their gazes. He felt like he was deflecting Superman's heat rays with a thin layer of beige crochet. So overcome was he with fear that he began to shake and then urinate. The immense fear gripped him so tightly that he couldn't breathe; the urine dripped off of his seat and onto the ground. They were so close that Stevin recognized them as the officers in the doorway when he 'took his dog for a walk.' He shook harder—uncontrollably.

"It's okay, sir," Bradley called from the passenger seat. Then, slapping Cesmat on the shoulder, he said, "Let's go. You're freaking that old guy out!"

"Have a nice day, sir," Cesmat offered as he smiled and waved, letting the car inch forward.

"Dude, that was bad. Maybe we better send Social Services over here for that guy," Bradley suggested.

"Let's focus on why we're here," Cesmat countered.

Stevin sat still. Time passed. What was fifteen minutes felt like fifteen hours. But after a while, his heart rate settled and he regained his wits. He started to feel the pain of the helmet in his back again. Still not wanting to move, he had to convince himself that he only had to go fifty feet to safety. He slowly got up, leaving the old clothing on, and moved across the road, pushing the chair.

Once on the other side and up the curb, with traffic flowing again, an older couple walking stopped and offered him five dollars.

"Please buy yourself something warm to eat," the woman said.

Stevin took the money like a Pony Express rider might grab a mail satchel, without so much as a nod or thank you, and walked into the building. Leaving the chair in the lobby, he climbed the stairs. His body gained some ground on the immense surge of adrenaline that had just washed over him, and he gradually regained his composure. He walked straight into the shower, turned it on, and stood there fully clothed for some time.

There is something refreshing about warm running water. It has a way of calming, washing clean both body and soul. Think what your life would be like without warm running water. For Stevin, it brought clarity. No longer would he attempt to wheel Taylor across the street—realizing that his luck was wearing thin. His brush with the police on the street shook him good, and the fear of being caught would now be his constant companion. It was time for him to move on and roll out his plan. Taylor would stay here. Stevin stepped out of the shower with new clarity and very wet clothes. After stripping down, he threw the clothes in the dryer. The dryer timer read 43 minutes.

Stevin walked out into the middle of the apartment, wondering what he would do.

"Forty-three fabulous effing minutes!" he said aloud.

Hands on his waist, he looked around for a moment and then realized what a scene this was. Here stands a naked man; there lies a dead woman; and over them both watches Bubbles. Who could ever conceive of such rowdy randomness? Stevin shook his head in disappointment and then walked to the window, all under the watchful eyes of the dog.

It was late in the afternoon—not dusk, but the sun was casting long shadows. Stevin sat at the window and watched the people below. An elderly woman across the street caught his eye. She was having difficulty pulling her trash cans to the curb. She seemed to have a large load of something heavy, probably glass.

"Old bag probably drinks like a fish," Stevin said to himself.

Just then her neighbor came out with his trash and effortlessly dropped it at the curb. On his way back, he stopped to talk to the elderly lady. Stevin watched intently as the two traded words. He could tell the lady was becoming very stressed and worked feverishly to get her load to the curb, while the man appeared to be yelling at her.

"What a prick!" Stevin said, continuing his commentary. Just then Bubbles jumped up and barked, as if to say *Let's get the bastard!*

Stevin stood up, looked at Bubbles, and knew exactly what to do. It was just what he needed as the first step of his grand test.

He raced to get dressed. His clothes were still damp, but he didn't care. He hastily packed his gear, not wanting to leave it behind, and headed for the door, but then paused. Turning around, he looked again at Bubbles. He reasoned that a toy dog was another good prop to have on hand, so he grabbed the leash by the door. When Bubbles heard the leash, she raced over and started jumping at his leg, not realizing that this walk could be very different and potentially very long. After getting her hooked up, Stevin just needed a piece of paper and a pen, which he found in the kitchen. After quickly writing something on the paper, the two were out, down the stairs, and across the street.

The old woman was nearly to the curb by the time they got there, but her neighbor was nowhere in sight.

"Can I give you a hand?" Stevin offered as he reached down and began pulling the trash the last few feet to the curb.

"Oh, you're a saint!" the woman exclaimed. "My Cleveland used to do this work, but he's been gone a couple of years now."

"It's no problem, ma'am," Stevin replied with a smile.

"Oh, I just love your little dog. What's his name?"

"It's a bitch...I mean, it's a she-dog," Stevin said, feeling very inappropriate. "Her name is Bubbles." He began to realize how lame he suddenly felt telling an old lady about his girl dog, Bubbles.

Leaning down to pet Bubbles, the woman began to talk to her at length, making Stevin feel even more awkward and very conspicuous.

"Okay," Stevin said, finally cutting her off. "You have a nice day now."

The woman thanked him profusely as she shuffled back to her door. Stevin waited until she was inside and then pulled out the piece of paper.

"Now let's kick some ass, girl," Stevin rallied Bubbles as he headed for the neighbor's door.

After three loud knocks, the neighbor finally opened. He was much bigger in person than Stevin had realized from the window, but nonetheless, Stevin was determined to avenge the old woman.

"Your neighbor told me you're a total dick and gave me this," Stevin said, handing him the piece of paper.

The man was confused and looked at the paper. "What the hell?" he replied angrily.

"I have no idea. What does it say?" Stevin responded, giving him a 'don't shoot the messenger' look.

The man looked down again and read *silence sometimes speaks,* and instantly collapsed with wild eyes of fear.

As he fell to the ground, Stevin spun around to see who was watching. He had to hold back the mighty war whoop that nearly escaped his mouth. It worked...again...flawlessly! As he surveyed the street, he casually pushed the body back into the house with the bottom of his shoe and reached down to recover the piece of paper. Then, looping the leash around the door handle, he pulled the door shut.

"You're out, f'er!" he mumbled to himself with a devious grin.

Stevin looked at Bubbles, and Bubbles looked back with big eyes. Prop or not, where he was headed was no place for a little dog. Stevin smiled and they both came to an understanding.

Walking next door, Stevin tied the leash to the door handle, bent down for a last hug and smooch, rang the doorbell, and slipped across the street to watch. The old woman answered the door, looked around confused for a moment, and then shrieked with joy as she picked up Bubbles. Stevin was impressed that there was no hesitation, no thought of 'maybe the man will be back' or 'maybe I should try and find her owner.' The lady seemed to know the intention, as odd as it was, and retreated into the house with pure joy on her face.

Stevin stood across the street for a moment, somewhat in a trance. He relished the feeling of doing something good for someone else, a feeling that he hadn't felt in a long, long time. It was refreshing, pure, and humbling. He pondered for a moment as if to consider the course of his life. The thought of being on the run with so much death around him weighed heavily on his shoulders. He felt lost. He felt hopeless. He felt dead, wishing his circumstances and choices had been different. He wondered where he would be if he simply hadn't taken the bat. After a few more ruminations of character, he realized he was still focused on the old woman's home, staring awkwardly at midday. What's more awkward was that a young girl walking a pair of dogs had come into his field of vision, and, at exactly the moment she glanced at him, the dogs stopped and became aggressively frisky with each other. Suddenly, Stevin felt as if he were naked on stage, and turned abruptly and started walking without daring to look at the girl again.

Heading north toward the water, he became über-conscious of his surroundings. He worried about being caught again in such a trance, only to snap out of it and be surrounded by police. He resolved to be more alert and dedicated to his cause, a decision that threatened the future of any more do-gooding. Until now, he had not contemplated what his cause was. *Am I a common thief? A cold-blooded killer? Where am I going with this?* All questions that ricocheted through his mind. The more he thought, the more he felt legitimate, telling himself he wasn't just anybody now. Now he had something that he could use—something that could bring him money, power, and respect. He began to realize the grandeur of his leverage, and he burst onto the bayfront with no inhibition. It was kickoff time, and he was ready to put the pigskin deep in the opponents' territory.

Crossing Marina, he noticed a man on a bike coming toward him, and he decided to just let it flow. Hailing the man, he said in his best Dutch accent, "Akcuz me. Help me little bit?"

"Sure," the man replied.

"You tell me...this say?" Stevin fumbled, starting to now sound Russian.

The man grabbed the small piece of paper and read. Then, with horror in his eyes, he looked at Stevin as if to ask, *How could you do this?* Stevin looked back with a blank stare and then, without hesitation, pinched the paper from his hands as the man collapsed in the street.

"You're out, f'er!" Stevin exclaimed with a smile as he stepped over the bike and into the park.

He walked a few blocks before sighting his crosshairs on his next victim. He didn't want the carnage to be too close, so as to not develop a trail. One after another they fell, reading the slip of paper and dying in horror. Some gasped for air, some reached for Stevin, but all fell with nearly no sound—except for the food vendor whose head slammed against his cart and startled a flock of pigeons just north of the Ferry Building.

Looking back up the Embarcadero, Stevin could see a flurry of emergency response activity. An ambulance here, a crowd there, police cars jackknifed as far as the eye could see—such coincidence the city had never seen. For Stevin, it was the perfect calling card.

It was dusk now. He sat on a bench and reflected on the day. It was a hard thing to do, because most of what he could remember revolved around Taylor. He could still feel her in his arms—her warmth, the way she smelled, her hair tickling his face—but at the same time, he couldn't help but remember the expression on her face when she slipped away, and the pain he felt for being responsible. It seemed like so long ago now. He had done some good, but the chaotic sound of sirens up the street reminded him of his horrific wake. With so many people around him and so much chaos, he needed to lay low for the night, and he knew just where to go—realizing he could probably go wherever he wanted. For now, something with a hot tub would be nice, and a pint...a pint of ice cream.

CHAPTER 8

RAMPING UP

Early the next morning, there was great tumult at the precinct. Everyone was so focused on trying to figure out what the hell was going on that all of the little things were set free.

"Listen up, people!" the Chief boomed. Chief Brenning stood on a desk with a bullhorn. "If you are here doing paperwork, stop. If you are on the phone, hang up. If you have someone in custody for anything less than murder or rape, let them go. All eyes on me!"

With that, basically everyone who wasn't on payroll stood up and headed for the door, including the scantily-dressed lady who blew the Chief a kiss as a small gesture of thanks. This caused the Chief to pause, but only momentarily. He continued: "As all of you know, we are at war. The morgue took in seventeen people from the Embarcadero last night. These are men and women, old and young. They are of every race. Some were walking, some were running, and one was biking. We have yet to find any trace of evidence. There are no bullets, no knives, no toxins; nothing more than people just flat-out dying. Now, mark my words. This is not a case of a random flock of blackbirds falling from the sky as an act of the Almighty. This is cold-blooded, heartless murder, and our number one person of interest is Stevin McDonald. I can't fathom why a group like you haven't been able to apprehend this criminal. Our delay just cost the lives of seventeen of our brothers and sisters. Seventeen! And I'm mad. I'm mad and I'm heartbroken. The thought of that crushes me. Do you people remember sitting in elementary school, and when your teacher asked you what you wanted to be when you grew up, you thought to yourself, *I want to be a police officer*? Why did you think that? Because police officers are heroes, and you wanted to be a hero. You wanted everyone around you to look at you with respect, with admiration, with trust. Look around you now. Here we are, heroes bound together in this war. Heroes for good, for justice, for every citizen outside those doors. Now I'm asking again. What do you want to be? What do you want to be? If that childhood flame still burns in your heart, if you still want to risk your life to save the lives of others, then stand with me. Stand with me and every other officer in this great city, and be a hero! Find Stevin McDonald and bring him here!"

There was majestic electricity in the station. No one moved, no one spoke, no phones rang. Chief Brenning slowly lowered the bullhorn to his side as intense resolve came over his face. He was Maximus, and he had just rubbed Coliseum dirt through his palms. Raising the horn again, he exclaimed, "Let's roll!"

With that, the legion charged.

Stepping off the table, the Chief motioned to Hibl and Howe. "You come with me. We're going to the lab to figure this out."

The city's crime lab was located a few miles south, toward SFO. Although the building itself was nothing special and was calcified with age, inside, it offered a wealth of technology, tradecraft, and touted examiners. In fact, for this particular state of emergency, the Mayor had called up—or rather reactivated—the city's most renowned doctor, scientist, and forensic magician, Dr. Johannes Verteidiger, or "Doc V" for short. In his prime, he'd helped solve many cases that most wrote off as dead or unsolved—his most famous being the Christmas Tree Murders of 1971, when he linked pine sap to a part-time Christmas tree-lot worker and crop duster from Rio Vista.

Doc V had incredible intuition in the lab, but his real strength was on the stand. For some reason, juries connected with and trusted him, and of course, DAs loved him. Maybe this was due to his insistence on always wearing a freshly pressed shirt and tie, which seemed to suggest a presidential aura rather than that of a forensic nerd. He also spoke with a not-so-faint German accent, somehow giving credence to his authority and always ensuring that all were fully concentrated on what he was saying. The last thing one wanted to do, however, was to interrupt him with a question of "What?" or "What did you say?" Such questions were usually met with a monologue of how the English language was derived from the German language, and the two shared so many similarities that any child could understand him. Needless to say, he took these questions somewhat personally.

When the officers arrived at the lab, they found several examiners and technicians in a conference room with a who's who of the city, and they felt a little late to the party. Behind the glass wall, they could see several gurneys parked like cars in the lab; seventeen of them, as a matter of fact. When they entered the room, they stood along the back wall, unnoticed. The deputy DA, Holly Jolley, was in a heated exchange with one of the examiners.

"How can this be? There are seventeen bodies out there, and no one knows how they died?" the DA stammered. "You've got to give us something!"

Just then, she noticed Chief Brenning in the back. He could feel the weight of her stare, and he knew her radar had just locked and a missile was zeroed in on his forehead. As luck would have it, at the same time, his phone started vibrating. He let the call go in anticipation of the DA's imminent launch.

"Chief Brenning, welcome. Maybe you can shed some light on this situation. What have you found?"

"So far, we have no leads other than I have the entire force turning the city upside down for our number one POI, Stevin McDonald," the Chief responded, hoping it was enough but knowing it wasn't.

"Do you have any leads, any evidence, any clue?" the DA burrowed further.

Deputy DA Holly Jolley was a slender woman of maybe 45 years old. Very attractive and deathly smart, she relished opportunities to pummel any and all clowns who so much as whistled anything remotely having to do with Burl Ives. As this was her given name, growing up, she'd endured a considerable amount of heckling, which wasn't all that bad because, after all, Christmas was her favorite holiday. Eventually, in her twenties, while traveling home for Christmas one winter, she'd heard something that helped her be at peace with her name. She was somewhere between Elko and Battle Mountain, Nevada, dying of boredom as the miles clicked by along Interstate 80. It was a time of deep inner reflection, and a time of poor FM reception. Out there, on that lonely highway, she was only able to find a very static AM station that was playing country and western music. The Lord's music, you know!

As she drove and was caught up in thought about her life and her future, she became mesmerized by the endless road. Her car drifted onto the shoulder and started to slide, which she overcorrected to the left and then overcorrected again to the right, like she was driving a slalom course at 75 MPH, or in one of those pointless car commercials on a dry lake bed. Luckily, the highway was basically empty as she got her old blue Volvo wagon straightened out. Now white-knuckled and fully focused on the road and her surroundings, the radio called out to her with the words, "It's that name that helped to make you strong." She glanced at the radio and listened intently to the last two verses of "A Boy Named Sue." Something about that song resonated with her. Granted, she wasn't given a man's name like Harold or Duane, but it was a similar enough situation for her to "come away with a different point of view." Now pummeling eager, neophyte comedians is more for sport than hatred, which she finds easy to do with her wit.

"I'm sorry," the Chief responded. "Nothing other than a tip from Stevin McDonald's wife." The Chief cupped his hand over his phone, which would not stop vibrating.

With that, the entire group fell silent, having no leads and no findings on the cause of death. All stood perplexed, wondering what the next course of action should be.

A junior examiner broke the silence and hypothesized, "Maybe there was a toxic gas cloud along the Embarcadero yesterday." Looking around for support and an atta-boy from her colleagues, all she found were eyes that seemed to say, *Seriously?*

What no one noticed was a tall figure in the lab moving slowly in their direction. In no apparent hurry, Doc V opened the door to the conference room and, once all eyes were on him, authoritatively exclaimed, "*Anfall!*"

Not understanding what he had said and not willing to question him, the entire group waited anxiously, except for the junior examiner who'd suggested that a toxic cloud had wafted up the Embarcadero and had randomly killed people. In a last-ditch effort to be a hero, she blurted, "Does that mean toxic cloud?"

Doc V's head slowly turned to face her; then he inhaled a large volume of air and began (to the incredible chagrin of everyone else). "Young lady. Are you familiar with your English language? Did you know that English descended from zah German language? With a little effort, one could certainly deduce that '*Anfall*' is rooted in zah word '*fall,*' which, when added to the word '*an*' in German or 'on' in English, means 'to assault', as in the military. Or perhaps 'attack'...wouldn't you agree? In zis case, an attack of zah heart. It was not, as you say, a toxic cloud. It had nothing to do with zah lungs. Zah cause of death for these seventeen poor peoples was a *Herzanfall.*"

"A heart attack?" Holly Jolley shouted, louder than she wanted to.

"You learn fast, Miss District Attorney," Doc V pronounced, as if schooling a fifth-grade class.

This revelation had everyone perplexed, because that was one of the first things checked when the bodies were brought in and readily ruled out due to a lack of damage to the hearts.

Doc V continued: "And in case you are vundering why zer is no damage to zah hearts,"—everyone in the room looked as if to say yes—"zah cause of zah attack was harmonic."

Again not wanting to ask any questions, everyone in the room stayed silent, hoping he would continue.

"As we all know, zah heart's rhythm is controlled by zah sinus node, which sends electrical impulses to zah left and zah right atria of zah heart. Zeez impulses generally range from sixty to one hundred per minute, and zat is why we have an equal amount of heartbeats. In special zircumstances, when zah sinus node fails or is disrupted, zah heart relies on its backup pacemaker caused by the ventricles. If by some abnormal zircumstance both of zeez actions fail, zah heart will not beat...and we all know what happens when zah heart does not beat. It is my theory zat, in each of zeez cases, a repetitive pitch of sound caused a perfect freezing of zah heart, which, as we know, brought certain and swift death to zeez poor peoples."

In an instant, nearly every hand in the room went up and then everyone began talking at once. Overwhelmed, Doc V continued: "Pleez. Pleez. Zomeone out there has zah key to certain death, and zey know it. How you find zem, I do not know. But you must find zem and find zem quickly. I want to examine zah officer and zah elderly man who vere brought in yesterday to support my findings. Are zey still here?"

As the room erupted in a fever of planning and discussion, Chief Brenning turned to Hibl and Howe with a face filled with disgust. All three of them knew that the longer Stevin McDonald remained at large, the more horrific this situation was going to become.

The Chief nodded his head toward the door, and the three slipped out of the building without being noticed. Once outside, the Chief had a few choice words with the detectives as they walked, furious that Stevin McDonald was still at large. Just as they reached their car, they looked up the road to see four news vans barreling down on them, with each van trying to overtake the other and arrive first in what looked like a scene from some old Burt Reynolds movie.

"Oh, shit," Chief Brenning mumbled, shaking his head and thinking what he might say to dodge their questions.

As he stood there ruminating, he heard someone call his name from the direction of the building. Looking, he could see it was DA Holly Jolley. He could see her still talking, but he couldn't quite make out what she was saying now that the news stampede had charged in. He motioned back to her with his hand cupping his ear, letting her know he couldn't hear her. Then she did something the Chief never expected: She came running straight at him. Normally, DAs are calculated and a bit reserved. This was far from either, and looked more like a game of *Frogger*, as she negotiated the news vans. As she got nearer, she looked so distraught that the three officers looked to see if someone was chasing her. She was yelling, "Get in! Get in!" as she ran.

Once they could make out what she was saying, the Chief pointed to Howe and said, "You drive!" And with that, all four of them jumped in the car, and Howe, in classic Howe style, let her rip, leaving the news crews in a cloud of thick dust.

"What is wrong, Holly?" the confused Chief turned and asked.

The DA was a quick wit with a fine figure, but wasn't necessarily a sprinter, so she had trouble answering. Instead of speaking, she passed the Chief her phone and motioned for him to answer. The Chief put the phone to his ear to hear a very agitated someone on the other end. "What the hell is going on over there? Listen, lady,

I don't care who or what you are; just put the Chief on!"

Upon hearing his name, the Chief chimed in, "This is Chief Brenning of the SFPD."

There was a long silence, so long that the Chief had to pull the phone away from his ear to see if the timer was still ticking away the call's seconds and minutes. Whoever was on the other end of the line seemed to be having second thoughts. He looked at Holly with a puzzled look on his face, and she bobbed her finger up and down, motioning for him to keep at it.

The Chief tried again. "Hello?"

Then came the response from the voice, which made the DA's frantic run seem as normal as blinking in the sunlight.

"This is Stevin McDonald. I understand you're looking for me."

From the backseat, Detective Hibl watched as the Chief's eyes grew to the size of eggs. The Chief spun in his seat and froze. His mind raced. He was caught totally off guard. Detective Howe glanced over from the driver's seat and, sensing something was wrong because he had never seen the Chief speechless, asked, "Who is it?", to which the Chief simply cocked a raised finger in the air, like a mother who's been on hold with the cable company's tech support for forty minutes and just when they answered, her four-year-old walks in demanding something to eat, yelling at full volume.

"Mr. McDonald. Thank you for calling. Yes, I would like to talk to you," the Chief replied, hoping to stall long enough to collect his thoughts and figure out how to milk clues from the conversation. He held back his laundry list of obscenities and accusations, something he probably wouldn't have done if he had been prepped for the call.

"Listen," Stevin continued. "I'm only going to say this once." He paused, realizing the situation he was in. It felt like it was out of the movies. Certainly his last line was. He smiled and almost started to laugh at himself. *How cliché,* he thought to himself. Again, he felt invincible. He had the Chief of Police on the phone and was going to issue a number of demands. It was, in fact, straight out of the movies. He wondered about asking for a plane with a suitcase full of cash and freedom for all the prisoners at Gitmo, or some other random request like Hans Gruber when he stormed Nakatomi Tower with his *Kameraden* and a brother with a drill.

Becoming impatient with Stevin's sidebar, the Chief interrupted, "Yes?"

Stevin snapped back. "Listen. I think you suspect that I have something that has the ability to kill people almost instantaneously. Obviously, such things don't go over well with people like you who are trying to defend the public and maintain calm in large cities. Think what would happen to law and order if word got out that something could kill you, but that nobody knew what it was or where it comes from." Stevin didn't realize it but the whole "only going to say this once" and generally going-to-keep-it-short thing was headed straight out the window. He continued: "I really don't think that is something you want, so here's what we're going to do. We're going to have a little arrangement." His voice was almost taking on a mob-boss falsetto. "You help me, and people can go on enjoying their beautiful lives. I want a bank account at Wells Fargo in my name. In that bank account you, the government, the DeBartolos, Denise Hale...I don't care who...is going to deposit one million dollars every Friday. That account will come with an ATM card, checks, and online privileges. The checks will be the ones with the stagecoach on them and have the carbon-copy page." Stevin was having a little fun, but his request was actually fairly practical...except for the stagecoach that was just for shits and giggles.

"In addition," he continued, "I want a U.S. passport in my name and privileges to travel at my discretion. Lastly, you will not harass me, arrest me, tail me, call me, conspire against me. I don't ever want to see one of your shitty cars parked across the street or some donut woofer in hyper aviators trailing me. You're going to want to leave me alone."

Chief Brenning didn't know quite what to say. If he was stymied before, he was certainly stymied now, but he managed to ask, "What's in it for me?"

"For you?" Stevin inquired.

"Well, not for me," the Chief responded. "What are you going to do in exchange?" he said, clarifying his previous question, with the other three in the car listening intently.

"For starters, I think people may stop suddenly dying," Stevin responded.

Just then Detective Hibl's phone rang. He questioned whether to answer it, but he decided to do so as quietly as possible.

"Hibl," he whispered into the phone.

It was Cesmat on the other end. "Hibl. Are you with the Chief?" he asked.

"Yeah."

"Tell him we got two more bodies. We got a call from a landlord a block away from 2200 Francisco. We did a wellness check and found a young girl on the floor. We got it locked down, but while we were out on the street, a neighbor approached us and asked us to check on her neighbor. We found him just inside the doorway. The old lady said she met a man yesterday who helped her with her trash and then left his dog at her door. I showed her a picture of McDonald and she ID'd him," Cesmat reported.

"I'll let him know," Hibl responded, then turned to Howe. "Howe, drop the DA downtown and head back to 2200 Francisco area. Lights on."

Hearing "lights on" was one of Howe's true joys in life. If ever there was a guy who loved the sound of squealing tires and feeling the back end break free, it was Howe. As soon as he lit the light bar, Chief Brenning turned back around and looked at Hibl, who held up two fingers and slid his hand across his throat to let the Chief know there were two more.

"Well, Mr. McDonald, I'm not sure I can trust you. Turns out we just found two more dead bodies," the Chief responded.

Stevin paused for a moment as he mentally reviewed the past couple days' carnage. He couldn't quite put his finger on who the Chief might be talking about.

Hibl chimed in with a whisper, "Chief, Cesmat says they got a lady who can ID McDonald."

"And it turns out, we have a witness that puts you at the scene," the Chief blurted into the phone, feeling the leverage slide his way.

Stevin continued to think. He couldn't believe they could have found Taylor so fast. But, if they were talking to the old lady who was now the proud owner of Bubbles, perhaps they had. His mind began to churn. *Okay, so I was there. There is no evidence of foul play. I didn't so much as touch them. Well, okay...maybe I touched the girl...a lot; but not to harm her! They have nothing on me. There is no law that can touch me.*

"Chief, I'm sorry to say that you have no evidence other than the bodies. Was there any sign of foul play? Any injuries? Any blood? Any gunshots, cuts, stabs, rope burns, toxins? Chances are you're beginning to realize that you have nothing, so there is really no reason for me to come to the station or be arrested."

"Listen here, you piece of shit," the Chief interrupted. "I've got a dead officer, and a dead author with his face smashed in. I've got a delivery girl whose life is hanging by a thread, and a firefighter and a cop who you knocked out, let alone a pile of dead bodies. Don't begin to tell me what I have or don't have. We're going to find you and we're going to park your ass in prison! So, yes, you *do* need to come to the station and have a little chat!"

"I'll tell you what. You have an ATM card with my name linked to that bank account we talked about with the manager of the McDonald's at the end of Mason tomorrow by noon, or you're out, f'er!," Stevin replied and then promptly hung up.

A feeling of being lost came over him as the Chief reminded him of the people he had hurt before he had figured out the 'phrase of death'—details he had long forgotten after being endowed with the effortless power to take life. All of a sudden, he felt like he had overplayed his hand, which led to the abrupt ending of the phone call and a bit of paranoia. For now, he needed time to fly below radar and more importantly, a place to do so. He had connected with the Chief rather obscurely, from a dummy Skype account he'd set up using a computer at the library on Green Street. When he had first tried the general phone number for the police and asked to talk to the Chief, the person who answered offered the assistance of one of the volunteers at the station, thinking Stevin to be some crackpot who wanted to vent about his cousin being in prison or about parking tickets—because you know everyone who gets a parking ticket is innocent.

When he suggested the Chief might want to speak with him, being Stevin McDonald, the officer on the phone hastily put him straight to the Chief's cell phone, but, as we know, the call caught the Chief in the crosshairs of the DA's interrogation at the lab. Stevin, becoming a little impatient at the time, suggested they try someone else, and the first thing to come to his mind was the DA. Bingo!

Having finished the call, Stevin exited the library, but only after disposing of the firefighter gear in a bathroom trash can. With so much attention during the day, and being in a bit of a funk, he felt his guise needed some freshening up.

It was evening, and again he found himself watching the city go by—people heading home, people picking up dinner, people meeting for drinks, and people walking dogs and closing shops. It was a time when neighborhoods and their streets became busy again, and Stevin wanted nothing to do with it, feeling very much like a ten-point buck in the middle of a large meadow at high noon.

He paused for a moment and considered what he really needed. First, he thought, was a place to stay, second was food, and third was money. *Certainly,* he rationalized, *someone with my power should have money*. Hopefully that money would come tomorrow from the city, but for now he needed something to hold him over and enable him to be on the run, or at least to hide out. Then he realized he was standing in basically the most expensive neighborhood in all of the city. Surely, he could accomplish what he needed here. He decided to go for a walk and look for a home.

It felt a little strange to him, strolling through a neighborhood looking for a home. Aside from the fact that he was the most wanted man in all of San Francisco, picking someone to die so you can take their house and steal their food and money just wasn't something he was used to. He was more of a fly-by-the-seat-of-his-pants kind of criminal than the calculated serial type, who might spend weeks or months researching and preparing. How would he pick? Who would he consign to die? Walking down the Embarcadero yesterday was more his style, like the sleazebags of questionable citizenship who hand out cards on the Vegas Strip: "Click, click. Here you go!" Now he was forced to plan, and he didn't like it.

He walked for a few blocks to figure out his strategy and then happened upon a gentleman pulling a trash can to the street. From a short distance, and by the clothes that he wore, Stevin could tell that the man was moderately wealthy, but it was the house that sealed the deal—a Victorian brick beauty prominently perched on a quiet corner with expansive blue-water views...an entertainer's dream! (Aren't for-sale descriptions always so sappy and stupid?) Stevin reached into his pocket and found his magic piece of paper, and he decided to go with the ol' 'your neighbor told me you're a dick' trick.

Walking up to the gentleman with a bit of hesitation, Stevin blurted, "Hey. Your neighbor told me you're a dick and gave me this!" and handed the paper to the man.

To which the man replied, in perfect West Country English, "I beg your pardon, sir!"

Stevin pushed the paper into the man's chest to force the handoff, but he was stymied for a moment by the man's accent. "Just read it," Stevin said in a reduced tone to try and diffuse the man's self-defense.

The gentleman looked down and read the paper. Then he looked up, puzzled, only to be volleyed by an even more puzzling and wide-eyed look from Stevin. Stevin was speechless. His mind raced. The effortless ability for destruction of yesterday had abruptly vanished, and he wasn't prepared for someone to look up after reading the magic paper. He thought he might just clobber the chap and get on with it, but, not wanting to cause more commotion and needing some time to figure it out, Stevin took back the paper, apologized, and hastily excused himself. He walked briskly to the corner, turned, and then ran a few blocks to a park bench, where he sat and racked his brain over what might have happened. The events of the day had Stevin a little off his game, and this was the clincher.

What the hell? he said to himself, as his leg bounced nervously on the bench. *Now I have no leverage. I have nothing!* Stevin wondered where he was going to go and what he was going to do, but more importantly, how he was going to keep up the arrangement with the Chief in the morning. He thought back over his failed attack... the man, the trash, the house. He even considered the weather, the fact that it was evening, the fog, the surrounding rumble of the city. He sat there for perhaps 15 minutes, going over and over the event. Then it hit him...the accent! The man was the first to speak differently as he read.

"That's it!" he shouted, jumping up from the bench. Several people looked in bewilderment from across the street, but he paid them no attention because Dr. Death, the Sultan of Silence, was back!

Stevin hurriedly crossed the street and began walking west. Things are always better in the west, they say. A couple of blocks down, Stevin came upon a charming neighborhood jewel with an aromatic and welcoming rose garden entry nestled amongst mature and lush big-leaf maples. This was also an 'entertainer's dream' because, well, they all are apparently! He felt bold and unstoppable as he rang the bell. The fact that he had figured out his dilemma gave him courage—at least, he was 99 percent sure he had figured it out. A few moments later, an elderly woman answered. Yet a few moments later, and Stevin was the newest owner in Pacific Heights, and 99 percent became 100.

CHAPTER 9

SATURDAY MORNING DRIVE

The next morning was brisk—the kind that gets people up and moving early in an effort to milk every last second of the day. No alarm clock needed; just let the bio-clock work its magic. Most Saturdays seem this way for some reason—perhaps because for many it's the one day you would like to sleep in but often never can, or the one day you have so much to do that you have no choice but to haul ass. Today was no exception for Stevin. After thoroughly rummaging through Francis Dunfey's home—who, by the way, was now sunning motionless in the solarium—Stevin was able to source the following items to aid him in his quest:

- $738 cash
- Sufficient food for a few days, including some nice cuts of steak in the freezer
- 2 pints of ice cream (which was almost better to find than the cash)
- 1 brown Mercedes-Benz 280 with cream interior
- 1 loaded Luger with 32 rounds of extra ammo
- 1 iPhone 6s Plus (gold case) with headphones

- 1 very interesting and authentic-looking samurai sword
- Various credit cards, complete with pin numbers on a Post-it
- Closet full of men's clothing

Stevin had about four hours until he needed to be at the McDonald's to get his ATM card and bank information. As he sat at the kitchen table surveying his booty, he wondered what he might do to pass the time. He held the Luger in his hand, knocking it against the wood table in time with the clock on the wall. He looked intently at it and was glad he didn't have to face it at the door last night. It was generally in good shape, despite its age. The clip was full, clean, and detached easily. The action was smooth. Stevin wondered why a distinguished lady would have this antique weapon, or any weapon at all. Then he remembered that he had just killed her, and everyone should have a weapon handy. Then there was the sword. When he first found it standing in the closet, he thought it might be a cane. He had grabbed it from the top and unceremoniously flipped it behind him, but when it landed, it made such a solid *thud* that it caused him to turn and see what it was. When he did so, he found it half unsheathed and half sliced through a vacuum hose that he had tossed just prior.

He stood and walked to the hearth over the fireplace, which was neatly decorated with pictures—some in frames, some just leaned against the frames. There were pictures of many children and people of all ages, but the one that stood out was Francis with a decorated war veteran. Stevin looked at the picture with great care and respect and suddenly felt melancholy. He realized he had killed the widow of someone very special. Looking further back on the mantle, he found more pictures of the man. There was one of him standing next to President Ronald Reagan, with a handwritten signature that read *Charlie, thank you! You're an ace!,* and another of the same man shaking hands with President Gerald Ford. Another of him on the Senate floor. It was quite clear that this man was a war veteran and senator and had a prodigious family. Stevin set the Luger down with reverence and shook his head back and forth. Just when he thought he was making progress, it was again spoiled by regret. In light of his current mood, he retreated to the large recliner behind him and thought about his past moves and his next moves. But then his stomach growled, and that was that.

He sprang up and headed for the kitchen, figuring he would scramble some eggs and make a proper breakfast if Francis had the fixin's. He really hadn't had a solid meal since Taylor's house, which he really didn't want to think about since it would turn melancholy into total depression. The fridge had plenty of eggs, bread, butter, jam, and even some bacon. Oddly enough, Stevin was no dunce in the kitchen. Although not a chef by any means, he could rally good meals at a good clip, like a line cook at Denny's, perhaps. After breakfast, he glanced at the time and still had three hours, so he decided to retire to the master chambers to clean up and perhaps try on some new, official clothing.

The master bath was a sanctuary of white—white tile, white walls, white towels, white rugs, and white soap dispensers. Just about the only thing that wasn't white was the pastel green curler set on the counter—the kind that plugs in and heats up. Stevin looked at it and smiled. He hadn't seen one of those since he was a kid, and it reminded him of his grandmother, who used to wear her curlers in public with honor and gusto.

He stripped down and eyed himself in the large mirror. He was a trim man and in decent shape—certainly not the Rock, but he fought his spare tire the best he could. A few cuts and bruises marked his adventure, but otherwise he had toned skin covered in light brown hair that wasn't overbearing. He sucked in his stomach and flexed, then pushed his pelvis forward and lightly slapped at his package to air it out a little and snap the private to attention for inspection. (Come on! All guys do this.) He turned and flexed his glutes a couple of times and then headed to the shower. Inside he found an array of shampoos, soaps, brushes, two shower caps, and a razor. Ready to relax, he turned the handle for water and, to his deathly shock, it came out instantly liquid magma hot! It was a rather small shower, so there was no room to stand aside and hold your hand out for testing, which resulted in his lower legs getting slightly scalded before he bailed out screaming all sorts of obscenities that are not appropriate to quote here. He looked at himself again in the mirror. His legs were now beet red but still had hair, which he had to bend over to verify because he couldn't see it in the reflection against the redness of his legs. Even more demotivating was the fact that his soldier had mostly retreated from the heavy enemy fire and excitement. But maybe that was a good thing in this case.

After some experimenting with the shower, he figured out that someone had installed the handle backward, so that cold was nuclear hot and nuclear hot was cold. With a little fidgeting, he got it just right and settled in for a long shower, feeling very refreshed by the warm running water.

Showering was great, but what he really wanted was to shave. He reached for the razor and examined it. It looked pretty standard except for the oval-shaped plastic guide flanking the blades. *What the hell?* he thought to himself as he lathered his face the best he could with a bar of soap. The first pass was fine, but the event quickly spiraled downward from there. The razor, obviously designed for legs, was dull and felt more like a rake in his hand than a fine cutting tool. By the time he was done, he had the appearance of a bombing victim. Blood streamed from his face and neck, as if he had been hit by a thousand pieces of tiny shrapnel. Perhaps we can say that this was Francis' revenge, or at least the best she could muster from the solarium. Actually, strike that; she's about to play her ace.

Stevin looked again in the mirror. "Are you shitting me?" he exclaimed. (Oh, the irony of that statement!)

After that, he didn't want to look in the mirror again. Each time he did, things just seemed to get worse.

He rinsed his face a number of times to try and stop the bleeding, then grabbed a towel off the counter to dry his face. This would be quite possibly the greatest horror of his life, because what he didn't realize was that Francis had had an issue in the bathroom just prior to his ringing the doorbell the night before. In haste, she'd used a hand towel, the very towel he was using, to wipe herself before she raced to the door. And not to exaggerate or be crude, and in respect for her being a well-respected lady with the greatest of social graces and etiquette, let's just say it's not something you would want within ten feet of you, or on your hands, or on your face or worst of all, on your *bloody face*. He dropped the towel and wiped the substance with his hands, smearing it to clear his chin. He looked desperately in the mirror to figure out what the hell it was, his mind not processing what he was touching and smelling because that just doesn't belong on a towel on the bathroom counter. Needless to say, the shrill and violent scream that erupted from the bathroom could be heard for blocks, like someone being slowly electrocuted or drawn and quartered: sheer and primal horror. Outside, many of the neighbors streamed out of their houses, expecting to see body parts in the street. Stevin raced back into the shower. Water and soap have never seen such violence. In the end, of the seven bottles on the shower floor, not one had a single drop of anything resembling a cleaning agent. The good news was that the bleeding stopped, but perhaps not in time for some sort of bacterial infection, and most certainly pink eye.

Stevin collapsed on the floor. His mind was reeling. He was exhausted and was determined to never ever look in that mirror again—and never, ever, *ever* to tell anyone what had just happened. With the shower done, and being quite obviously extremely unsuccessful, he picked himself up and moved on to the closet to figure out if he could come up with something to wear. He was going to need some sort of disguise in order to pull off the McDonald's visit. He didn't want anything too flashy, but certainly a hoodie with dark glasses wasn't going to cut it. The closet was still divided into 'his' and 'hers' sections. He swiped through the men's clothing and decided to try some pieces on to get a general sense of fit. All of the clothes were dated, not by a few years but by a few decades.

"A blue polyester three-piece suit? Really? Wow, I'm surprised they don't have an Aries K parked in the garage," he mumbled. Then it struck him. "Old clothes. Old car. I'll go grandpa style!"

Things were looking up, and he had a plan. The blue suit fit well enough. The hem of the pants needed to be longer, but that allowed the orange and brown socks and brown wingtips, which actually fit perfectly, to really shine. He found an old gold watch, a hideous sweater that he chose instead of the vest that came with the suit, and a stiff grey homburg hat. Luckily, the closet door had a mirror where he could admire his style. He was only missing a cane, which he found in a bucket in the corner. Strangely enough, the Luger would be a perfect piece to compliment this look. Grandpa, yes, but more like retired *Stasi*. He admired himself and role-played a few lines, trying to make his voice sound old, but he felt the pressure to get going. He headed downstairs and collected the Luger, money, phone, and ammo, and then walked out to the garage to get the car.

The car, it turns out, was a mint-condition 1970 Mercedes-Benz 280SE convertible. Stevin had always wanted a convertible, so he decided to roll with the top down. Donning Francis' glasses, he opened the garage and looked up and down the street for anyone who would suspect foul play when he backed out. The street was pretty quiet despite the earlier torture audio.

He eased the Benz back and then cruised east toward the McDonald's. What he didn't know was that he was headed straight into the tightest and most armored perimeter the police had ever set up in the history of San Francisco. But Stevin was oblivious in his new outfit and country cruiser, so much so that he pulled in for gas about three blocks away and saddled up right across from an unmarked Explorer with four officers inside. Remembering that he was "old," he forced himself to move slowly with a hitch, just to be on the safe side, and moseyed into the store to pay cash. The officers were more intrigued with the car than with the driver and paid no attention to him. When Stevin walked in, he was greeted kindly by an attendant with a heavy accent. He glanced his way, thanking him, and then turned back and stopped in awe. In front of him, getting a Gatorade from the cooler, stood himself—or at least a man who looked very much like him.

Instantly Stevin's mind flooded with plans, actions, steps, and executions. He immediately approached the man.

"Excuse me, sir," Stevin grumbled in his best elderly falsetto. "Could I bother you for a favor?"

"Sure," the man replied a little hesitantly as he soaked in Stevin's outfit.

"I've left my passport and bank card at the McDonald's just down the street and I just don't have the energy to get down there. I had my hip replaced about eight months ago and it's just terribly hard to get around these days. Normally I would have the missus help me, but she passed recently. It's been very lonely without her. Could you help me by running down there real quick and collecting them for me?" Stevin asked, deliberately going overboard on the explanation, as lonely people generally do.

The man paused for a moment and then replied, "I'm sorry, sir. Maybe you can find someone else to help you."

Stevin sensed that he was close to convincing him to do it as the man was clearly thinking it through in his mind, so Stevin pushed further.

"I can give you a few dollars," he said as he pulled a wad of cash from his pocket and pretended to fumble with it. "I've already rung the manager and he has it ready. It would be very easy."

The man looked at the money and thought for a moment, and said, "Okay, but I'll need two hundred for the trouble."

"Done!" Stevin exclaimed, almost breaking his cover. "Just collect my things and meet me back here."

Stevin gave the man $100 and told him he would give him the other $100 when he got back. For some reason, Stevin felt relieved not having to go down the street. This would be the perfect test run to see if the Chief was going to go along with his wild request, or if it was just a perfect setup for a trap.

Stevin sent the man on his way, paid the attendant fifty dollars for Pump 3, and hustled back out to gas up. Once done, he backed the car into a parking spot just off the street and across the station from the Explorer. There, he decided to detail the car rather than do something obvious like read a paper. He figured people with cars like this, in this condition, are probably always wiping them down and cleaning them up. To pass the time, he thought he would check the oil and fluids as well. After finding a microfiber towel in the trunk, he began polishing the hubcaps, making sure it appeared difficult to bend down, and making sure he used slow and deliberate strokes. With very little else to do, the officers across the lot watched passively, and must have felt a little sad for the old man.

Farther down the street, things were clipping along at a much more intense pace. The delivery man pulled into the McDonald's parking lot right about 10:45 a.m., in plain sight of about 200 eager eyes. All law enforcement radios immediately lit up. There were eight undercover officers in the dining room, reluctantly eating a third meal, and another six SWAT members in the kitchen. The manager had been replaced by a SWAT member who would grab for his wad of key as a signal if someone were to come in and ask for their passport and bank card.

"Potential suspect just arrived in a black Prius. West side of lot. Exiting car now," the report came over the radio. "Snipers ready. All teams on alert."

The Chief was anxious—very anxious. He watched from a scope down the street.

Another voice came from the officers in the lot. "Suspect matches description. Very likely our boy." Everyone involved was tense, not knowing what they were up against. The fact that a suspect would casually stroll into something like this either meant he was completely stupid or had the utmost confidence in his weapon and escape plan, which could be very dangerous for all involved.

The man walked in and up to the side of the counter, unaware that four rifles from deep in the kitchen had crosshairs on him. "Can I speak with the manager, please?" he inquired. "I left a few things here." The worker looked at him with wide eyes and then hustled to the back office. About a minute later, the SWAT member emerged in a manager's uniform, complete with a heavy wad of keys.

"Sir, how may I help you?" he inquired cautiously, broadcasting the conversation across all radios.

"I'm here to pick up a passport..."

At the word "passport," the sky fell. The manager drew a pistol, put it in the man's face, and started screaming for him to *"Put your hands up! Put your hands up!"* The man froze instantly, which caused the officer to scream louder. Before long, and before he could even say a word, the officers from the restaurant happily left their food and all eight of them dogpiled on the perp right in front of the fryer.

About this time, up the street, Stevin was feeling antsy, so he slowly packed up. He could hear the distant echoes of chopper blades and the Explorer randomly started up, which he then noticed for the first time. It was going south, and he knew it. Time to go.

He forced himself to slowly get in the car. As he made a left from the parking lot, he looked to his right down the street and saw a massive offensive of police and police vehicles collapsing on the McDonald's. He watched from his rearview mirror and was grateful he'd sent in bait. The whole idea made him mad, though. The Chief had not followed through, and Stevin was determined to make him pay for it. He turned toward the Bay, away from the house, and found the first payphone he could, which took a while. Payphones are almost as hard to find these days as crooks dressed as grandpas! He dialed 911. Michelle answered.

"911. What is your emergency?"

"This is Stevin McDonald. Please put me through to the Chief of Police," Stevin politely requested, not wanting to appear heated in public.

Michelle paused, and then Stevin heard a whispered "Oh, crap!" just before the call was transferred. This made Stevin smile. After a few rings, Chief Brenning answered.

"Chief Brenning."

"Stevin McDonald," Stevin responded. The line was silent for a long while, which Stevin loved!

"Mr. McDonald. How can I help you?"

"Big mistake today, Chief. Huge!" Stevin calmly said, and then slammed the phone back on the receiver, a bit of a 'mic drop' moment. Adjusting his homburg, he hobbled back to the car and headed home to take lunch with Francis in the solarium.

CHAPTER 10

SATURDAY AFTERNOON DRIVE

Stevin was by no means computer-savvy, as was evident during his interlude with Taylor. But with a little time and a lot of effort, what he could produce was half-decent; such was the case now, having commandeered the house computer and printed three simple pages. Page 1 read "SILENCE," Page 2 read "SOMETIMES," and Page 3 read "SPEAKS." The biggest challenge for Stevin was figuring out how to print each page in landscape so the 200-point font size would fit and the words would be visible.

It was time for him to go for a drive around the Bay and drive home his demands for a stipend and a passport. Stevin knew that if this plan worked, it was going to be of epic proportions, so he took some time to think it through. Spooning through a pint of New York Super Fudge Chunk, he began to develop his route. He would start at the Bay Bridge, then head south for a bit, come back across the San Mateo Bridge, and then head back up to the house. He reasoned that he might not have much time left at the house, because it probably wouldn't be long before the police were able to interrogate his stunt double, get the video from the station, and run the plates from the car. Thinking about this made him regret not pulling the plates off altogether before driving to the gas station, but there was nothing to do about it now. He would have to be very cautious coming back, though.

With the pint readily consumed and papers in hand, Stevin headed to the garage to get under way. He was able to find some packing tape, along with a couple of bottles of water for the drive. He opened the garage and once again peeked out to check the street for trouble. It looked sleepy as ever, so he cautiously backed the car out, this time with the roof up. He drove slowly, as an old car would be driven by an old man. With Francis's phone in hand, he was able to use mapping apps to coordinate his route and stops. Getting this set up as he drove down Van Ness caused him to drift back and forth in the lanes, which added to the charade of an old car and an old man. Several honks and birds from bikers later, and he was stopped at the southwest corner of Bryant and 5th, just short of the onramp to Interstate 80 and the Bay Bridge.

He climbed out of the car and got to work. What he didn't realize was that his plan would start almost immediately, almost before he got the last piece of paper fully taped to the back bumper. Right as he was applying the last piece of tape, a gold Camry whizzed by him, narrowly missing a fire hydrant, and drove straight into the concrete corner of the St. Vincent Building. I guess that's one way to donate a car! The crash sent several people on the street running for cover. But where to run? Not two seconds later, a minivan went through the intersection, veering left, and leveled the onramp sign. It hit so hard and fast that the entire backend of the van lifted high in the air and came down with a squealing thud, the tires still under power and digging in the dirt. It was as if Stevin was standing in the street and shooting people as they drove by. Still in back of the car, Stevin quickly turned off the death trap by kneeling in front of the bumper and blocking the words in order to collect his thoughts. People were shouting and running in every direction. He could hear someone across the street yelling "The driver is dead!" Stevin realized that he needed to go quickly a) because the place was going to be crawling with police in about three minutes, and b) because he might become trapped if it caused a big enough pileup, and I guess c) he didn't want some guy with 20/10 vision to read it a block back and then plow into him! So much for the old-man routine! He jumped up and Luke Duked it into the driver's seat, got it started, and then headed up the ramp and onto the freeway.

With what had just happened, Stevin would need to get enough speed to stay ahead of the shock wave. Sure enough, as soon as he got up top of the Interstate and got going, it started. Stevin looked in the rearview mirror and time seemed to slow, at least in his mind, like this would be a scene that the director would do in slow motion. There was a car going dead left and another going dead right. Both slammed against the concrete barriers and then were directly plowed by cars behind them. Of all that ensued, the most impressive was the Prius that somehow got airborne, flying low over Stillman Street, and then disappeared behind a stand of trees. There was no explosion, though, like in the movies when helicopters always seem to crash where you can't see them, and the explosion comes from behind the hill.

A few seconds later, Stevin found himself alone in the back of traffic. The freeway behind him was jammed. Glancing at the streets below, he could see police cars coming up the Embarcadero and turning inland. He waited in the back for a mile or so and then slowly made his way forward. As he did, sometimes several cars would wreck and sometimes none of them would. The cars ahead had no idea what was happening behind them, and Stevin found that looking forward was a very typical day on the road but looking back was twisted and mangled. He wondered who the people were who were reading the sign and why others weren't. Of those who didn't crash, he wondered if they were all Brits or of some other nationality. He certainly didn't intend to get everyone, but he did want to send a message. As it turns out, his message on the Bay Bridge was about a thousand times that of Mancow Muller's. Not only was traffic stopped, so were hearts and lives.

Having plowed and planted five miles of roadway with death and destruction, he decided to turn it off for a bit and assess. Once he got across the bridge and headed south, he exited at 5th in Oakland and quickly backed into a parking space against a fence at a gas station. What he didn't realize at the time was that in the process of exiting the freeway, he sent a semi truck further south with a dead stick, killed the driver of a minivan on the offramp, and claimed another bicyclist right in front of the gas station. Once he was parked, he looked up at the deck of the freeway and could see people running on the road.

"Holy shit, this is bad!" he actually said out loud as he watched people scramble to help the bicyclist just a few hundred feet away. He realized that it was fortunate he'd stopped, because above him, helicopters circled. And not just Bonnie Bimbo doing the news. These were police helicopters scrambled from every corner of the Bay. He wondered if they were looking for a brown Mercedes yet. He thought it best to keep moving without the sign for a while, so he pulled the papers off and headed farther south. Then he figured he would just destroy bridges, not with bombs but with traffic and destruction. That should get the Chief's attention.

He pulled over again just before the San Mateo Bridge entrance and thought he would like to have a way to turn the sign on and off without having to stop, so he decided to tape the papers to the back of the convertible roof. Of course he would have to slow down, but that was better than stopping and having to back up to a fence or to some bushes.

On the San Mateo Bridge, he tried to keep a steady pace. Cars were building up quickly behind him and it didn't take long for the copters to figure out something was happening on that bridge, too. They fell in right behind him, but at a slight angle and over the water.

At first, he was worried, but then he realized all he had to do was slow down a little so that no cars were behind him, which made everything calm. Then he remembered that no one knew what was causing this, so he decided to have a little fun with the police. Every few seconds, he would speed up slightly and cause an accident. Then he would change lanes and cause an accident. Then he would slow down, and it would be calm. He laughed as he imagined what they might be saying as they tried to make sense of the whole thing. Looking back, he could see great pillars of black smoke on the bridge and the choppers circling, looking for any sign of cause.

Stevin then decided to go for broke. Both hands clutching the wheel, he dropped the hammer. The old car hesitated for a second. Stevin feared she would die the same sudden death as those in his wake, but then she mustered a stroke of power that happily surprised him and caused him to squeal in boyish glee. Off he went in this lane and that, roaring past unsuspecting motorists in a great asphalt surf session. It was a surprising fete for an old car to go from 55 MPH to 85 MPH and keep it there even as the road elevated over the shipping channel, but Mercedes motors are known for torque, even if this one was just 2.8 liters. The result was brutal, because his surge caused such a big scene, like he was running from a wall of St. Helens ash or was a terrorist with a trunk full of explosives (because, you know, terrorists always seem to prefer old Mercedes). Actually, he *was* a terrorist, except instead of explosives he had three pieces of printer paper and a few feet of tape, which everyone looked at and most people read.

He kept the pedal to the metal clear through the run out at the end of the bridge, took the first exit, and as soon as he was going slowly enough, put the roof down. He turned right and ducked into an industrial park. He could hear sirens in all directions and jokingly said to himself, *I wonder what's going on? Let's go find out.*

Climbing out of the car, he walked up the overpass on Foster City Boulevard. At the top, he looked east. He stood in amazement, as he could see clearly the western slope of the bridge as it found land. Vehicles were scattered everywhere in the westbound lane, as well as several in the eastbound lane, from the top of the bridge to where he was standing approximately a quarter-mile from the water. It appeared like a squadron of Warthogs had strafed the bridge, or as if 200 cars were playing red light-green light and green light actually meant 't-bone your neighbor'. Stevin was in shock. He knew while he was driving and looking in the mirror there was great calamity, but one doesn't fully take in a scene like this unless surveying it on one's own feet while hearing the intense noise in one's own ears and seeing the black smoke in one's own eyes. Even for Stevin, who had caused it, the scene was overwhelming.

He stood on the overpass, deep in thought. Rescue vehicles raced beneath his feet and cars started to slow behind him on the overpass, some stopping to see the cause of the smoke. Within a few minutes, all cars on surrounding surface streets had slowed due to ensuing gridlock. He again pondered the events of the last couple of days and regretted that with every random act of violence, his wake of destruction continued to get wider and deeper.

Why couldn't they have just given me the money? he reasoned. But he knew that this was all him. Not the Chief. Not the police. They say money is the root of all evil; it certainly was in this case. For one man's greed, many gave their lives on this day.

Unnoticed by Stevin, a black sedan had pulled up behind him and stopped, engine idling. It looked like an ordinary four-door sedan from a distance. Okay, it was German-made, so maybe a little nicer than your standard four-doors-and-four-wheels, $199-per-month, nothing-down people-mover. If you knew cars, you might have noticed the carbon ceramic brakes and the burly gurgle of an upgraded exhaust, aside from the obvious oversized wheels and low-profile tires. It was black with dark-tinted windows. The driver feathered the throttle a little, which cut loose a vicious growl, catching Stevin's attention. He turned to look and didn't quite know what to make of it. It certainly wasn't an unmarked police car, and he had no idea why it had stopped just behind him. Just as Stevin was about to turn back around, the window cracked a few inches and a black-gloved hand offered a business card. Stevin was again clueless, but curious nonetheless. He leaned forward to see inside, but as he did, he heard the driver simply say, "In case you need a ride...old man." Then the window rolled up, leaving the card stuck outside of the car. The car then began to roll, and Stevin reached for the card, grabbing it just before it got away. He watched as the car headed down the street and slipped through traffic. Stevin was impressed by how effortlessly it drove away despite the commotion. He looked down at the card, which simply had a phone number.

Well, that was really weird, Stevin contemplated.

The fact that the driver said "old man" spooked Stevin, like he knew who Stevin was and what he had just done. Stevin put his head down and moved slowly back to his car. He actually wanted to run, because he felt like he was being watched, but he used caution and continued with the "ol' timer" shtick.

Once in the car, he fired it up, top down, and worked his way north to the 101 using 3rd Avenue, noticing the vivid beauty of windsurf sails slicing back and forth in the bay from the Point. Once on the freeway, he kept a low profile all the way back to the city, driving slower than usual. He thought he was done for the day and actually forgot about the papers on the convertible roof. That was, until he was back in his old neighborhood en route to his new house.

As he made his way up Divisidero, his slow, methodical driving finally caused a guy in a yellow Camaro stuck behind him to tilt. The driver just couldn't take anymore driving red light to red light at 30 MPH and decided to try and persuade Stevin to just let him pass by flashing his bright lights and honking. At one light, he even rolled down his window and began yelling, to which Stevin responded by rolling down his window and hanging out a regal bird. This obviously made the guy irate—so irate, in fact, that he got a little too aggressive at tailgating and actually bumped the Benz's bumper. Stevin's calm demeanor changed, much like the Hulk's when you make him angry. At the next light, Stevin had had enough. As soon as his car came to a stop, he raised the roof. For all of you clubbing types, this meant that he literally raised the roof, or, in other words, pulled the convertible roof closed—but not for long. Just as the edge of the roof hit the top of the windshield, he put it back down. When the light turned green, he pulled away to the sound of many horns honking—this time not at him, but at a yellow Camaro that had mysteriously stalled at the light. So much for being in a hurry behind a mass murderer.

When Stevin got within a few blocks of the house, he found a space on the street and parked the car there. He wanted to walk the rest of the way in order to scope out the situation at the house to see if he had been made. All seemed quiet, so he went back to the car, drove home, and parked in the garage. Inside, he was eager to turn on the TV, and it didn't take long to find what he was looking for. It seemed to be on all channels—news coverage of what the media was calling Bridges of Death. He had seen glimpses of what had happened while there, but it wasn't until he saw footage from the news helicopters that he really understood what he had done. Hundreds of cars where involved, and even more people. The news had already begun running stories of people and families who were affected: mothers, brothers, children. Family members were being interviewed. Wives wept. Beyond the human aspect of the scene, what caught Stevin's attention most were the National Guard Humvees posted at the bridges. Apparently, bridges are prime targets for terrorists, and to Stevin's surprise and disappointment, the initial news reports suggested this was an act of terrorism by radical Islamists. He began to realize that he had taken it a little too far. A few fatalities in the park probably would have gotten the Chief's attention. Now the entire nation was reeling from a massive attack, and ironically, Stevin and his seventeen victims in the morgue were yesterday's news.

Stevin wondered how he would take responsibility for the event without taking responsibility for the event. Then he realized that maybe it wasn't so bad to have a bit of freedom and be out of the limelight. With time, the investigation would certainly determine that heart attacks had caused it all, but it would likely take a few days to really pin that down. There were many heart attacks, but there were also many collateral deaths from car crashes and drownings, as it turned out, so it probably wasn't going to be clear at first.

He turned off the TV, and then all was quiet in the house. The silence was awkward and unnerving. For the first time in several days, Stevin had absolutely nothing to do and nowhere to go. He contemplated how long he might be able to stay in the house, and he guessed that it would be quite a while unless someone called the phone or came to the door. So far, no calls had come in, and he'd been out all day, so no telling if someone had stopped by.

One thing he did know was that he was hungry, so armed with a few hundred in cash, several credit cards, and the Luger, he decided on Italian. One of the beauties of living in a big city is the ability to walk to many of life's necessities, which is what Stevin decided to do. Again, he walked slowly, with a little hitch to play the part, and it didn't take long to find a small Italian restaurant on Fillmore. He sat by himself and ordered lasagna. It was lonely, even though the restaurant was full. He hated playing "old man" when he'd rather be checking out the talent in the place. His waitress came by to see how he was doing. She was very cute. Probably too young for Stevin even without the costume, but he was enamored nonetheless.

"I'd be doing a lot better if you were sitting with me," he said without thinking.

The waitress giggled.

"Oh, you're so cute!" she said as she put her hand on his shoulder.

Stevin watched as she moved on to the next table. He realized he could get away with a lot more as an "old guy" than as his real self.

After he finished, she brought the check. Stevin figured now was as good a time as any to try the credit card, so he put one in the black receipt holder and waited for the waitress to come back, hoping there would be no issues. When the waitress came back, she had a bit of a bewildered look on her face.

Holding the card in her hand, she inquired, "Francis?"

Stevin, being a quick wit, replied, "Just call me Frank. Francis was my father."

"Oh, I thought it was a woman's name," the waitress responded.

"Now you're bringing back memories of high school. It's actually both," Stevin replied.

"Oh, I'm so sorry," the waitress responded with an embarrassed laugh.

As Stevin signed the receipt, he pushed his luck. "Maybe you can make it up to me with a kiss on the cheek?"

The waitress was timid at first, but then looked both ways and quickly gave him a kiss and scurried in the back. Stevin smiled, not so much that a cute girl had just kissed his cheek, but that he was learning how to step over boundaries with his new self.

Full and satisfied, he headed home for the night—at least he thought for the night. Not three minutes after arriving back home, the doorbell rang. In his mind he saw a SWAT team with a battering ram on the front porch. Slowly turning around to look at the front door, he found no flashing lights outside, and no one was barking at him from a megaphone, so maybe it wasn't the police. He moved cautiously to the door and looked through the peephole. He saw a middle-aged couple outside, speaking with each other. He turned on the porch light and answered the door, not thinking what he might say or how he might explain Francis' absence.

"Hello," the woman said cautiously. "Is Francis home?"

"No. She's actually in Tallahassee," Stevin said without thinking, actually surprising himself. He wondered why he chose Tallahassee, of all places.

"Oh...Tallahassee?" the woman inquired.

"I'm her cousin, Frank. We've switched houses for the month. She wanted a little sunshine, and I wanted a little fog," Stevin said with a believable laugh.

"Oh, wonderful! I'm so happy for her to travel. We wanted to check on her with all that is happening. We live next door. I'm Laura and this is Alejandro," she said, pointing to the man.

"How are you?" Alejandro said, extending his hand.

Stevin paused, and then answered by saying "Mooey beeann!" in the worst Spanish he could muster. All laughed.

"It's nice to meet you both. Thank you for stopping by," Stevin offered, trying to send them on their way.

"Well, we hope to see you again soon, Frank," Laura said. "In fact, a few of us neighbors are having a little get-together tomorrow night at our house—the one just here to the right. We'd love to have you over and get to know you better. Can you stop by? You wouldn't have to stay long, if you didn't want to. But since you're here for a month, you should know who your neighbors are."

The gears in Stevin's head turned. He knew once he closed the door, he really had nothing to do. These two were obviously buying his story and his outfit. He wondered if the other neighbors would too. Then he figured that if things went bad, he could just figure out a little game where everyone reads a fun, three-word phrase.

"Well, why the hell not? Maybe I'll find a wife!" Stevin replied loudly with a wink. This caused the couple to laugh hysterically.

As they walked away laughing, Laura called out, "See you around 6:30."

"6:30?" Stevin questioned, furthering the joke. "That's my bedtime!"

This caused the couple to laugh even more, and Laura to stumble.

"Well, then," Stevin said to himself as he closed the door. "New home, new car, and new friends. This could get interesting."

CHAPTER 11

THE BIG BALANCE

The next morning, over a stack of hotcakes and thick cuts of bacon, Stevin decided that he needed to do two things. The first was find money someplace other than from the police. With the way the events of the previous day had played out, the hunt for Stevin McDonald became somewhat "back burner," and he wanted it to stay that way as long as possible. The second was that he needed a better disguise—an old suit and hat just weren't going to cut it at a neighborhood party. Perhaps he could orchestrate a bit of reverse Benjamin Button and somehow get younger and more like his real self in a very short period of time. Nonetheless, these minor details were trivial without first finding more operating money, so that was paramount.

After finishing his breakfast, he decided to take inventory again of the credit cards he had found. He was not able to find any checks or checkbooks, so he was going to have to figure out how to survive with the three credit cards and what he had left in cash. He looked at the credit cards. He hated the idea of using them, because they were so easy to track. He reasoned that the SWAT team would probably storm the house long before anyone tracked the cards, but the idea still didn't sit well with him. He wondered what their balances might be and how much runway he had, which led him back to the computer.

Within a few minutes, he found bookmarks for two of the cards and, using the magic Post-it with its series of passwords, was able to log in to each of the accounts. Both had $0 balances, and together had $55,000 of purchasing power. Stevin's eyebrows rose and a little smile cracked. He could work with that. It was a start, but he knew without some sort of identification, he wouldn't be able to buy much in person—maybe some smaller items and groceries. The third credit card was a little different. It read *Morgan Stanley*. Finding the link to this card on the computer was a little more challenging; the bookmark was labeled "Investments," but the password was readily available on the Post-it. When the page loaded, the balance read $5,622,310.45. He sat back in the chair, stunned. Excitement turned to worry as he wondered how he might access the funds. Almost $5.7 million at his fingertips, but all very restricted...*unless*. Unless he could mastermind a way to somehow shuffle it all online. He was so excited about it that he almost forgot about the upcoming neighborhood party and his plans of either a transformation or a better disguise.

"I've got to figure this out later," he said, now standing with his hands trembling from excitement. He almost didn't want to log out for fear of never being able to get back in.

He sat back down and navigated to Amazon. This was really his only hope. He'd have to find what he needed here and pray they could do same-day delivery. A grey wig and glasses and a bolo tie would be nice. Maybe a decent mustache too. He could probably pull that off without anyone noticing he didn't have one yesterday.

He mostly found what he was looking for, except for the wig. No wigs on Amazon could get there in time. Maybe he could just wear a hat. But the homburg was too big and clumsy for an intimate neighbor setting. Maybe he would just miss the party and claim he had diarrhea or hemorrhoids. You know how older folks love to tell of their illnesses with no discretion. Certainly, the neighbors would understand. Then an idea hit him. He remembered that up in the closet was a much smaller hat that would work. He also remembered a funny hat a friend once wore which had pieces of hair sewn around the back, so that when you put it on, it looked like you had hair...or longer hair.

Stevin jumped up and ran into the kitchen. Grabbing the scissors and chopping them in the air, he exclaimed, "Time for a haircut, dear!" Then he headed out to the solarium.

No one should ever disrespect the dead. Just being in the presence of a body would creep most people out, let alone cutting their hair. Stevin entered cautiously. The sun shone brilliantly through the windows and lit the many plants in the room. It was actually quite peaceful there, and it surprised him how much just entering the room impacted him. He paused at the door and took it in. Francis was in the chair, hunched to one side as if in thought. Stevin's irreverent tone evaporated, and his heart was backfilled with solemnity. He sat down on the floor next to Francis and gazed out the windows into the garden.

"I never wanted this to happen. It just got out of control and before I knew it, I was in too deep," he reasoned, speaking to Francis. "Isn't it funny how life throws you curves? A few days ago, I was somewhat happily married and working to get my life back together. Now I've thrown my life in the dumpster and lit the whole thing on fire. Boom! Gone!"

Stevin was quiet in thought for a few minutes, and then he

continued, "Do you think God exists?

Yes. He does.

"I guess you know, now being there...wherever there is. I wish you could tell me what it's like."

Oh, it's beautiful!

"Someone once told me that grapes are bigger in heaven. I wonder if that is true."

No. They are the same but taste much sweeter.

"I guess I'll never know, because surely there is no forgiveness for someone like me, who has done so much bad."

There is always forgiveness, my dear.

"Maybe I could plead ignorance or insanity!" he said, knocking the back of his hand against the chair as one does when cracking a joke. He laughed a little at first, but then it trailed off and he put his head down. "You know. I once had an uncle who was the religious type. He told me that even the worst of sinners can be forgiven...if they change."

Yes. He was very right.

"Imagine that. I don't know; if I were God, if I could do such a thing, I would probably take all the murderers and rapists and assholes and just fry their souls with thunderbolts from my fingertips or something. Maybe it's like a hotel, and the really good people get the penthouse, the nice people are on floors five through ten, the not-so nice people are on floors one to four, and the devils like me are in the basement with the boiler."

Stevin looked down at the scissors in his hand and realized he had lost all interest in cutting Francis' hair to make his hat.

He continued, "I guess life threw you a curve, too. One minute you're at home minding your own business, and the next, the doorbell rings and you read a stupid piece of paper and your heart stops. Ain't that just tragic? Maybe I should just read the paper and put an end to this whole thing. It certainly would be easy. But then there's the nearly six million you have in the bank. Wouldn't it be a shame to not have a little more fun? Speaking of fun, how about that towel you left for me in the bathroom? I've got to give it to you. If there was ever a way to get revenge on the guy who killed you, that would be it. Shit...literally, shit! Wow, I can't even—"

Stevin stopped talking. Not because he didn't have more to say, but because he couldn't speak. The thought of the towel, the smeared gooey feces on his face, the smell of it, produced a visceral reaction. The acrid odor had lodged itself in his mind, and any thought of the event brought the horror back to his nose and mouth. And with the smell came the gagging and uncontrollable sweating. He jumped up to walk it off, leaving the room.

Mustering a few words, he yelled back, "Fran, honey. I think it's time you got some fresh air. Tonight let's take a one-way trip to the garden, shall we?"

I'm with my honey now. You'll have to go alone.

After something cold to drink, Stevin was able to compose himself and decided to get back to work on freeing up some working capital. He logged back into the investment account and was thrilled when it opened—much like the same anxiety one has when opening college-application responses or letters from the I.R.S. He spent a fair amount of time examining each and every link on the page. Most of the assets were held in stocks, mutual funds, and bonds, but there was a cash account with just over $700,000 in it. Stevin assumed that these funds were available by using the card. He found all sorts of things he could do online—buy, sell, transfer, et cetera. He thought that it would be fun to try a sell order and see if he could grow his cash fund, so he decided to sell $25,000 worth of stock. The order was placed, but the cash balance did not increase...at least not yet. What did happen was that the phone rang. On the screen, Stevin saw the words *Morgan Stanley.*

"Oops!" he said, pushing himself away from the computer. There was no way he could answer, so he let it go to voicemail. Once the message was saved, he played it back.

"Mrs. Dunfey. How are you today? This is Jack at Morgan Stanley. I got a notice that you want to sell seven hundred shares of Intel. That's not a problem, although I wouldn't recommend it at this time. If that is not the case, please call me back immediately. I will be executing the trade in the next fifteen minutes. Thank you."

"Blow me, Jack!" Stevin yelled, as he held the phone close to his mouth, taking on a Happy-Gilmore-versus-Bob-Barker arrogance. "Just make the trade, Jack!" Then he laughed at himself. Any residue of the towel incident was now gone, but it reserved the right to come back at any time with no warning.

Stevin put down the phone and headed into the kitchen for more to eat. The food stock was getting a little thin, so he slid back to the computer and placed an order on Amazon Fresh using one of the credit cards, and then settled into a sandwich using the last of the turkey in the fridge.

Isn't it amazing how the computer has changed the world? From your own home, you can order just about anything to be dropped on your doorstep the next day; do your banking; keep in touch with a thousand friends; and sell someone else's stock. Actually, it's more than just the computer. Really, it's the internet. The internet has revolutionized life as we know it. No telling what wonders will come in the next ten years. For Stevin, he was more worried about the next two hours because he had a party to go to and nothing to wear. It was about time for the Amazon godmother to transform him from a guy with some ratchet old clothes to a svelte Southern gentleman.

He walked to the front door and checked the peephole. Nothing stirring on the street, but he still needed to be cautious. He didn't want to be seen by anyone who he couldn't give some sort of explanation to. Opening the door, he surprisingly beheld a large man bending down and dropping off boxes. It wasn't so much seeing an unexpected man that caused him to quickly shut the door, or the fact that he didn't want to be seen. It was the man's burly plumber's crack. Such hairy sights conjure no reference to easy dialogue, so it was just better to close the door and let him go with no words exchanged.

Upon hearing the door rattle, the man turned to say hello, but found the door closed and then lumbered back to his truck and left. Stevin watched again through the peephole, and then grabbed the delivery once the man left. In the boxes, he found his ordered items and was thrilled to see that they were better than expected. Within minutes the doorbell rang *again* with his food order, but this time he didn't open it until the driver left.

Now Stevin had his disguise, he had food, and he had quick access to nearly one million dollars. More importantly, he had a little time to relax and regroup. Maybe not long, but at least enough time to consider whether or not he would continue his attempt to strongarm the authorities for money, or just try and slip away with as much freed-up investment funds as possible.

Stevin hustled upstairs with his new accessories and began getting dressed. He took a little time in the closet, doing his best to find the nicest suit, erring on a modern style as much as possible. He found a belt and socks, a watch, and a decent shirt. Then he saw his pièce de résistance—a brilliant pair of black Lucchese cowboy boots in glorious mint condition.

"Oh, hell yeah!" Stevin shrieked. With a little effort, which is normal with boots, his foot slid into the world-renowned Luccheses and found a perfect fit. Nothing like a nice pair of Lucchese boots to boost your confidence, especially in San Francisco, where you might be the only person with a pair!

After putting himself together, he surveyed his work in the mirror. It wasn't Hollywood standard by any means, but it would do in a pinch. Plus, people have no problem overlooking flaws of the elderly. A hole here, a rip there, mismatched socks, an untucked shirt, or unruly hair is all of no concern. Although getting old is not necessarily fun, it does have its perks, and not worrying about impressing others is certainly one of them. After brushing his teeth, he made his way to the neighbor's with a bottle of wine in hand.

The house next door was a little shabbier than the Dunfey residence. The window trim showed weathering and the yard was unkempt. Nonetheless, surely some 20-year-old software wizard would pay $3,000,000 for it, if it were ever sold. Stevin could hear voices inside as he approached the door, his boots solidly striking the brick walk. He pushed the doorbell, took a deep breath, and thought of six million dollars. This rigorously boosted his confidence.

"Well, hello!" Laura said with a grand smile, opening the door.

"Howdy!"

"Here he is, everyone," Laura said, turning to the crowd huddled in the kitchen. "Everyone is excited to meet you. Come on in...and thank you for the wine!"

Stevin handed Laura the bottle and walked straight toward the crowd. He figured if he was going to send it, he was going to do it with guns blazing. There were about ten people in the kitchen sipping white wine and nibbling on cheese and crackers. Most looked to be around his age...his *real* age, so as an elderly gentleman he was definitely the oldest.

"Hello, everyone!" he said, breaking the ice. "Thanks for letting an old codger like me parachute in on your party."

Everyone started to excuse his insinuation of being a burden, but then Stevin spoke over them loudly.

"Alejandro, you ol' coyote!" he said, recognizing him from the day before. "Has *la migra* caught up with you yet?" he continued with a bold laugh. Alejandro snickered for a minute and then his attempt to play along and be cool faded.

"Somebody pour me a drink. I feel like I'm at my own funeral!" Stevin joked, shaking off the nerves.

After he settled in a little, he realized that he may have played his entrance a little too boldly: something like Al Czervik walking into Bushwood. Finding cover with his drink, he sat at a barstool and immediately noticed one of the other men approaching him.

"Hi, Frank. My name is Burt Shields," the guy said, extending his hand.

"Burt. Pleasure."

"So, you survived the terrorist attack, I see," Burt said, breaking the ice.

"And 'Nam!" Stevin responded jokingly, not realizing exactly what Burt was saying.

"What a terrible thing, right? I saw on the news that a minivan full of kids plunged into the Bay and they had to send divers down to unbuckle the bodies from the car seats. Just so sad. Whoever would do such a thing?" Burt asked rhetorically.

Stevin could feel the sweat bead on his forehead and his body temperature rise. He foolishly hadn't planned on this topic at the party. He was more prepared for talk of business, golf, and this year's vintage from Sonoma County. The last thing he wanted was to talk about the events of yesterday, but this, ironically, was to be the topic for just about the entire time he was there.

Stevin mustered a response to Burt. "Yeah. Terrible. Boy, I'd like to shoot the balls off the asshole who did that!"

"Exactly!" Burt responded. "Well, they'll get him eventually. I hear they are starting to think it's related to the seventeen people who died along the Embarcadero. Damn, there are some crazy people in the world today!" After a moment of reflection, he continued,

"The good news is that with all the excitement, my daughter's case has been put on hold."

"Oh, yeah? What did she get into?" Stevin inquired. "Runnin' guns, booze...exotic reptiles?" he joked.

"No," Burt responded with a smile. "Just a little trouble with a fake ID."

"Was she trying to change her name to Brooke?" Stevin quipped, continuing his irreverent humor.

"Funny," Burt responded, a little perturbed. "Her name is Amy. She was just trying to get into a club, apparently. Her friend got caught and the officer bluffed my daughter into admitting hers was fake as well. He told me later that her ID was perfect; even withstood his blacklight test. Kids...it's always something."

The mention of a fake ID sent the gears in Stevin's head spinning and he zoned out for a moment. He realized that with an ID in the name of Francis Dunfey, he could basically start anew. He could travel, at least domestically; he could access more of the investment funds; and it would help him stay incognito for much longer than running around in, say, firefighter's gear or a leisure suit. Suddenly his mind was washed with visions of tanned waitresses serving him cocktails poolside and misting him as he blistered in the sun, but then he snapped back to the conversation.

"Hey, Burt. I'd like to shave a few years off my age. You know, with the ladies and such," Stevin joked as he nudged Burt with his elbow. "Do you have the name of the guy who made her the ID?"

Burt paused and gave Stevin an inquiring look. Stevin, realizing that he may have crossed the line and, not wanting anyone questioning his motivation, immediately changed course.

"Ha! Had you there, friend!" he ribbed.

After a few more pleasantries with Burt and a few more short conversations with others in the room, Stevin could think of nothing else but getting the heck out of there. He was afraid he was going to blow his cover, and also found himself staring more and more at one of the blonde ladies wearing a tight dress that was entirely too short for a woman of her age. Luckily, she had not picked up on his attention, but the last thing he wanted was trouble with his neighbors, even if it meant he had to fly solo for tonight. Besides, he would have to break character to even have a chance, which wasn't going to happen—but that didn't stop the blood from rushing.

"Well, it's time for this ol' cowboy to mosey on back to the ranch," Stevin said as he stood and adjusted himself, not wanting a Ron Burgundy moment in his polyester pants.

The group bid him farewell and promised to visit in the next couple of days. As Stevin closed the door, he paused to see if he could hear them talking. Almost immediately, he could hear Burt speaking prominently, and was able to make out the words "old saddlebag" and "lazy moustache," which caused him to check and make sure the thing was still there. Muted laughter erupted from inside.

Whatever! Stevin said to himself as he headed home to move Fran into the yard. *I can do whatever the hell I want, and they'll love me for it. Why? Because I've got a huge bank account and I'm wearing sweet-ass boots!*

CHAPTER 12

SANTA BARBARA

"Santa Barbara!" Stevin declared reluctantly. "Oh, crap!"

Stevin leaned back in his chair at the computer and wondered how he was going to pull this off—a road trip to Santa Barbara in an old Mercedes, and as one of the most wanted men in the country. As he thought about it, though, he grew to realize that maybe it wasn't going to be so bad. He certainly did not want to troll Craigslist to find someone to make him a fake ID, and maybe it would be nice to get out of town. He looked back at the screen to study his target.

Amy Shields, he read from her Facebook account. *From San Francisco, student at UCSB, worked at Unique Tan.* Tanning? *Perfect,* he thought, *guess I'll have to come up with a new disguise. Or, maybe I'll rock a g-string with my new boots. That oughtta get her attention! We'll find out tomorrow, won't we, dear?* Her resemblance to her father left no doubt that this was Burt's daughter.

Stevin started laughing hysterically, which felt really good. He hadn't had a good laugh in a long, long time. Maybe it was because he was on the run. Maybe it was because he had a little subconscious guilt about what he had done. Maybe it was because he'd lost Alexes and Taylor. Whatever the reason for his drought of happiness, he found himself laughing harder at himself laughing than laughing at his ridiculous comment—like a simple DOS program that loops back and repeats forever and ever. He sat there and just let it out. All of it. The more he thought about himself sitting there, the more he laughed. He started to have trouble breathing, and then came the tears, one after the other, streaming down his cheeks.

"Good hell!" he exclaimed, finally standing to shake off the giggles. "I need to take a walk."

It was late, but he decided to stroll up to the corner market and see if he could get a few munchies for his road trip and give the ATM a whirl with the Morgan Stanley card. He was going to need more cash despite his healthy credit facility, especially when he encountered Ms. Shields and her Deep Throat ID maker. He put his jacket back on and headed out the door.

The market up the street was a typical late-night neon trap with a narrow barred door leading into a den of overpriced items. Stevin looked incredibly out of place. He perused the aisles looking for things he might like along the way. Of course, first and foremost was beef jerky—the go-to staple of any road trip—followed closely by CornNuts.

CornNuts have the amazing ability to never be seen, heard of, thought about, or craved until someone is on a road trip; then they magically appear in your mind and you start to taste that salty goodness, and they lure you out of your soft car seat like little golden sirens of tooth-breaking delight. Maybe it's the smell of gasoline and the excitement of clicking away miles that triggers it. At any rate, when Stevin got to the counter, he had compiled a healthy menu of snacks and drinks, including some random-flavored Mountain Dew, which is another road trip phenomenon. You always see this wacky-flavored stuff in the case, but never have the guts to try it until—yes—you're on a road trip!

After making his purchase with one of the credit cards without a hitch, he swung over to the ATM by the ice freezer. Ever suspicious of ATMs, especially the kind you see plugged into the wall that feel like they are simply a ruse to get your card number and PIN or send a code-red signal to the police, Stevin reluctantly put the card in. He had memorized the PIN from the Post-it note at the house, which was basically the same PIN for just about anything and everything he needed a PIN for. He didn't want to overdo it and ask for something stupid like $5,000, because he knew it would tilt this machine, so he decided to get $300 now and then try for more tomorrow. As the bills slipped out, his grin got wider and wider, like a winner at a 20-dollar slot machine.

With food and cash in hand, he made his way to the door, but noticed the attendant watching the news, so he stopped for a moment. The screen showed yesterday's bridges jammed with cars and smoke and then a reporter interviewing terrified people. After a moment, it switched back to the anchor at the studio, who spoke for a minute or so. Stevin couldn't quite make out the words, but then the screen lit up with a picture. His picture! He immediately put his head down, found his limp again, and scurried out the door. His little reprieve was apparently over, and he needed to fly south as soon as possible, which meant that his plan to leave in the morning now meant 12:30 a.m. instead of 9:30 a.m.

Heading back to the house, he stopped about a block away to see if there was any activity down the street. It was quiet as a church. He decided, just to be safe, to slip in through the back, so he made his way home scooting from shadow to shadow.

Once in the house, he began packing. He didn't feel like this time he would be coming back, so he grabbed as much as he could, including the Luger, and jammed it in a large purple suitcase that he found in the master closet. He loaded the car and was just about to start it up when an idea popped into his mind. He had been thinking and worrying about driving all the way to Santa Barbara without getting pulled over, and he remembered coming face-to-face with the police at Old Man Bornstein's house and what he'd done to avoid them. He smirked at the irony that his current alias was "Frank," the same name as the very deeply sleeping dog he'd had at the time. This triggered an idea that would be much easier than digging a hole in the backyard, and it wasn't long before Frank was on his way south for a little R&R with his soulmate, Francis, sleeping soundly in the passenger's seat.

Stevin made his way down Van Ness. The streets were surprisingly active at this time of night. Even the bums had yet to retire, shuffling along the streets. At California, he was surprised to see the taillights of what was probably the last trolley headed east. He rambled onward, making the most of the stoplights, and before long, he was near the onramp to the 101. Francis was quiet and peaceful. In fact, the only thing out of place was the occasional waft of putrid air that Stevin couldn't quite zero in on because he had never encountered it before. He did have the windows down, so maybe it was sewer fumes rising from the access holes in the manhole covers. Maybe it really was time to offload the old ball and chain, but rather than traveling alone, Stevin felt safer with her in the car. This was especially true about an hour later.

Unlike his departure in the city, the highway south in Palo Alto was mostly vacant at 2:00 a.m. Stevin felt like he could really drop the hammer, but he hesitated, because he was tired and the car was old. He didn't want any issues, and he needed to get to Santa Barbara and find cover as soon as possible. But despite his cautious demeanor at the wheel, a tire still managed to blow.

"Crap!" Stevin exclaimed as the rear end dropped and the car slowed. He knew just what had happened.

I am so tired of just getting by, he mumbled to himself. *As soon as I can, I'm getting a new car...and not just new to me. A new car, complete with new-car smell, random stickers that don't come off, and free fucking XM Radio! Do you hear me, Francis?*

Yes. I still hear you, but you need to focus on what's important in life, dear.

Stevin pulled off the freeway and commenced the work of repair, which wasn't pleasant because it was the back left tire. Changing it required him to hang his ass in truck traffic, like John Stockton boxing out Shaq moving at 70 MPH. Then his luck worsened. Red-and-blue lights flashed from a few hundred yards up the freeway and a highway patrol car swerved in behind him. Stevin felt the sweat bead on his forehead, but he had a plan. In fact, this was the exact situation that he had hedged against by inviting Francis to come along. After a while, the officer climbed out of the car and walked up with his flashlight.

"Everything okay?" he inquired.

"As long as we don't wake up the missus, you and I are going to be just fine!" Stevin blurted, trying to talk over the nerves.

The officer flashed his light through the hazy plastic window of the convertible and could make out someone sleeping in the passenger seat.

"Oh, right!" he said as he took off his baton and squatted down to muscle the lug nuts. "Let me give you a hand and get you on your way."

Stevin stepped back, never intending for this to happen. Not only would the officer not recognize the most wanted man in the state—and probably the country—but he would actually change his tire for him. Still, there was risk. Stevin kept close to the baton on the ground in case he needed to bludgeon and bail. He thought of doing it anyway, but he decided that this game of cat and mouse was more fun. He got such a thrill from being so close to his enemy, yet undetected, and he remembered that he had heard somewhere that one of the highest acts of bravery among Indians was to touch your enemy and escape.

Stevin looked down at the officer making short work of the tire change.

"Oh, what the hell?" Stevin whispered rhetorically to himself as he timidly put his hand on the officer's shoulder.

"Thank you, officer. I don't know what we would have done if you had not come along." His hand was shaking due to the nerves, but this seemed to support his disguise.

"No problem, sir. I don't like to see elderly people on the highway this time of night. By the way, why in the world are you driving this late?"

"Our daughter is in a bit of legal trouble in Santa..." Stevin paused, not wanting to tell him where he was headed, and then found a city that worked. "...Cruz. We need to be there early in the morning for a meeting."

"Well, careful down 17. They don't call it Blood Alley for nothing!"

A few minutes later, the spare was on and Frank and Francis were on their way—but not after Stevin burst out in laughter as he pulled back onto the road. Driving was smooth and uneventful from there on out, except for periods of drowsiness, which Stevin combatted by singing, eating CornNuts, and playing brisk games of pocket pool— nothing like a little dopamine and adrenaline to wake you up!

Francis even pitched in by really starting to stink. Sometimes it wafted over and shocked Stevin so bad that he had to roll down the windows and stick his head out in the wind, Ace Ventura style, which was a little peculiar on a freeway at that time of night. It was all he could do to combat the quiet lull of the endless passing lights of the freeway, which came slowly but passed in a steady blur.

When dawn broke, the happy couple were just south of Carmel, the gateway to Big Sur—California's rugged cousin to Hawaii's Nā Pali Coast. The stoked fire of the morning sun raged in the mountains to the east, and eventually broke free of the peaks and rushed against the wall of cool morning mist on the water. By Bixby Creek Bridge, the wall of fog had all but crumbled, leaving nothing but the blue brilliance of sea below.

Stevin had never been to Big Sur. But that morning, Big Sur made a big impression on him. As he drove onto the bridge and over the gorge, he felt as if he had been washed clean, like he was seeing with new eyes, like a young bird leaving the nest. A new day meant a new him. Did he want to kill again? No. Did he need to kill again? No. Everything felt fresh and new...that was, until Francis gurgled.

Most people ignore gurgles, unless you're a kid. In that case, they are just about the funniest sound you've ever heard. But this gurgle was actually very startling, because it was coming from a dead person. One could only assume that her insides where being cored out by decomposition, which would explain the smell, too. This was all very off-putting in this moment, and Stevin's demeanor changed instantly from a pure angel of white floating over the clouds to a no-bullshit garbage man at the end of an eight-hour shift. Stevin slammed on the brakes, exclaiming "You're out, f'er!"

The old car shuttered for a full 80 or so feet until coming to rest, and by some miracle, the donut spare held up. It just so happened that at exactly the moment that Francis gurgled and Stevin went from Jekyll to Hyde, they happened to be directly in the center of the bridge.

Without hesitating, Stevin got out, walked around the front of the car, opened the passenger door, grabbed Francis by the armpits, and heaved her over the rail like a bullfighter tosses his cape to his side to avoid the bull. Stevin leaned over the rail to watch her go. Francis' body cartwheeled toward the canopy of trees below, much like how movies depict people slowly drifting off into deep space. At impact, her body split in half before disappearing in the vegetation.

In disgust, Stevin stepped back from the edge. He wasn't expecting the body to be blown apart by tree limbs. Decomposition was obviously well underway. As he turned to close the door, he noticed a puddle of something on the passenger's seat.

"That woman does not give up!" Stevin fumed, gesturing at the seat. "First, shit in a towel. Now, I don't know what the hell that is!"

He grabbed the towel in the trunk, put a little water on it, and did the best he could to clean it up, then pitched the towel over the rail too. It didn't suffer the same fate as Francis when it hit the trees.

When he got back into the car, he put the top down and grabbed the biggest piece of beef jerky that would fit in his mouth, hoping the strong pepper would chase the smell from his nose. With the sun up, Francis dashed to pieces below, and the top down, what Stevin had in front of him was pure driving bliss. All he needed to make it surreal was a better car and a smoking-hot passenger in a tight white camisole and bright red lipstick.

From Bixby Creek, the Pacific Coast Highway, or PCH, winds its way along the coast to its terminus near Dana Point in the south, or in the tiny town of Leggett to the north. Either way you go, from Big Sur, the highway turns inland at times and also gets wound up with Highway 101 for some of the way, like when it crosses the Golden Gate Bridge. Wherever it might be, nowhere is more famous or well-known than here, where it starts in Big Sur, being carved from enormous seaside cliffs with prison labor.

Stevin clicked away the miles with wind in his hair, enjoying panoramic postcard views at every curve and stopping only for gas and bathroom breaks. By lunch, he had arrived at his destination, near UCSB, and he pulled in at a taco stand across from the tanning salon. He was wiped out from the stress of the party and then driving all night, especially down the PCH, which is a demanding drive for even the most robust of drivers.

He decided to find a place to stay and sleep for a few hours before attempting to contact Amy. But without any form of ID to match the credit cards, and not having been able to stop at an ATM, he wanted to find somewhere cheap and easy—somewhere where the person at the desk wasn't likely to ask many questions. He looked around the area from his seat at lunch and didn't see anything, so he grabbed the phone and did a quick search. There were a lot of options nearby, but none that he could find that fit his parameters, so he filtered the search to one-star motels. Bingo! Using the phone was much more modern than flipping open a phone book to find Navin R. Johnson, but the result was the same. He found his target.

At the motel, Stevin drew the shades and surveyed the room. It wasn't much to look at, and he prayed that there were no bed bugs. Even worse than bodily fluids, nothing sent more shivers up his spine more than the thought of waking up in a pile of bed bugs sucking his blood. He lifted the mattress to look, but he didn't see much in the dim light. At that point, he was almost too tired to care, and he fell into the bed, lifeless. Before he passed out, he thought about his strategy to connect with Amy and his plan to get her to give him the name of her fake ID dealer. He hoped money would talk. That was his only plan, really. He would approach her, throw down a wad of cash, and ask for the name, but he wasn't sure if he would just barge in and do it or if he would play it cool and go through a tanning session first. As he contemplated how this might play out, his eyes closed and his breathing slowed; his body randomly convulsed with a hypnic jerk, and he fell deadly asleep.

CHAPTER 13

WHITE LACE

Press conferences are never fun when things aren't right, especially early morning ones that you set your alarm for but wake up hours before, thinking and stressing about them—much like finals, work meetings, and trials. Such was the case for Chief Brenning. With the Mayor, the FBI, and just about every citizen of the city hanging on his every word, he found himself fielding some very difficult questions.

"Now that the event has been ruled to not involve terrorist ties, what is the police force doing to protect the city?" one reporter asked.

The Chief responded forcefully: "Any tragedy, like the one we endured this week which took so many lives, is definitely terrorism in my book. Terrorism isn't confined to radicals who climb out of caves in the Middle East and bomb civilians. Terrorism can be homegrown, as we feel strongly is the case here."

The Chief pointed to another reporter.

"Chief Brenning, first, exactly how many lives were lost, and, secondly, has any organization claimed responsibility?" she asked.

"Total lost is 123, 52 of whom suffered acute heart attacks very similar to the other fatalities we have from the Embarcadero. The other 71, we believe, were collateral fatalities caused by vehicular accidents, fires, and, in some cases, drownings. In addition, just over 400 other people were injured to varying degrees," the Chief responded and then paused, overcome with emotion at some of the horrors he'd witnessed on the bridge.

Then he continued. "We are faced with a very silent and cunning enemy, and all of our efforts are now aligned with the FBI and other law enforcement agencies across the country to locate and apprehend Stevin McDonald, our number one person of interest. We attempted to apprehend Mr. McDonald in a raid two days ago, but were unsuccessful."

"Chief, Chief, Chief!" a third reporter clamored from the back. "Are you saying that all of this—the bridges...the Embarcadero--may be the work of one man?"

"Yes. We feel strongly that he is responsible," the Chief replied.

With that, the room burst into a frenzy. On everyone's mind was a quick calculation of other attacks by a lone wolf. No one could recollect an event with so many fatalities by a single attacker, even thinking about attacks abroad and back in history. Gunmen might get 10 or 20, and bombers might get 80 if they were lucky. But 123—working alone?

"Listen!" the Chief boomed over the tumult. "Listen. You here in this room have a lot of power at your disposal, and you have a decision to make. Normally people like me give you answers like, 'I'm not at liberty to comment on that.' But today I'd like to try something different. Because the bottom line is, you and I are standing in front of a new face of terrorism. So I'm not going to deflect and stay silent. I'm going to ask you, are you going to do what you normally do and report blood and horror with headlines like 'Mass Killer on the Loose!', which will undoubtedly drive our city into chaos, or are you going to help me and work in harmony with law enforcement to apprehend Stevin McDonald by plastering his picture on every news bulletin, website, and broadcast across the globe? The last thing we need is hysteria in the streets and immortalizing of this murderer. We should not give him what he wants. I've talked to this man on the phone. He knows what he wants, which so far has just been money, and he acts decisively in that pursuit. Knowing what I know, I believe it's very likely he's still here in the city. I would expect him to call with his demands before he terrorizes again. He is waiting for our next move. Let's be unified in letting him know we will not bow down; we will stand unified in demanding justice and peace!"

Several hundred miles south of the press conference, our silent and deadly mastermind was just emerging from a peaceful night's sleep. What Stevin had planned to be a quaint catnap before heading to the tanning salon had turned into a small coma. Now, 20 hours later, he sat up in bed and stayed there, very still, looking around the room. He knew where he was and what he was doing, but something felt *off*. It wasn't until he looked at the clock that he figured it out. A peaceful smile came over his face. Each new day brought a wave of joy over him, and this day, he felt, was going to be a good one.

His plan was to first to get breakfast, which was always nice in Santa Barbara on sunny days like today. Then he would assault a proper ATM and see if he could get $1,000 or so before heading to the tanning salon.

After getting ready, he checked out of the motel, assuming he would be able to get his ID and find something better later on. Either way, this place certainly wasn't going to sell out, so he could always fall back here. He made his way to the shopping center near the tanning salon and found a place to eat. There also happened to be an ATM at a proper bank branch which gave him $1,500. He figured he would keep increasing the amount until he hit the limit, so next time he would try for $3,000.

His seat at breakfast gave him a good view of the tanning salon. He watched people going in and coming out. Most were women, and most of them were blonde. Every now and then, a man showed up. The men seemed to be cut from the same cloth—military haircuts, sunglasses, flip-flops, tank tops, and muscles of suspect origin. Stevin wondered what his best approach would be. Based on the existing clientele, going in as an old man might be awkward. He needed to age in the opposite direction, which was going to require a radical haircut and a bit of shopping. Although he didn't have muscles like the other jocks, it would certainly be easy to copy the rest.

As he walked out of the restaurant, he looked around for a place to get his hair cut. There was nothing in the center where he was, but across the road he spied a monument sign with a simple *Salon* written on it. Perfect!

He found the small salon tucked back in the corner of the center, adorned with typical posters of wild hair from the '90s. A small bell rang on the door as he entered, and a petite Asian girl came whisking out from behind a black sheet that covered the back door. Stevin imagined a small room behind the sheet with a computer on top of a microwave on top of a refrigerator—a typical mom-and-pop break area.

"Can I help you?" the girl asked in perfect English.

"Ah...yes. I'd like to get my hair bleached and cut," Stevin responded.

"Bleached? You want to be blond?" the girl inquired hesitantly.

"Yes," Stevin responded boldly. "I think it would fit better in Santa Barbara. Don't you?"

"Sure. No problem," the girl answered, shrugging her shoulders.

She led Stevin back to a small sink and asked him to sit. Then she proceeded to wash and bleach his hair. This wasn't an easy task. Even at middle age, his hair was thick and sturdy, and was probably his greatest facial asset. Washing it took effort. It soaked up water and shampoo like a sponge and challenged even the strongest fingers to scrub it clean.

Once washed, rinsed, bleached, and toweled, Stevin sat in a chair and admired himself in the mirror. The first thing he noticed was how strikingly dark his new bleached hair made his eyebrows look. He appeared like a cross between Eugene Levy and Glen Plake. He hadn't considered the rest of his face in making the decision to bleach his hair. It was quite obvious now that he was a person of brown complexion with dark hair who had chosen to go blond. But it helped set him apart from the mugshot on TV and the guy everyone was looking for. For the cut, he envisioned some sort of surfer buzz on the sides and back, leaving the top long and wild.

When he was done, he determined that he looked more like a pro wrestler than a surfer, which wasn't so bad considering his plans at the tanning salon. After a quick shopping trip at the discount store across the center for a tank top and flip-flops, he was ready to get baked and bronzed.

The tanning salon seemed quieter now. He decided he would tan first, which would allow him to build some rapport and scope the place out. In his pocket he had a wad of cash, which he hoped to use to bribe the name out of the girl. How he was going to go from a tanning customer to a guy wanting the name of her counterfeiter, he didn't know. He was just going to have to shoot from the hip.

He walked into the salon to find the sparse lobby devoid of any personnel. He could hear people speaking in the back, and determined that some other customer was getting directions, so he decided to have a seat and wait. As he sat, he noticed his heart was beating a little faster than normal, and he realized he was really anxious about this situation. Here he was, a guy who had put a world of hurt on an entire city-even blowing the top three floors off a building and closing down two major bridges—and now he was giddy about asking a twenty-something for a little help.

Maybe it was the fact that she was a girl. Were he here looking for a guy, he would probably just march straight up to him and say something simple like "Hey man, can you hook me up with the name of your fake ID contact?" No introductions would be necessary, and perhaps not even any cash. The low-key bond among men allows for such a no-nonsense, just-get-it-done kind of protocol, whether talking to another man or doing work...like pitching old ladies off bridges.

To talk to women requires calculated planning, surges of anxiety, repetitive practice, ample role-playing, and enough time to analyze and prepare for each and every possible outcome, response, facial expression, hint, suggestion, no-means-yes-or-does-it-mean-maybe-or-maybe-it-means-no possibility, and/or total rejection. Case in point: Stevin had changed his entire hairstyle, gone shopping for new clothes, drained the ATM, and played out the event a hundred times in his mind—all of this, only to find himself in an empty lobby of a lowly tanning salon waiting for someone to walk out and not even knowing if it would be the girl he was looking for.

Despite his incredible preparation, Stevin still didn't know what he was going to say, and this made him especially jumpy. Just then, the noise of sliding metal rings on a curtain bar made him spring out of his seat. He tried to get the words rolling from within, but fear had clamped his lips shut. As he turned to face his captor, he met Jason, which sent the huge weight of Stevin's anxiety sliding off of his shoulders and shattering on the floor.

"Oh, hey man!" Stevin exclaimed, as if he was meeting a long-lost friend.

"Ah. Hello! Can I help you?" Jason answered and scurried behind the counter, fearing an awkward hug was coming from someone who seemed a little off.

"Yes. Yes," Stevin said, settling down a bit. "I would like to sign up for tanning."

"Great! But we only take women," Jason responded jokingly, making Stevin turn pale. Stevin hadn't planned for that scenario and, being caught off guard, failed to remember all of the guys he had seen coming and going just a few hours earlier. "Just kidding, sir," Jason offered when Stevin didn't respond.

"Oh, right! I get you," Stevin said awkwardly, but then collected himself. "Listen, just give me a package of ten and get me set up. I don't have much time today."

"Perfect. I'll have someone come up and show you to the bed," Jason responded.

Turning to the phone, Jason hit the intercom. "Amy, can you come up and show a gentleman to Number Three?"

Stevin's heart began to race again, but at least he knew he could just play it cool, and a simple "Hi" would suffice until he got settled. About a minute later, Miss Amy Shields stepped into the lobby. Just over 5'10" with long, shimmering, nearly black hair and rich brown skin, she was truly a vision. Stevin remembered briefly meeting her mother at the party, and he could now see her mother's Indian ancestry culminating in her daughter's splendor. Amy's short skirt and tight T-shirt helped reveal the intriguing curves of her body, which was thin and well-proportioned. All of this certainly didn't help Stevin focus. Although she was probably half his age, Stevin couldn't help but be a little awestruck. As he followed her to the back, he shot a look at Jason as if to say, *Are you kidding me? If you haven't tried, you're a damned fool!* Jason volleyed with a look of *Get going, you psycho!*

Amy led Stevin down the hall to Room 3. Inside was a simple tanning bed and a chair by the door. The bed was still a bit dirty from the previous client, so Stevin stood at the door and watched as Amy bent over to clean it. He fought the urge to stare and get caught up in fantasy. Besides, this was his buddy Burt's daughter! Sheesh!

Amy turned and inquired, "Do you need goggles?"

Stevin contemplated making some joke about not needing *beer* goggles, but it was too much of a stretch. Not wanting to think too long, he managed a simple "Um...sure." He tried his best just to roll with it and not seem like a rookie tanner, despite his pale skin.

Amy handed him a set of small goggles with black lenses in the middle and no straps, like something a rabbit might use while welding in a Tim Burton movie.

"You're all set! When you're done, just check out with Jason at the front desk," Amy instructed.

Stevin didn't want to let her go, for several reasons—the obvious one being that he needed a name. As she was about to close the door, he made his play.

"Um...before you go, can I confess something?" he asked.

Amy, having faced this sort of scenario many times before with eager men, smiled and answered simply, "I'm involved."

"No, no," Stevin urged. "I need to ask you something."

Amy was intrigued and came back in the room, closed the door, and sat in the chair.

Stevin continued, "I'm not sure how to say this, but I follow the local crime report, and your name came up recently."

Amy's eyes grew wide and then settled into a skeptical squint.

"Listen. I'm not a cop. I'm not a pervert," he said, crossing his fingers. "You're very beautiful, but that's not why I'm here. I'm really just hoping I can convince you to give me the name of your guy. I need a little work done myself, if you know what I mean."

Amy cracked a smile, and Stevin could see that he had a really good shot at pulling this off, but he had no idea just how good of a shot he had.

"Armin Hassan. You can find him at ETHOS tonight. Tell him I sent you, and he'll help you out," Amy offered without any reservation.

Stevin was dumbfounded: So much anxiety for such an easy thing! He wasn't quite sure what ETHOS was, but he was confident he could find it later. Amy got up and opened the door to leave without waiting for a response.

"Wait!" Stevin said, grabbing her hand and sitting in the chair. "I want to thank you. Normally I would press my luck and ask you out, despite the fact that I'm old enough to be your dad. Actually, now that I think about it, let me be your dad for a minute and help you out."

Stevin reached in his pocket and pulled out a wad of twenty-dollar bills.

"Take this," Stevin said, not taking the time to count it out, but he figured it was damn near $1,500. It was nearly three times what he was planning to give her, but she was so pretty, and he really did want to give her a strong thank you for so effortlessly revealing the name. Of course, such generosity is always easier with access to nearly six million of someone else's money in the bank.

Now it was Amy who was dumbfounded. She massaged the bills in her hand, trying to comprehend the amount of money she held. With over seventy twenty-dollar bills, it wasn't easy, but she knew it was a lot.

"Oh, my gosh! Oh, my gosh! You don't know what this means to me!" she squealed.

"Well, I guess that makes two of us who were really lucky today!" Stevin said, feeling very altruistic.

Amy, still ecstatic, looked at Stevin on the chair and then jumped in his lap, straddling him as if starting a certain dance. Stevin leaned back as she sat down. Her short skirt parted, revealing white lace panties, which made a poor effort at coverage. She pressed his head against her chest and said, "Thank you! Thank you! Thank you!", then immediately got up and walked out.

Stevin sat in the chair as a statue, his mouth wide open, his arms hanging to his sides as if to demonstrate his innocence before a firing squad. There was no thought of tanning now, just wishing he could call her back and that he had another $1,500 in his pocket. He breathed heavily and closed his eyes, trying desperately to burn her image in his mind. After a few minutes of mind-etching and realizing that he didn't have much else to do until later, he forced himself to strip down and climb into the bed. He turned the dial. Electric blue light filled the room and glowing warmth covered him. As he donned the goggles and closed the lid, he exclaimed, "In my next life, I'm going to college...for twenty years!" Then all was silent, except for the hum of the bed and the ticking of the timer. Tick, tick, tick...

CHAPTER 14

FIREBALLS AND GHOSTS

ETHOS wasn't hard to find. Such places are famous in college towns when the sun goes down. Once Stevin figured it out, he sighed in frustration. He wasn't a 'shopper' by nature, but he knew more shopping was necessary if he was going to a dance club full of students. Certainly the gear he borrowed from Charles Dunfey wasn't going to work; cowboy boots only work on two-stepping dance floors with plenty of room. If he still had his firefighter gear, that might be a hoot. But, alas, he didn't, so new clothes it would be!

When you think dance clubs you either think a) rapper elite in corner booth with a bottle of Bollinger brut flanked by several seductive ladies, or b) more the rave flavor with packed dance floor, quirky DJ, fog, and stomach-churning light shows. Based on the demographic in the area, Stevin was planning on option b), which actually was a little easier to shop for. A nice shirt, expensive jeans, and shoes should do the trick. He needed it to be a little edgy, so instead of the mall, he would take a drive downtown and see if he could find a few hole-in-the-wall shops to fill the order. ETHOS was down that way anyway, and there was nothing more he needed near campus.

Walking to the car, he remembered that he still had the spare tire on it. This was a minor inconvenience. It still worked fine, but it made him stand out, even more than his new hair and eyebrows. He would have to drain another ATM to get cash to replace the tire, because he wasn't comfortable using the credit or debit cards without proper ID. He would need money for Armin anyway, so once he got downtown he looked for a bank with another proper ATM. He was anxious about trying for $3,000 this time. His personal limit had always been $300, which never seemed to be enough. After finding a bank, he pulled through to the ATM. Inserting the card, he typed in $3,000, but was denied. A wave of fear rolled over him and he wondered if the police had finally tracked him to Francis's house and had frozen the cards. He tried again; this time for $2,000. The machine started to hum, and he could tell that it was counting the cash inside. Always a good sign! A few seconds later, it pushed out the money; this time it was mostly fifties, with about $400 in twenties.

Stevin felt rich. He had never been able to pull thousands of dollars a day from an ATM. In fact, he couldn't even remember the last time he had a thousand dollars that wasn't headed for rent or food or bills. Having money gave him comfort, and the more time he had with it, the more he slipped into his worry-free life in Santa Barbara.

Downtown, he was able to also find a tire shop just prior to closing, and luckily enough, they had a tire in stock. He hadn't considered the possibility that a tire would have to be ordered for this older car. Apparently, the folks in Montecito produce enough demand for classics and exotics that the shops keep them in stock. While the tire was being repaired, Stevin strolled down State Street toward the water. Mature trees flanked each side of the street, hinting at its age, but modern stores with modern storefronts filled the old buildings. Stevin looked up. Through the canopy of the trees, he could see brilliant blue sky, still energized by the warmth of a sleepy sun. Down below in the evening shadows, there was a hint of autumn. The air was still warm, but a slight rustling of leaves and crisp air hinted at a turn in the seasons.

After an hour or so, Stevin had sourced a few new pieces of clothing, including a bold, designer t-shirt that read *Porn is for Pussies*. When he first saw it, he thought it quite an obvious statement, but the more he considered it, the more he grew to love its double entendre. In fact, he loved it so much that he found himself converted to quite the opposite perspective of his first impression, and felt like he could wear it with confidence.

With the car done and some new clothes, he took a break at an inviting café along the street. Downtown was beautiful at night. Golden lamps lit the streets and buildings, and the hustle of cars gave way to the bustle of people moving past him on the sidewalks.

As he sat there, he thought back to San Francisco and how different it was. The last time he was on a street like this in the evening, he was dodging in the shadows and chasing down a poor girl with a bat. Tonight, he soaked in freedom from a vaulted perch, out in the open with a pocket full of cash. An air of mightiness and elegance settled on him, sitting there in his new clothes as he cut his filet mignon and rubbed it through the rich wine sauce. He loved how those passing by observed him alone at his sidewalk table, like the king taking supper while looking down on the rabble, ready to sentence some to the stocks for no reason at all other than they didn't move fast enough. He wondered if he could just stay here forever—just go dark and hope that no one ever asked about Francis Dunfey and that Chief

Brenning found some other villain to harass and that the money never ran out. As he considered how he might unwind history and vector into an alternate future, the waiter interrupted with the check. Stevin looked up and smirked as if to say *Don't trouble the king with such miniscule and banal botherings.* Then he pulled the wad of cash from his jacket pocket, dropped down three crisp fifty-dollar bills without even looking at the check, and motioned his head to say *Be gone with you!* Talk about tall hat and no cattle! Well, he did have six million in the bank...sort of.

Four blocks from the café was ETHOS. From the outside, ETHOS looked like a bomb shelter, or a building that was trying too hard not to be noticed, but inside it was many things: a club, a lounge, a dance floor, an event center. When Stevin got there at 8:00 p.m. sharp, the bouncer looked at him with a bit of confusion, but he let him in without any trouble. What Stevin didn't realize was that the place opened at 8:00 p.m., but no one really showed up until about 10:30.

Inside was absolutely empty except for a middle-aged woman who was preparing one of the rooms for a party. He felt awkward being there, so he quickly settled in a booth and got out the phone, pretending to attend to some important business. Isn't it quite normal these days for people to pull out their phones with just seconds of downtime, like bikers and drivers at stoplights or churchgoers during hymns? Holding a phone is somehow the equivalent of being 'on base' while playing tag, and no one can touch you. Being obviously older than the normal clientele and the only soul in the place, it wasn't long before the woman approached him out of curiosity.

"Are you here with the Sieck party?" she inquired, then paused and smiled while reading the print on his shirt.

"I didn't know Sikhs partied!" Stevin responded quickly with a chuckle. Bada bing! "Actually, I'm looking for someone named Armin. You don't know him by chance, do you?" His eyes stayed fixed on her. Up close, she was much prettier than he'd realized, having only glanced at her when he walked in.

"Yes. Actually, I do. He'll be here around 10:30. I'll have him come by and say hi before he goes on," she offered.

"Goes on?" Stevin asked.

"He's our house DJ. Talented kid. Sometimes *too* talented, if you ask me. It's a miracle he's not in jail for hacking Taylor Swift's cell phone or something," she answered and started to walk away.

"Thank you, Miss...?" Stevin responded, fishing for her name.

"My name is Catherine Little. I'm the manager of ETHOS," she responded politely with a smile, and offered her hand. "What is your name, Mister...?" she asked a bit smugly, with extra emphasis on "Mister" to let him know she recognized his obvious lure.

"Dunfey. Francis Dunfey—but call me Frank. Francis makes me feel 85 and female!" Stevin joked. Both giggled and stared in each other's eyes as they shook hands for a little too long.

Stevin hadn't felt his heart flutter this way about someone since Taylor had opened the door in her pajamas, and it was much more than the surge of dopamine he'd experienced earlier with Ms. Shields. His budding feelings and attraction to Catherine were genuine. She was very near his age, as best as he could tell, and was very intriguing. He sensed that she was feeling the same about him—bleached hair, eyebrows, and all.

"Okay, Frank. Nice to meet you," Catherine acknowledged with a little flair in her voice.

Not wanting to let her go just yet, Stevin invited her to sit with him a while. Catherine was hesitant and stood for a moment, seemingly running through the pluses and minuses of sitting with this stranger named Francis. Had she only known the endless length of the minuses!

"Okay. Fine. But just for a few minutes," she answered, and slid in the seat opposite him.

Stevin was surprised that she actually took him up on his offer, and a few minutes turned into an hour. The two talked of their pasts, their families, and their former love lives. Of course, Stevin had the benefit and the burden of making up just about everything he said. He didn't want to lie—not with this new friend who he liked a lot—but he wasn't ready to totally let his guard down just yet. It turns out that Catherine had lived in San Francisco for a few years, so Stevin was comfortable talking about the city—restaurants, hikes, traffic, concerts—and it gave him opportunities to actually tell the truth, which felt good. Being there, talking to Catherine, made Stevin want even more to be free of his sin. He really and truly could now see that he had failed until this point to live a good life, even before he'd walked out on Alexes and became a terrorist.

There was something spiritual and joyous about loving other people and helping them. As Catherine talked, he reflected on how he had helped the old lady with an ass for a neighbor and then gave her Bubbles, and how he'd made Amy so happy with a few Andrew Jacksons. He then started to think back on his life, on all the good that he had done, trying desperately to see if by any chance the good could offset the immense amount of bad—like he was drafting the pluses and minuses of his own life. Staring into Catherine's eyes and watching her beautiful mouth as she spoke, and feeling rays of warm joy fill his heart, awoke in him a great desire to help her.

He wasn't sure exactly what she needed until she mentioned vacation by saying something to the effect of "Someday I'll find a way to sit on a beach and not have a care in the world." Candidly, Stevin had planned to travel to somewhere like South Beach once he had an ID. Wine, women, and song would be his calling card. He would rent a Ferrari—a yellow one, because con men are always enamored by yellow Ferraris or Hummers—and throw money around like it was rice at a wedding. But sitting here now with Catherine changed all of that, and it felt good and right and true.

As the couple talked, the room filled, and once Catherine realized it, she jumped up abruptly to get back to work.

"It was so nice talking to you," she said apologetically. "I'll find Armin and have him come over." Then she was gone in the crowd.

The crowd was made up mostly of young men, with a few young women here and there. That was, except for the Sieck party. They were a rowdy bunch of hard-charging girls that almost overtook the noise of the house music. Most in the club were likely students or twenty-somethings eking out the last few years of their glory days. Stevin stuck out noticeably, but not awkwardly. His new haircut and clothes made him look younger and hipper, and his money gave him youthful confidence. While he waited for Armin, he decided to have a bit of fun, so he motioned for a waitress.

"Hello," the waitress said seductively, which was more part of her job than anything else.

"Yes, I'd like to send a bottle of Fireball to that party of ladies over there," Stevin said, smirking and nodding and pointing to the girls.

"An entire bottle?" the waitress inquired. "Shall I send an ambulance as well?"

"They'll be fine. They look like they can handle it," Stevin estimated with a smile.

"Shall I tell them it's from you?"

"Sure. Why not?" Stevin said, still feeling altruistic.

Before long, the waitress returned with the bottle of whisky and ten shot glasses, and she announced her arrival at the party. Stevin watched as she talked and pointed at him. He leaned back in the booth and flashed a peace sign in return, trying to play it cool while making rain, to which all ten girls stood up, shook their fists in the air, and screamed exuberant obscenities, generally ending in "Yeah!" What Stevin didn't plan on was that the party moved to his booth, so that when Armin showed up, Stevin was surrounded by ten young and very happy girls.

"Looks like you've got this place figured out!" Armin said, admiring Stevin's entourage. "I'm Armin. Cate said I should stop by."

Stevin shook off the girl on his arm and jumped up. "What did Cate say?"

Stevin's response took Armin by surprise. He was expecting Stevin to get right to business, but instead, he seemed more interested in Cate. "Uh...all she said was, 'The older gentleman in the booth wants to speak to you before you go on,' so I just came over," he said, feeling a bit interrogated by Stevin's eagerness.

"Yes. The old guy. Right. Listen..." Stevin said, wrapping his arm around Armin's shoulder like he was doing him a favor, "I need to talk to you about my ID. I seem to have misplaced it. A Miss Amy Shields suggested I stop by and talk to you about helping me find it."

"Listen, guy. You don't need to talk in code here. We're all cool. Amy's cool, too. If you need a fake ID, just meet me out front at 2:00 a.m. and we'll go to my place and make it happen. Good?"

"Uh..." Stevin hesitated, again surprised at how well this was going. "Sure!"

"Great," Armin said, undocking himself from Stevin's arm. "Stick around. I'm going to lay down some sick beats."

"Sounds swell, Daddy-O!" Stevin responded cynically with a thumbs-up. Armin rolled his eyes and headed to work.

When Stevin turned around, Cate was standing there, waiting for him. "I wanted to make sure Armin found you," she said anxiously.

"And did you?" Stevin responded suavely, with a straight face, this time calling her out on her intent to see him again. Cate laughed and looked at her feet in guilty embarrassment.

"All right. You got me. Looks like some others found you too," she said, looking up and over his shoulder at the ten Fireball infernos behind him.

"Just weak opening acts for the headliner," Stevin countered, doubling down on the cheese.

Cate smiled a seductive smile and backed up a few steps, then turned and walked away. Stevin stood and watched her. He admired her jeans and her thin figure, and how her legs didn't seem to touch clear to her waist, something he found really sexy. Once she vanished again, he settled back in the party and spent the next three hours laying down sick lies to Armin's sick beats. The girls loved him; he was so funny and clever and cute, but they especially loved his credit card, which had no problem keeping up.

At 2:00 a.m., when the music went down and the lights came up, the revelers cleared out to the sidewalk and started their risky journeys home. Most walked up the quiet street, but some hailed cabs and Ubers. Stevin found a bench and waited for Armin. After ten minutes, he emerged from inside the door.

"You ready?" he asked.

"Yep," Stevin said, standing.

"You got the cash?"

"Yep," Stevin responded, not actually knowing if he made it out of ETHOS with anything but his clothes. But, he was pretty sure he did have the money.

Armin made a call, and a minute later, a black Rolls-Royce pulled up and stopped next to them. It was the most beautiful car Stevin had ever seen. It was black with a matte black hood and matte black wheels. It slipped up the street like a ghost, making almost no sound, and pierced the night with laser-like LED lights.

"Is this yours?" Stevin asked excitedly. It seemed so contrary for a young guy to be in a Rolls. Usually one envisions these cars moving at half the speed limit and being driving by old men who can barely see over the dash and have to squint to see their 38-year-old blonde wives next to them. "It was like a ghost coming up the street."

"It is a Ghost. And, yes, it's mine," Armin responded, opening the door and motioning for Stevin to get in.

Inside the car was more impressive than the outside. Even though a king at dinner, Stevin felt a complete peasant pitted in the plush red seat. It stole his confidence and he started to wonder what he had gotten himself into.

"Let's go home," Armin said to the driver, and then rolled up a leather-wrapped barrier between them.

"So. Let me just tell you how this works," Armin said, turning to Stevin.

"Okay," Stevin responded, feeling very small.

"Normally I don't just take random strangers off the street, but since Amy gave you my name, you're cool and I'll help you out," Armin continued. "I know she got pinched by the cops, but they know nothing of me. And why is that? Because my clients don't roll on me. Now don't get too excited; we aren't selling warheads here. This is pretty simple stuff and they probably don't even care about hocus pocus with fake IDs. But just keep in mind that we don't know each other, and the ID came from the DMV, right?"

"Right!" Stevin responded very obediently.

"You'll get the finest product available and be on your way."

The ride to Armin's was quiet. The streets were empty, and the large car made short work of Barker Pass Road and the surrounding climbs. Stevin thought about the events of the night. He wanted nothing else but to legitimize himself with an ID and then to find Cate. He wondered if Armin knew Cate very well; he reasoned that Armin must know her better than he did, if nothing else because they worked together.

"Tell me about Catherine—or Cate, I mean. I really liked her," Stevin said, breaking the silence and lowering his guard a little.

Armin smiled, and Stevin could tell that he had broken some ice along with the silence.

"Cate and I have been work associates for about four years. I owe everything to her. She was the one who gave me a chance when I was just a freshman geek at school who knew how to run a turntable. I guess she saw something in me that I didn't see myself. Since then I've been DJing clubs all over the world—Paris, Ibiza, Moscow, Stockholm, Bangkok. I live here because I like to keep grounded and remember where I started. Cate is beautiful and amazing, but she's been mistreated a lot." Stevin's heart began to sink in guilt. "Maybe that's because of the industry. In her younger years, she had men in her life who were real pigs. It's ironic that she had so many chances at love, but she is still single—all because most guys are just dicks. You aren't a dick, are,,,"

"No!" Stevin blurted before Armin could even finish the question. But, in his mind, Stevin regretted not being in better 'dickless' circumstances.

By this time, they had arrived at Armin's house. Armin did not invite Stevin in, but rather escorted him to a small garage adjacent to the main garages. Stevin could tell the house was very nice and probably very expensive. The pool alone, which he caught a glimpse of behind the main structure, was probably worth more than most people's entire houses.

Inside the small workshop was an array of computers and work tables. It resembled more a CIA war room than a place where you might keep your lawnmower and leaf blower.

"Sit there. We'll take a picture first," Armin instructed.

Stevin sat and continued looking around while Armin got ready. When Armin returned, he set up a background and took a battery of pictures, which caused Stevin to be a little uneasy, being the most-wanted man in the country—or so he speculated. Armin then moved to a small computer and asked Stevin a series of questions: name, address, birthdate, etc. Stevin pulled out Francis's driver's license to make it all match. This was critical. The picture of a man who looked 50 and a birthdate of a person who was 71 might pose some problems, but it was going to have to do. In another minute or so, a printer lit up and began working. It was different than most, which was evident when it spat out a perfect driver's license.

"Wow! Where did you get that printer?" Stevin asked naively, admiring his new ID.

"It's time for you to go now," Armin suggested without answering and holding his hand out for payment.

Stevin reached in his pocket and pulled out a wad of cash. This time he counted it out to $500 even.

"I'll have Javier drive you back to your car. And remember what we talked about...especially regarding Cate," Armin instructed.

Stevin strolled back to the front and slid into the Ghost. With his ID, he was now legitimate. He wondered if he should have asked if Armin did passports too. Nonetheless, with a driver's license, he would have much more freedom to travel, to purchase, and to access his vast funds. But all of this was ironically uneventful, because he couldn't stop thinking about Catherine and his overwhelming desire to do something for her. He thought about what she'd said about vacation and wondered in his mind what he could do. Somewhere near Soledad Street, when the lights of the city illuminated the cabin and his mind, it hit him. It was risky because she could say no, but he would only be out a couple thousand or so. He pulled out his phone and frantically searched for flights on Kayak. He needed a little time tomorrow for a few special errands, time to convince Cate, and time to get to LAX, so something in the evening was necessary. When he finally found what he was looking for, he was thrilled. It felt so right, and he was so excited. By the time they reached his car, he had two first-class tickets west. Stevin tipped Javier fifty bucks, and, walking back to his car, exclaimed, "If it's a beach she wants, it's a beach she shall have!"

CHAPTER 15

WORK IT, OWN IT

Today's magnificent sunrise brought with it endless possibilities for Stevin. He was a man on a mission, again jumping through an incredible number of hoops in hopes of talking to a woman. But this time, he was aided by nearly $800,000 of liquid cash. By 9:00 a.m., he had showered, eaten, and was waiting in the lounge of Santa Barbara's Mercedes dealership. His attempt at a new life would start here, and he was hoping dearly that he could pull it off.

The dealership was quiet, at least in the showroom. He had come in eagerly through the service wing only to find absent-minded managers more focused on getting their coffee just right than selling cars. He decided to sit in a plush brown leather chair until someone noticed him. About 15 minutes later, someone did.

"Sir. Have you been helped?" a portly man, who had strolled up from behind him, coffee in hand, asked.

"Not yet. I'd like to trade in my car," Stevin answered.

"Oh," the man responded, surprised, thinking he was there for service. "Most of the sales people come in around 10:00 or so, but let me see if I can find someone who can help you. What kind of trade do you have?"

"It's a Mercedes," Stevin said, a little perturbed that the rest of the world wasn't sharing his sense of urgency.

"Well, that should make it easy. Stay put and I'll be right back."

Once the man was gone, Stevin decided to stroll through the showroom. He loved cars, especially fast ones, and he was still dreaming about Armin's Rolls-Royce from last night. Near the end of the showroom floor, he caught sight of a sleek black sports car parked on a ramp just outside. It looked Mercedes-ish, but was very different. He glanced around for a door to get outside and take a look.

"Ain't she a beauty?" a voice said, again from behind him. Stevin turned to find a very slender man in a suit. At first glance he was quite presentable, that was until one noticed his shoes, which were dull and worn. But his demeanor was more pleasant and innocent than most salesmen's, and Stevin instantly connected with him.

"Well, yeah. I don't know if I've ever seen that model! What is it?"

"It's what they call an AMG GT," the man responded. "Let me show it to you."

The man led Stevin to a door in the middle of the showroom and, along the way, introduced himself as Dennis Wimmer. Of the people Stevin had met so far at the dealership, this chap was certainly the Stan Laurel of the duo. Once at the car, Dennis opened the driver door and Stevin slid in, like he was a buttery hand sliding into a glove.

"Oh, I like this a lot!" Stevin gushed, with hands firmly on the steering wheel, giving away much of his negotiating power.

"We just rolled it out this morning," Dennis said, beginning his pitch. "She's got 503 horsepower with a hand-built motor, and she will get you from zero to sixty in about three seconds and has a top speed of over 190 miles per hour. You can take on Lambos and Ferraris, and for only a third the price! This is the S model, which has an upgraded engine and also comes with better suspension and brakes. Take a look under the hood," Dennis continued, reaching for the lever.

Stevin climbed out to see the enormous V8 shrouded in carbon fiber and aluminum. He leaned in to read the inscription on a little plaque.

"These motors are hand-built in Germany. The tech actually signs his name," Dennis explained.

"*Thomas Alby. Mercedes-AMG. Germany,*" Stevin read. "Sounds official!"

"Shall we go for a drive?" Dennis asked, with a sinister look on his otherwise honest face.

"Let's work out the deal first with my trade and see where I'm at. I know I'm going to love it, and I don't want any surprises," Stevin countered, shutting the hood.

"Okay. Let's go see what you have," Dennis suggested.

Stevin felt a little uncomfortable with the idea, since he knew only a little about the car and he feared that it still smelled horribly. "Let's do this," Stevin suggested. "Here's the key. You go take a look, talk to your manager, take it for a drive...do whatever you need to do. Then come back with a complete package, trade-in and new car, and let me know what I owe. That's easier for me. I'll sit back in my leather seat and wait for a bit. But know that I have a flight to catch at LAX tonight, so I'm hoping to get this done in the next couple of hours. Make it fair and we can make it happen," Stevin instructed.

"Will do!" Dennis said anxiously, feeling a new pair of shoes coming.

Stevin handed him the key and sat back in his seat to plan his next move. He needed new clothes, a suitcase, a swimsuit, a razor, flip-flops, sunblock, sunglasses—just about everything one would pack for a beach vacation—and reasoned that the most efficient way to do it would be to bomb Nordstrom or Bloomingdale's. Then it would be off to save Cate from the dance dungeon and whisk her to the beautiful beaches of Kauai.

He felt sleepy waiting there in the soft leather chair. He wasn't used to such revelry deep into the night and getting up and going early certainly didn't help. He had thought about the possibility of getting caught impersonating Francis, but with so much fun on the docket today, he discounted the risk and slipped easily into a nap.

Outside, at his brown convertible, there was a bit of bustle. No one had ever suggested trading a classic like this before, and there was much debate as to whether they would even want to risk taking it. Doing so required a call to the dealership owner, who, luckily for Stevin, was interested in owning the car himself. After some serious number-crunching, phone-calling, and researching, they agreed to lowball the value a bit just to be safe. Dennis, with deal in hand, headed back to find Stevin and see if he could convince him to trade his classic at a less-than-thrilling price for a brand-new AMG GT S. He wasn't optimistic.

"Sir. Sir," Dennis said, shaking Stevin's shoulder.

"Yes," Stevin said groggily.

"I have the deal. Can I go over it with you?" Dennis asked.

"What time is it?"

"About 10:45," Dennis responded.

"Perfect," Stevin said, standing and wiping the sleep from his eyes. But he wasn't groggy long. The excitement of the day was a strong, warm wind in his sails.

After giving a long and arduous disclaimer about the value of the 280SE, and how rare it was, and how great of shape it was in, Dennis settled in for the punch line. "So, we'll give you the AMG GT S with tax, license, and all fees, and a check for $27,336.41," he said hesitantly.

"That's fine. Can I give you a credit card for the 27 grand?" Stevin responded, without quite understanding the deal.

"No. We are going to write *you* a check—or send you a wire. Your car is worth more than ours," Dennis explained, resolved not to tell his manager that they'd shot too high.

Stevin sat there with a blank stare. The gears in his mind were turning, but with significant effort from the hamster. Then his face lit up with a smile. If anything would foretell the magic of this amazing day, certainly a new missile and a $27,000 check would. Stevin was now convinced that he was going to make his flight and, more importantly, make it with Cate.

"Let's do it!" Stevin declared, feeling like he had just hit the lottery.

There really is nothing like rolling off the lot in a new car, especially one like this. The engine note itself was enough to turn heads, let alone the sleek lines of a car that not many people see every day. Stevin feathered the pedal through the lot and beamed with every look and finger pointed in his direction. The king was in his chariot, setting off to vanquish all foes! In a way, he felt equal to Armin now—that is, except for his clothes. Driving in this car dressed like he was made him look like a regular Joe Blow wearing a Canal Street Louis Vuitton belt. If he didn't have the full package, people would see through his façade, so he needed to get outfitted fast. He headed for the freeway, trying to get somewhat familiar with all of the car's high-tech features and anxiously awaiting an opportunity to open it up—and what better launch pad than the onramp to a freeway?

As he made the turn to enter the 101, he floored it, but not before he had finished the turn. For those of you who have had powerful rear-wheel drive cars, you know what happens next. It's the same thing that happens to a lot of young kids who get behind the wheel of powerful cars, and you read a headline in the newspaper that reads something like TEEN TOTALS NEW VIPER TWO BLOCKS FROM HOME.

As Stevin stomped on the gas, the car hesitated for a split-second, emitted a dragon-like roar, and then spun the rear wheels into blender blades and whipped the back end toward the concrete barrier. Luckily for Stevin, he had owned a car with this kind of power before, so he was somewhat familiar with how to harness its horses without crashing, which, most of the time, means keeping those wheels burning even when you're sideways.

Steering slightly right and keeping his foot down, he laid down an impressive 80-foot skid—uphill, mind you—before the wheels caught traction. Oh, how we love Mercedes torque...and an ESP button! Stevin came up onto the freeway like Toothless on a village strafing run, only to find that the freeway traffic was basically at a standstill. Now Stevin had both feet and his heart on the brake pedal. God bless automakers who pair massive brakes with massive engines...and Gabriel Voisin for ABS brakes!

The car came to rest on the shoulder so abruptly that Stevin felt a little like Iron Man landing on stage—every eye across all three lanes was on him. He gave a curt wave of his hand, and added an innocent smirk, then merged in.

About lunchtime, Stevin arrived at the downtown mall to shop, and valeted the car to the oohs and ahhs of all who heard him coming a block away. Climbing out at the valet stand, he still felt out of place in his clothes, and was eager to shop and get back over to ETHOS. He headed to Nordstrom and marched straight to the first salesperson he could find.

"Can I help you?" the chicly dressed man asked.

Stevin hesitated for a second as he recalled the scene from *Pretty Woman* when Edward takes Viv shopping, then responded smugly with, "I'm going to be spending an obscene amount of money in here, and I am going to need someone who can do a lot of sucking up to me, because that's what I really like."

The salesperson was a little lost at first, but then, by some miracle, seemed to recall the scene himself and countered, barely able to keep a straight face, "Sir, if I may say so, you're in the right store—and the right city, for that matter!"

Stevin paused in amazement and then both men burst out in laughter. Truly a friendship had never been struck so fast or so oddly. Again, Stevin's mojo could not be fazed—at least not today. It was as if he was in the front row at *Oprah,* and she was about to announce her favorite things.

"My name is Jonathan. I can help you. What do you have in mind?"

"I basically only own the clothes I have on. I'm headed to Hawaii later tonight and need the full kit and caboodle: clothes, toiletries, swimsuit, shoes, watch, sunglasses, umbrella, suitcase, and anything else you can think of. I'll be gone about four days, and really want to dress to impress," Stevin said somewhat reverently because he really needed help.

"Oh! I'm your guy for sure! We're going to need a cart for this," Jonathan said as he led Stevin to the storage area and sourced a cart.

Looking at Stevin, Jonathan eyed him for sizes and style.

"Let me see. You're middle-aged, with a good build. Most likely you tend to be more conservative, but your hair suggests otherwise. I've got some ideas. And you're probably a 42 long, maybe a 44 long in a jacket. Maybe a 36 in pants. Probably an XL in shirts. Size 12 shoes?" he asked.

"Wow! You are the man. Yes, 12 in shoes," Stevin answered, happy to know he was in good hands.

"Let's start with suitcases, and we'll pack as we go to make sure it all fits. Then we'll head to shoes, because shoes are the most important item of your wardrobe."

With that, the two blitzed the store like they were robbing it—Jonathan spending Stevin's money, and Stevin spending Francis' money. It was a win-win, except for Francis, but she no longer cared, did she? In all, the spree took three grueling hours. Shopping is much more tiring than one might think. There is trying everything on, and walking to different departments, all while basically standing the entire time. No wonder most men hate it. Perhaps their distaste also comes from their tee-shirt-shorts-flip-flops, good-to-go mentality. For Stevin, this would not do; he was eager to shop, and anxious to reveal his new self.

At the register, Stevin watched as Jonathan rang it all up. Jonathan's eyes got really big at the last item he scanned, but when he turned to Stevin, he was cool and collected and matter-of-fact.

"Looks like your total today, 'Mr. Lewis,' is $11,256.29. Would you like to use your Nordstrom card?" he asked.

Stevin smiled and declined, and handed him the Morgan Stanley card.

"Mr. Dunfey," Jonathan read from Stevin's card. "Can I see your ID, please?"

Stevin pulled out his freshly minted driver's license and handed it to Jonathan.

"Thank you," Jonathan replied, handing it back.

Stevin watched with baited breath to see what would happen. He was poised to run at any sign of a declined card. Seconds seemed like hours as he watched for the receipt, but to his relief, the little machine came to life and started printing.

"Thought I was going to have to get the change in my pocket!" Stevin said jokingly, and a little too loudly, because of nerves.

Jonathan rolled the suitcase from behind the counter and handed Stevin his business card.

"Thank you for coming in, Mr. Dunfey. I hope to see you again soon."

Stevin thanked him for his help and then headed for the dressing room to change into something new. After a few minutes and a complete metamorphosis, he emerged like David Gandy, ready to shoot a Dolce & Gabbana ad. People would look at him differently. He exuded legitimacy and commanded respect, and this went to his head a little bit...or a lot.

Stevin was focused and prepared on the outside, but on the inside, he was suddenly very nervous again about talking to a girl. When he arrived back at ETHOS, he found only one car in the parking lot, a newer-model BMW X5. He prayed that it was Cate's. Funny thing about nightclubs is that they are quite opposite in activity to most other businesses, and to catch someone there during normal business hours is nothing short of a miracle.

Stevin walked to the front door not knowing exactly how to ask what he was going to ask. When he got there, he hesitated, but then turned to see his new car and smiled proudly. The thrill that it was his gave him the nudge he needed at the door. He rapped with vigor, then heard some shuffling inside. He could tell someone was behind the door looking through the peephole. Whoever it was, they were in no hurry to open up.

"Cate, if that's you, I need to ask you something," Stevin pleaded.

Still no luck.

"Cate! I need you! Please open the door!" Stevin pleaded, surprising himself at how bluntly he was speaking.

The door crept open. There stood Cate like a schoolgirl, knowing she was going to be asked to prom by the captain of the football team, but not believing it could be real. She looked different than from the night before—more simple and genuine, but in Stevin's eyes, even more beautiful. He was speechless for a moment, looking at her with a blank stare. Deep down, he struggled with the conflict of living a lie and potentially breaking this woman's heart. The way she looked at him, he knew she was going to say yes, but he had to decide now if he was going to do the right thing and walk away or give in and try to outrun his horrible history. He struggled for the words, being more like a freshman trombone player trying to ask out a varsity cheerleader.

"I want..." he stammered, closing his eyes to compose himself and taking a deep breath. This was really difficult. He felt very strongly for Cate, so much so that he couldn't stand to be without her. But he also didn't want to start a relationship on a lie. He didn't know what to do, but at long last, he buckled.

Conjuring a smile and settling into her eyes, he looked at Cate and asked, "I don't know quite how to say this, but last night you mentioned getting away to a beach. I have two first-class tickets to Kauai tonight from LAX. Will you come with me?"

Now it was Cate's turn to freeze in fear. She really didn't know this guy, but she liked him. He looked amazing. His car looked amazing. Certainly he was legitimate. Certainly he was real and wouldn't crush her like all the others. She decided to play it cool and probe a little to be safe.

"Wow! That's quite an offer...and quite a car!" she responded. "Frank, why were you here last night, looking for Armin?"

Stevin hadn't anticipated a question like this. He was ready for things like, "I have to work" or "I have nothing to wear." His eyes grew a little wider and he wondered how to respond, but he decided to graze the truth with a more-or-less accurate explanation.

"I needed a fake ID with a different birthdate. You know what that's all about, right?" he explained.

"Well, that's a stroke of honesty I wasn't expecting! I know all about fake IDs, and all about Armin's specialty print shop, but usually it's 17-year-olds trying to be 22 You are clearly not 17, so please explain," she asked, now settling into the role of investigator.

Stevin didn't want to lie, but she boxed him into a corner. "It has to do with my father, who recently passed away. I can't access his bank accounts without an ID showing our shared name with his birthdate. It's a mess, and just a lot easier to sort out with a fake ID and passwords to his accounts. Otherwise, I have to wait months for probate court and the attorneys. You might have to just trust me on this one."

Cate's countenance changed. She liked the fact that he was honest, even though his explanation was a little shady. She changed her line of questioning.

"So, where are we staying?" she said with a cute smile and a darling tilt of her head.

Stevin paused again. This was like a chess game where each player has to consider the outcome of every move before actually moving, and he sensed that he had just moved into checkmate.

"Wait...so you'll go?" he blurted, unable to contain his joy.

Cate leaned against the doorframe, starred in his eyes, and kept smiling.

CHAPTER 16

BIG IZ

There is something about stepping off a plane in Hawaii that automatically dials one's normal anxiety of ten down to about a three. It goes away altogether if you're there long enough. Maybe it's the heavy, humid air, or maybe it's knowing that you're in for something special. Most special for Stevin was the fact that he could travel as one of the FBI's ten most wanted without worry or care, which was followed closely by how truly special Cate was. The flight seemed like 20 minutes. And even though they were both tired, they couldn't help but talk the entire time, which bothered most of the others in first class including the flight attendants. But these two were oblivious to what was around them, speaking on topics of childhood, past relationships, religion, and plans for the time that they would be on the island.

Kauai is known as the Garden Isle, and for good reason. On the eastern and northern slopes, it truly is a tropical paradise—just as you would imagine, with lush tropical jungles, waterfalls, and white sand beaches. Expansive vistas are viewable in many places along the highway, and as you stand at each, you feel like you might see a T. rex from *Jurassic Park* or King Kong himself come crashing through the jungle. The southern and western exposures are more arid—not a wasteland by any means, but noticeably different. Great canyons and mountains adorn the center, and rain becomes an instant switch that turns on the many waterfalls cascading from its peaks. Most of the island is accessible by meandering two-lane roads, except where the roads end at either side of the Na Pali Coast in the north. For two people falling in love, it was the perfect place. And dirtbag or not, Cate was willing to risk her heart on Stevin just to indulge her whim of checking out on a beach somewhere.

After landing, a black Escalade met them at the airport and drove them north, nearly to the end of the road, to Princeville, where the expansive St. Regis Hotel soaks in views of Hanalei Bay and the jagged peaks of the Halelea Forest Reserve. It was late, just after midnight Hawaii time, so much of the island was out of view during the ride, except for the occasional floodlight illuminating crashing waves. Cate became more reserved as the car wound its way north on the mostly deserted highway. Tiredness had set in and she dreaded the uneasiness of arriving at the hotel and dealing with any 'expectations.' She figured it would be better to tackle it head-on now, before they arrived, rather than when they were awkwardly alone in the room, staring at the bed.

"Frank, are you awake?" she asked.

"Yes."

"What are you thinking about?" she said, probing for an entrance to her topic.

Stevin squirmed a bit and took a big breath, then responded with a categorical shift from his normal modus operandi. "I really want to be honest with you, so I'm going to tell you what I'm thinking about without discounting it. Now that we're here and almost to the hotel, I want you to know that I'm really happy to be here with you. I am really excited about getting to know you better. But, that being said, I think it would be wrong to rush. And as much as I want to be with you, I feel like it would be better to get separate rooms."

He sat up and shifted in his seat to face Cate as he waited for her response. He hoped he didn't come off as regretful or uninterested, because his feelings and intentions couldn't be further from that. He waited for a moment in silence for her reaction. Cate was overtaken with surprise, but then, feeling that a prayer had been answered, she turned to him with a warm glow and smile and put her hand on his cheek. Stevin smiled back and just stared in her eyes. Without words or explanations or motions or force, they sat opposite each other in love, trust, and respect. Stevin felt like he had not only eased her anxiety, but also had also passed a great test. His love for her was growing exponentially and he also felt hers for him. With the rules laid out, they could relax and let their relationship grow deep roots, and it wasn't long before they were both sound asleep in their own rooms.

The next morning, Stevin awoke early and wanted to get in a little exercise before breakfast. He slipped a note under Cate's door, letting her know where he was heading, and then found his way to the lobby and the gym. In the lobby, Stevin caught his first glimpse of Hanalei Bay, an almost perfect half-circle cut from the coast like a great sea monster had taken a bite out of the island. He stepped onto the terrace to get a better view. Across the Bay, in the far distance, he could see cars skirting along the Bay's western edge. Below, on the beach, eager guests were already dragging kayaks and stand-up paddleboards to the water. What floored him, though, were the mountains. He had never seen anything like it. Great spires of dark green rose from a lowland valley across the Bay. He could see three waterfalls pouring from their peaks, as if they weren't peaks at all but volcanoes of spring water. While there were puffs of clouds in the sky, he wondered what fueled such a scene, and came away thinking that it must rain here every day to produce such wonder.

To the left of the main lobby and down a half flight of stairs was the hotel gym. It wasn't big by any means, but it was sufficient for tourist traffic. Stevin found himself alone there and decided to warm up on one of the treadmills. After about thirty minutes, and just when he was settling into a good stride, he was startled by the door flying open and a large and boisterous man entering the room.

"Richard Spencer. How the hell are you?" the man yelled over the hum of Stevin's treadmill.

Stevin couldn't believe he was talking to him, but since no one else was there, he responded with a simple, "Fine. Thanks," while trying to stay focused.

The man jumped up on the treadmill next to Stevin and continued his introduction.

"My friends call me Dick. Think you can remember that?" the man asked and then laughed full-heartedly.

Stevin smiled and shook his head. He couldn't help but laugh a little, not so much at the joke, but at the audacity of this total clown.

"Shouldn't be a problem," Stevin responded, sarcastically.

"Where are you from?" Dick continued, trying to engage Stevin in a conversation.

"Santa Barbara," Stevin responded, hoping to be done.

"We're out here from San Francisco for the week. I haven't seen you yet. Did you just arrive?" Dick prodded.

"We got in last night."

"Nice. It's a beautiful place. Lots of tail...and young tail, too!" Dick suggested, and then laughed again, slapping Stevin's arm.

Stevin was about done with this guy. He was starting to feel angry, and he caught himself scanning the room for a pen and paper.

Dick continued, "Well, with all that is going on back home in the city, we thought it best to get out of town. You heard about the lone terrorist we have, right? They think it's some guy named Stevin McSomething-or-other. We're hoping that they get the bastard soon, so we can go home. I'm about broke buying $20 hamburgers here!"

Stevin's demeanor changed. His guard was up, and he was mad about it. After a day or two with no care in the world, he was now forced to care.

"Yeah, I heard about it," Stevin responded while getting off the treadmill.

Stevin wanted to play it cool, but he also wanted to run. On the off chance this guy recognized him, his whole life could change real quick. His mind spun with contingency plans, and he realized that maybe an island with a single airport wasn't the best place to be when you're on the lam. Then it got worse.

"You actually kind of look like the guy," Dick said, becoming curious and sensing that Stevin has headed for the door. "Hey. I didn't catch your name."

Stevin thought he could get out without any further discussion, but chose to humor the guy a little, hoping it would quell his curiosity. "Haywood. Haywood Jablomi," Stevin shot back with a smile and then left.

"Haywood...huh," Dick said to himself. "Interesting name."

Back up in the lobby, Stevin was beelining it for his room when he ran into a very well-rested and casual Cate.

"Hey, turbo!" she said. "You're running like you're still on the treadmill."

Stevin collected himself and relaxed, telling himself there was no imminent threat. "Oh, I had a feeling you might be up, and I didn't want to leave you waiting," he said quickly.

Cate smiled and gave him a hug, then turned to look out the window. "Wow...it's absolutely beautiful here!"

Stevin was calmed, but he didn't feel comfortable standing in the middle of lobby. "Breakfast?" he asked abruptly.

Cate lit up. "Yes!" she exclaimed. "I'm starving."

The breakfast terrace was set overlooking the Bay and the mountains. Cate couldn't get enough of it, and, despite being very hungry, couldn't focus on the menu. Stevin watched her intently, knowing exactly what she was feeling, because he'd felt it just a bit earlier. The magic of Kauai was sinking in.

"What did we decide to do today? I can't remember if it was hit the beach or go exploring." Stevin asked, eager to have some fun.

"Explore...and we're going to need a car!" Cate exclaimed.

"That sounds incredible," Stevin said as he reached out and held her hand.

After breakfast, Stevin worked with the concierge to rent a bright orange Jeep Wrangler, and when it showed up, he worked with the valet crew to take the top down. Then he showered up and met Cate back in the lobby an hour later.

"Wait until you see what I've got!" he said, giddy with excitement.

When the valet pulled the Jeep around, Cate exploded with joy. "Yes!" she screamed, which caused all the men in the *porte-cochère* to look with bright eyes and regret immensely not being the one who would leave with her.

Cate bounded in almost before the valet brought the Jeep to a full stop, then leaned over and gave him a big kiss on his cheek. While she felt like a teenage girl again, he got the best tip of the day—one he wouldn't have to, and really couldn't, share!

Stevin watched Cate with pure joy. He reflected on where he was in this moment and how he got here. He thought how a near-endless well of money had made this possible. Everything was effortless with money. He didn't have to care about $20 hamburgers, the cost of an extra room, paying for the rental car to be delivered... anything, really. It helped, too, that he hadn't had to spend years earning it; it had just fallen in his lap. Actually, in a way, he did have to earn it; let us not forget how hard he worked at leveraging his dumb luck, his quick thinking, and his having no respect for life! Poor Francis was still in the Big Sur—dashed to pieces in the canyon below the bridge, like someone was chumming near the shore and then the tide went out, leaving all the scraps washed up in a gory heap. Well, at least her money was of comfort to those she'd left behind.

The drive from the hotel first makes its way to the main road through a battery of timeshares and condos. At the junction, there is a retail center with the area's main grocery store, a gas station, and other smaller shops that sell clothes, set up tourist excursions, and scoop ice cream. When they got to the junction, Stevin had to abruptly slam on the brakes about 100 feet short of the stop sign to allow a lone chicken to cross the road.

"Someone lost their chicken!" Cate exclaimed, laughing.

"I think a lot of people lost their chickens here. They are everywhere in Kauai!" Stevin explained.

This became a running joke for the weekend. Every time they saw a chicken, Cate would yell "Chicken!" Then they would both laugh. Sometimes Stevin would tease her by swerving the Jeep toward the otherwise solitary birds, just to get her to scream and laugh. They even bought a bumper sticker with a picture of a chicken and the island that read, *Ruler of the Roost—Kauai State Bird.*

From the chicken and the junction, and after ice cream at Lappert's, they made a right and drove the winding highway through lush green hills and valleys and over rivers with single-lane bridges to Hanalei, where they stopped for a while to investigate local shops and gear up for the beach. From Hanalei, they continued west to Wainiha, and eventually to the end of the road at Ke'e Beach.

While Ke'e Beach is incredible in and of itself, it is also home to a few amazing caves, and serves as the eastern terminus of the Kalalau Trail—an eleven-mile nail-biter of a trail that crosses rivers, negotiates sheer sea walls, and claims several lives every year. Today, Stevin and Cate were interested in only the beach, wanting nothing more than to spend the rest of the day lounging in the Hawaiian sun. They left the Jeep and waded barefoot into the warm sand of the beach, then worked their way around the point until they found a secluded stretch near an outcropping of rocks. Once settled, both melted into the moment. The warm sun and sand and the gentle lull of the waves finally convinced them that it really was real, and not a dream.

After a few minutes of rest, Stevin slyly turned to look at Cate. His dark glasses gave him the opportunity to see her entire body in her bikini unnoticed. She was absolutely incredible, and much more toned and fit than he would have guessed. This made him a little uncomfortable, because he wasn't all that, although the rigors of being on the run had allowed him to drop a few pounds along the way. He noticed how dang cute her feet were. He normally hated feet, especially his, but her feet were perfect, especially wrapped in the white sand of the beach. Her legs were almost as big as his but, again, beautiful and toned and long! Her butt was nearly perfect, and Stevin concluded that twenty years ago it probably was.

As his eyes moved up her body, he could see her pubic bone slightly raised over her hips, which he prayed weren't lying. The sight sent a shot of love potion through his body. His eyes stayed there for a moment, then he noticed how low-cut her bikini bottoms were over her flat stomach. There was hint of a tattoo near her hipbone, but he couldn't quite make it out from his vantage point. He did notice, however, how sweat was starting to bead on her body. Stevin was becoming so charged that he couldn't decide whether he should keep looking or just pounce! His eyes kept moving up, now at her bikini top. He stared at her chest for a while and fought the urge to touch her—something that seemed so natural. He hesitated, not wanting to get too excited and *Tommy Boy* his biscuit this early in the trip. He sighed heavily, hoping not to give away his sensual survey. He continued up and admired her lips and face and hair. From top to bottom, she was far more than he could have hoped for or even dreamed about. Initially, he was struck by how well he and Cate hit it off when they talked, but her being a bombshell was an ever-so-delicious icing on the cake. Eventually his eyes let her go, and he rolled onto his stomach and sighed again.

"What's all the huffing and puffing over there?" Cate asked without moving, somewhat suspecting a wolf was prowling.

Stevin thought of a million responses, all of which didn't quite seem to fit or were just too lewd as he struggled to break from his prior life in word and deed. He decided to play it cool and responded simply, "Just relaxing."

Upon hearing this, Cate erupted in laughter, which caused Stevin to sit up a little startled.

"What?" Stevin said, feeling a little embarrassed.

"You're a terrible liar!" she said as she reeled up on her elbows, still laughing. Then she looked Stevin straight in the eyes and without a wince asked, "Are you going to do something about that erection, or just leave me out here to roast?" Such a tone might be a tad forward for some, but apparently middle-aged daters often feel they don't have time to beat around the bush.

Needless to say, Stevin was speechless. He looked down at his swimsuit and, sure enough, there was no getting out of this one.

He countered back, "I think that question is more suited..."

Before he could finish, Cate sat up, embraced him with one hand between his legs and one hand behind his neck, and then pulled him to her lips and down to the sand.

That afternoon was one of the greatest of Stevin's life. He had everything he wanted: money, freedom, a beautiful woman. He never wanted that day to end. He never wanted to let Cate go. Sitting there in her arms, he was overcome with emotion. He attributed these immense feelings of joy and love to his effort at attempting to do what was right, to telling the truth, to being honorable, which was all contrary to how he'd lived prior to walking into ETHOS. He regretted that he had not realized it earlier. He certainly wished he had met Cate earlier, but somehow, he knew that he would have churned and burned her just like many of the others in his life. With every kiss and every smile and every hug and every caress, the anger and pain and hate sloughed off him. He could feel his heart changing, and it killed him to know that there was still the chance that he would have to atone for his previous misdeeds. This cut him to the core, because he knew all too well that if such a thing were to happen, he would be alone again, and all that he had now would vanish. He soaked in as much as he could, registering every touch, every sound, every feeling.

After a few hours of rolling in the sand, the tide began to tickle their feet and the evening crept upon them. Looking at the sea, as clouds scattered high overhead built a backdrop for the day's last rays of light, they could tell that Kauai was soon going to put on a magnificent sunset. Reluctantly, the love birds flew back to the coop to get cleaned up for dinner, which began together in Cate's room and ended with Stevin in the hallway en route to his room with only a towel.

With fresh clothes on and the top back on the Jeep, they doubled back down the dark road to Tahiti Nui, a restaurant they'd spied earlier in the day. From the parking lot, they could hear the melodic sounds of slack-key guitar and traditional Hawaiian music coming from inside. Cate smiled at Stevin and took his hand as they scampered in just as the rain started to fall.

Inside was small but comfortable. The dinner tables and those on the patio were arranged to take full advantage of the stage. As they sat at their table, the guitarist started speaking, still strumming his guitar.

"Aloha, everybody. Thank you for joining me tonight. My name is Michael Keale. I'm sure happy to be here with you. The next song I'd like to play was made famous by my cousin, Israel Kamakawiwo'ole, or Big IZ, as he was called, before he passed in 1997. I think you'll recognize it. It's one of my favorites. 'Somewhere Over the Rainbow'."

When the song started, a rush of emotion overtook Stevin. As he watched and listened, his eyes welled up. He couldn't remember ever feeling this way, and he didn't know what to do other than keep watching and weeping. His heart was full of gratitude, pure love, and joy, and he wanted nothing more than to be free of his past. He turned to Cate, desperate for help. Cate looked at him as one would a puppy that was lost.

"What's the matter?" she asked in a soft, caring voice.

Stevin could hardly speak. There weren't words for what he was feeling and thinking, so he just took her hands and stared into her eyes. He loved her more than he had ever loved anyone or anything. And more than that, those tears washed his eyes clean, and he began to see with new vision the beauty of life around him. He grasped Cate's hands as if hanging from the edge of a cliff, hoping she would never, ever let go.

Then he closed his eyes to wish and hope, letting the song guide his mind...

Someday I'll wish upon a star

Wake up where the clouds are far behind me

Where trouble melts like lemon drops

High above the chimney top

That's where you'll find me

Oh, somewhere over the rainbow, way up high

And the dream that you dare to, why oh, why can't I?

CHAPTER 17

BORROWED TIME

Stevin woke the next morning as would a napping mother who'd just remembered she needed to pick up her child at school. His eyes opened widely in an instant and his breathing was near-panicked. He didn't dare move as he lay still in bed, grappling in his mind with exactly when and where he was. Next to him, Cate was sound asleep. Her soft breathing put him moderately at ease, enough to allow for some modicum of rational thinking. Still lying motionless, he glanced up. Her long brown hair cascaded from her pillow, and he could see a sliver of her shoulder peeking out from beneath the covers. He smiled a calm smile and sighed a calm sigh. All was well. He lay there watching and listening to her peaceful sleep.

Beyond Cate, at the window, the morning sun was prying its way through the heavy curtains. Stevin looked at the light and it beckoned to him. His courage was growing, and so was his tomfoolery. He ever-so-gently rose to see the clock—it read 8:33—then settled back on his pillow. *Perfect!* he thought to himself. It was just late enough for him to actually want to get up, and still early enough for him to have the entire day ahead for fun. He slid out of bed and ninja'd over to the curtains. With one finger, he parted them to see outside, but was blinded by the brilliance of the sun. Then, right at that moment, the air conditioner at his knees kicked on and startled him so much that he inadvertently flung one of the curtains open. For an instant, the entire room electrified as if Ellen Griswald had flipped the switch in the basement. Then the curtain swung back and all was black again. Stevin held the curtains tightly together, hoping that Cate hadn't stirred; he turned to find her still peacefully floating in the clouds. This was perfect. As she was facing the curtain without an eye mask, he could now commence Operation Blinding Light (he also thought about calling it Operation Carol Anne). Looking down at the floor, he grabbed one of her shoes, then excitedly blew the curtains wide open. Between the sunlight burning through the windows and the shrill noise of the curtain rollers, one would have thought this would be the worst of it. However, the worst was yet to come. For, in his hand, Stevin held his 'microphone', and he began to sing:

Tiny bubbles/(whispering as if a background singer) *tiny bubbles*

In the wine/(whispering) *in the wine*

Make me happy/(whispering) *make me happy*

"What the hell is happening?" Cate erupted, half asleep and completely blind.

Stevin continued, thrilled as fox in a hen house, and adding a little footwork:

Make me feel fine/(whispering sensually) *make me feel fine*

Tiny bubbles/(whispering sensually, now with an Asian accent) *tiny bubbles*

"You're out of you mind!" Cate yelled, trying to keep from laughing and still trying to see in the light.

Stevin moved to the foot of the bed and then climbed up, so he was standing over her:

> *Make me warm all over*
>
> *With a feeling that I'm gonna*
>
> *Love you till the end of time*

With the last phrase, he dropped down on all fours on top of her and beamed from ear to ear.

"You're dead!" Cate mused.

"Oh!" exclaimed Stevin. "Says the slumbering princess pinned under the sheets!"

With that, Cate exploded her right knee through the sheets, straight into Stevin's gut. It didn't hurt him, but it sure surprised the hell out of him. Stevin sprung off the bed and onto the floor. Apparently, he was actually going to need some ninja training. Cate was up in a flash, clothed only with fiendish eyes and wild hair, but armed with a feather bundle of mass destruction. Her first swipe caught Stevin square in the side of the face. Operation Blinding Light was against the ropes and dimming fast! The good news was that he was finally able to make out her tattoo, which was a small hummingbird.

Stevin lunged in and swiped her feet from under her, so she fell flat on her back on the bed. She was so stinking beautiful, lying there naked and wild, that he paused for a moment to consider whether to jump on this croc Steve Irwin-style, or go for the other pillow...and the other pillow it was! Now armed himself, he was ready to brawl. Cate was up again, and on the other side of the bed. She took a moment to look down, and noticed that she wasn't wearing any clothes, so she held the pillow in front of her for cover.

"Are you surrendering?" Stevin asked assumptively.

"Never!" Cate shouted, and jumped onto the bed with pillow now loaded for launch.

Stevin met her there, and they traded blows until their arms could hardly swing anymore. Finally, they collapsed on the bed, laughing between deep breaths. Stevin stared at the ceiling for a moment and had a bit of Zen clarity. He realized that he was truly happy—and, oddly, for a strange reason. It wasn't the money or the trip or Cate's beauty that made him feel this joy. It was the realization that his decision to try and choose the right had led him here. This was in stark contrast to his previous choices, which had led him down a dark path, riddled with deceit and death. He started to feel immense regret for all the people he had hurt—all of the innocent people who had lost loved ones or who were, perhaps, still recovering in the hospital. He thought of Alexes and wondered, if he had chosen differently during their marriage, whether or not he could have had this same joy with her—something akin to Tom and Rita, Mike and Karen, Paul and Ali, or Mitt and Ann. As he sat there thinking with his guard down, Cate took a cheap shot—a little payback for him blinding her with the curtains and, more importantly, defiling her shoe with that crooning! The force of the blow was enough to pop his nose, which gushed blood.

"Oh my gosh! Oh my gosh!" Cate yelled, jumping to his rescue.

"Yes, I was hoping to get you to say that, but I had something else in mind," Stevin said sarcastically, and then laughed with blood dripping into his mouth.

"Come on, Don Juan. Let's get you cleaned up," Cate ordered, taking his hand and leading him to the shower.

Good days often begin with friendly banter and brawling. From the bedroom, the pair funneled their energies into further exploration of the island. First was a stop at Anaina Hou Community Park, where they rented bikes and rode the Wai Koa Loop Trail through vast mahogany groves to the Kilauea Stone Dam. Then it was pizza for lunch at Kilauea Bakery, and then on to the lighthouse at the point. Secret Beach was just down the road, and, even though they had spent most of the previous day at the beach, the name of this one was intriguing. After a few wrong turns and vague directions from a local, they found the beach hidden down a steep, unmarked trail behind a set of large houses—the beach could basically be their expansive backyard.

While on the beach, the weather had turned cloudy and rain was imminent, which is typical for tropical afternoons, so sunbathing was probably not in the cards. But today was a day to experience as much as they could. Down on the beach, they found quaint tidal pools and a beautiful waterfall, at which Stevin insisted on taking a picture of Cate with his phone. Before long, rain drove them away, drenching them by the time they got back to the Jeep. It was a warm rain, though, and thrilling to be in, as they darted through the lush vegetation of the trail.

They were beat at this point and yearned to be back at the hotel for a hot bath and decompression before dinner. But the hotel would have to wait a bit; there were chickens to slalom and Lappert's to assault on the way.

When they finally returned and pulled into the valet, Stevin saw something he didn't like at all—more accurately, some*one* he didn't like at all.

"Fu…!" Stevin resisted saying the entire word in an effort to not only clean up his actions but also his words, and he ended up holding the *u* for quite some time before he settled on an appropriate replacement. "Fudge!"

This caught Cate a little off guard because, until this point in their trip, there had not been a single glitch, and it had seemed to truly be a slice of heaven.

"What's wrong?" she inquired.

"*Dick* is getting out of the car in front of us," Stevin said, perturbed.

"Who's Dick?"

"He's an obnoxious guy who was all over me in the gym yesterday. He wouldn't quit talking, and I don't want to get caught talking to him again. And I told him my name was Heywood Jablomi," Stevin admitted.

"You *didn't!* Well, you can't have all the fun!" Cate said, laughing, and then jumped out of the Jeep just as Dick was handing his keys to the valet. Dick's wife, a bit unnoticeable, was bent over in the car, reaching for some bags.

"Hey, Richard!" Cate said seductively, with a little wave in his direction and a little toss of her hair, and then she walked into the lobby.

Dick, so exhilarated by the attention, lit up with excitement and watched her—along with the rest of the men in the valet—saunter through the drive with her short-shorts and her bikini top.

Stevin was mortified. Cate didn't know the real reason Stevin disliked Dick, and he wished dearly she hadn't done that. He watched Dick's wife pop up like a prairie dog at the first sign of danger, turn, and give Dick a look that no man would ever want from his wife or any woman he was involved with. Dick's facial expression changed from dreamy bliss to that of an outlaw with a noose around his neck. Stevin heard him plead and stammer and explain that he had no idea who Cate was, while his wife walked away from him under the gaze of all present. Then Dick turned and looked Stevin straight in the eyes. Stevin couldn't move, and he certainly didn't want to get out. All he could muster was an innocent shrug of his shoulders. Stevin hoped that Dick was hell-bent on catching his wife to smooth things over and that he wouldn't waste time pressing the issue with him. However, Stevin's hope to ride it out in the Jeep was foiled by the valet, who opened the door.

"Welcome back, Mr. Dunfey. May I say, you are one lucky man!"

Stevin felt like melting into a puddle and washing into the storm drain to escape the attention. He could only muster "You have no idea," and then walked around the Jeep toward the lobby, where he came face-to-face with Dick Spencer.

"You got a problem with me, Hay...wood?" Dick inquired forcefully.

Stevin could tell by his tone that he had figured out the joke, which was incredibly bad timing. Stevin didn't know quite how to respond—whether to apologize for his lewd joke or for Cate's lewd actions. Either way, he didn't want to be anywhere near a guy who thought he looked like Stevin McDonald.

"Hey, look. I'm sorry. I was a jerk yesterday, and, honestly, I don't know what got into my girlfriend. If you would like me to talk to your wife, I'm more than happy to straighten it out," Stevin said, trying to diffuse the situation, which wasn't looking good.

"I don't want you, your girl, or anything 'straight' of yours near my wife!" Dick exploded.

Stevin withdrew, continuing to launch chaff. "I'm sorry. We'll stay out of your way."

Dick's face turned red, and Stevin fully expected him to throw a punch, but he just raised his fist. He looked like a person who might do such a thing and say 'Try anything else and you're going to get it, buster!' Stevin stood his ground now, and was unfazed by Dick's audacity. Dick was a good six inches shorter, and his pasty white skin and pudgy build critically discounted any real threat. Dick then walked away and into the lobby.

Stevin waited a few minutes, and then made his way to the lobby bar balcony to regroup. He knew he needed to play it off as if Cate had done something really funny, but he also knew it would take him some time to get into that mindset. After two drinks, he felt loose enough to see Cate again.

Up in her room, Cate was waiting for him. He had taken longer that she'd expected, which was agonizing because she couldn't wait for him to compliment her on her performance. When Stevin knocked, she opened the door sheepishly and waited for the grand ovation.

Stevin had rehearsed what he would say to give her the full benefit of the moment and not tip her off to his dark secret.

"You...are...*dead*!" he said with a huge smile, quoting her from earlier.

Cate erupted in laughter, so extremely proud of herself.

"You should have seen the look on his face...and the look on his *wife's* face!" he continued.

Cate abruptly stopped laughing. "Wait...wait, wait! His wife? His *wife* was there?" Cate asked, horrified by the implications.

"You didn't notice his wife? Yes...*his wife!* His *wife* was there and about pummeled the poor guy right there in the street," Stevin explained. He felt relieved that Cate hadn't seen the wife, because it would be easier now to explain how awkward it was, which was more in line with the truth.

"Oh! *Oh!* I'm so sorry! And I left you there right in the middle of it!" Cate said with her hands over her face, feeling remorseful.

With the tide moving in his direction, Stevin quickly used it as leverage for sympathy. "Yes, you did. I thought he was going to hit me!"

"Oh, baby! I am so sorry! What can I do to make it up to you?" she asked sincerely, her hands on his cheeks.

"Well," Stevin said with a grin. "I have an idea that involves the shower."

Cate smiled and then stepped back a few steps. Still looking in his eyes, she unbuttoned her shorts and slid both her shorts and bikini bottoms off. Stevin's heart surged. Before long, her bikini top joined the bottoms on the floor, and Cate ran her fingers through her long hair, teasing up the volume. She truly was a vision. Stevin stared at her, and she let him. Something inside pleaded for him to keep admiring her beauty and not move. After a few moments, Cate playfully walked up to Stevin and pulled his clothes off, turned him around, pushed her body to his from behind, and walked them in tandem to the shower.

Outside, the rain continued to fall, creating a harmonious hum of tiny drumbeats on the balcony and the broad leaves of the tropical foliage along the building. The sun had set beyond the horizon of Hanalei Bay, but again illuminated the underside of broken clouds above. Evening storms in the tropics have a soothing effect on the soul. Those who have spent a fair amount of time in such a climate love this phenomenon. Each day usually dawns with a brilliant blue and clear sky above and exploding green below, a time when Mother Nature allows for fun and play. Then the sun sinks and the clouds roll back on stage for a dazzling evening show, often with lightning on the open water. Such was this evening: electric without and electric within.

After some time in the room, it was time for dinner. While only 8:00 p.m., it felt deadly late by mainland standards. Were it not for their hunger, Stevin and Cate might have just ridden out the storm deep in the caverns of their covers. However, Stevin had heard of a famous teriyaki tuna steak at a restaurant along the river in Hanalei that he was dying to try. He called for the Jeep and they made their way down the road to the Dolphin.

The Dolphin was a local institution. Positioned on the Hanalei River, the building was open and inviting, but at the same time dark and clubby from the rich exotic wood used in construction. The entire structure opened to the outside, and the galvanized steel corrugated roof panels made for deafening white noise during heavy rains.

A thin hostess led them to their table, and just as Stevin sat in his seat, he looked up to see Dick Spencer and his wife at a table across the room. Cate had her back to them and probably wouldn't have recognized them anyway. Stevin knew that he had to play this very carefully, or it was going to develop into a situation that might involve the police, which was not an option. Dick hadn't noticed them, at least not yet, so Stevin used Cate as a shield to block Dick's view, hoping he wouldn't remember her beautiful hair from the *porte-cochère.*

Dinner was uneventful and actually very nice. Stevin ordered the teriyaki ahi and Cate tried the beef tenderloin. Stevin loved that Cate had the guts to order steak at a fish restaurant. She never ceased to amaze him. Even the littlest things made him admire and cherish her more each minute. Then came dessert. They decided to split the homemade Dolphin ice-cream pie, which was the restaurant's take on a mud pie, with coconut, macadamia nuts, and banana. It was so good, and Stevin ate so much of it, that they had to order another.

However, before it arrived, Cate had to use the restroom. This meant that Stevin was exposed. He had actually forgotten about Dick and his wife, assuming they would have left by now, but when Cate got up, there was Dick, staring directly at him. Stevin's heart sank. He didn't want any trouble. Dick looked at him in such a way that Stevin could tell his blood was boiling. Dick raised his fist again and shook it. Stevin paused for a moment, and then felt his own blood begin to boil. He could feel the Hulk coming on. But then there was Cate in the bathroom. He didn't want her to come out to a bar fight. Stevin wondered what he might do. He watched as a waiter dropped Dick's check at his table. Then it hit him.

"I think it's time for this Dick to go limp," Stevin mumbled under his breath, and he stood and walked to the bar.

"Hey, do you have a small piece of paper and pen I could borrow?" he asked the bartender.

After carefully writing his favorite three words on the paper, Stevin made his way to Dick's table. As he approached, Dick was caught by surprise and reared back in his chair, which allowed Stevin to slip the paper in the thin wallet that held the dinner check just before he spoke.

"Excuse me, sir. I just noticed that your beautiful wife dropped some money on the floor," Stevin said, holding two $100 bills. "I thought I would grab them before someone else got them, so you can pay for dinner and not be washing dishes all night!"

Mrs. Spencer laughed wholeheartedly, but then paused, trying to figure out where the money had come from. Dick's demeanor changed slightly and he played along, not wanting to alarm his wife.

"Thank you, sir. We really appreciate it," Dick said, biting his lip and keeping it short.

Stevin smiled and nodded and went back to his table, arriving just before Cate, who was oblivious to the exchange. Their dessert had been delivered, so they dug in.

About a minute later, Mrs. Spencer stood and started screaming. Other guests rushed over to her table, including Stevin. Stevin looked down at Dick, who was on the floor. His wild, yearning eyes were still open and staring at the ceiling. Stevin kneeled down, pretending to assist, but instead took back his piece of paper, which was lying on the floor. When Stevin stood back up, he melted into the crowd and watched as others called for help and attempted to revive the poor helpless man. Cate stepped up beside him.

"Oh my gosh! What happened?" she asked.

"Looks to me like a heart attack," Stevin answered, and then convinced Cate that they should leave after paying their own bill.

On the ride back, Cate was melancholy and mostly quiet, but then did speak up near the turn to the hotel.

"Oh, that's so sad. One minute you're having dinner with your husband and the next he's gone," she lamented. "Did you see his wife and the horrible lost and lonely look on her face? I hope I never have such an expression on my face. I don't think I could bear such a thing."

"I hope you never do either, love. I hope you never do either."

CHAPTER 18

BRING A BARF BAG

Chief Brenning lay in bed, unable to sleep. The clock on the nightstand read 2:33 a.m. He watched as it turned, minute by minute—the longest minutes since recorded time. Lying awake at that time of night is tricky. On one hand, you know you're dead tired and want desperately to sleep, but on the other, you're so wrought with anxiety about being awake that you can't sleep. That, of course, in addition to the relentless three days of sorting through the events on the bridges. He and his force had worked almost nonstop for the last 72 hours, dealing with the fallout from the event with incredible demands raining down on them from just about every bureau, guard, agency, and department one could think of—let alone the barrage of calls from the public. But, in the end, and despite the reservations of others, the more the Chief pieced it together, the more he knew it was Stevin McDonald's retribution for the ambush. The last words Stevin had said to him rang in his ears—ringing that still hadn't stopped. In about nine hours, he was again going to be in front of a firing squad of interrogators, wondering what progress he'd made on finding Stevin. The truth was he had no idea where Stevin was, and in his correspondence with the other agencies working the case, he knew they didn't have much either. Stevin had, in essence, 'gone dark.' This frustration had chased the sleep from the Chief's eyes for the last several nights.

He rolled over and stared at his wife's solemn face, framed neatly by her pillow, and watched as she breathed little breaths, certainly far smaller than his frustrated huffing and puffing. He thought back to his one chance to catch Stevin, thinking he had done everything possible to build an inescapable trap. He winced thinking about how everyone was duped by a lookalike dummy. *Jason Henley. Jason Henley. Jason Henley,* the Chief thought to himself. *What am I missing?* The chief went over in his mind the two days they'd held Jason, making absolute certain he actually was Jason Henley and then milking every last detail from his story—how he was approached at the gas station by an old man and told to go to McDonald's and ask for a passport. Jason had done his best to detail the account, but, in the end, there really wasn't much to go on. There were recordings from overhead cameras of the meeting at the gas station, but Stevin had given nothing away except for showing off some old clothes and a broad-brimmed hat. Honestly, it was a stretch to even prove that it was him in the video. When the Chief watched the video for the thousandth time, he, along with his detectives, waited for that moment you see in the movies when someone notices a wrapper, a sound, a label, or something that becomes the tipping point in the case; but alas, nothing ever materialized. The closest thing they had was the account of the four officers in the Explorer, who remembered seeing an old guy, but they couldn't agree on almost anything else about him, including the type and color of his car.

Missus Chief Brenning kept breathing, and he kept watching. In and out. In and out. Watching her was calming. She made him feel safe. He knew he could get through whatever happened in the morning because he would be right back here by her side for bedtime, and this gave him peace and confidence. In and out...and out. Sleep finally came.

In the morning, the all-hands-on-deck meeting was held at City Hall, where there was a large, theater-like training room that could accommodate the approximately 30 people in attendance. The Chief sat next to the Commissioner, DA Jolley, the Mayor, and the Governor. If POTUS had been there, the Chief would have been sitting near him too. The Chief was more or less in the hot seat, and there was no way out of it.

On the street outside was a mob scene of news reporters and the public, which was demanding answers and justice. There were news crews from many different cities and countries, as the event had made national headlines and was being followed across the globe.

At 11:00, Chief Brenning reluctantly began the meeting.

"On behalf of the Governor of California and the Mayor of San Francisco, I'd like to thank all of you for coming today. I am Samuel Brenning, San Francisco's Chief of Police. This meeting has been called in the spirit of cooperation in our joint effort to apprehend the number one person of interest of our city's worst act of terror, Stevin McDonald. I will start with the police report. I will then turn the time over to Special Agent Daily of the FBI. After the FBI, we will hear briefly from forensics. At the end of each of our reports, we will field questions from the group; then, at the end of the presentations, we'd like to review our action items moving forward."

With the introduction, the group settled in for the police briefing. Chief Brenning didn't know what more to say without coming right out with the fact that the trail had gone cold, so he reviewed some of the key points of the case as a bit of smokescreen.

"Our suspect is a white male, approximately forty-five years old. He has brown hair and brown eyes and a fit build. He has several prior convictions, including spending four years at San Quentin on a second strike for larceny and assault. He was released two years ago after serving his full sentence and has been quiet, until ten days ago, when he killed Martin Bornstein in his apartment and nearly killed Val Ma, a delivery girl—who, by the way, I hear is doing well and is on the road to recovery. From there, as you all know, we have a series of mysterious deaths, which culminated in the death of one of our own; 17 on the Embarcadero and the 123 lost on the bridges. We believe..."

"Chief," a voice called from the front row.

"Yes?" the Chief responded, pausing to look up. It was Special Agent Daily of the FBI.

"May I?"

"By all means, Special Agent," the Chief said as he stepped aside, relieved, and let Agent Daily speak.

Special Agent Daily was as clean-cut as they come—a Boy Scout, if you will. He was known for playing by the book. While many might take a little heat for being so rigid, Agent Daily rarely had to, largely due to his immense size. At 6'6" and 270 pounds of muscle, with the ability to conceal a much larger weapon than others, most fellow agents heeded their scruples when wondering whether or not to question his rigid dedication. A top graduate of the Academy and a top agent, he commanded respect in every way, even from those who didn't subscribe to playing by all the rules. When he spoke, he did so with confidence, despite a slight lisp.

"I have some intelligence on the case, which I just received and would like to share. I think it is something we should all focus on, and is very time sensitive. Over the past three days, we have been feeding our field officers with up-to-date information on the case, with special attention given to any and all heart attacks. We've had a couple very interesting and intriguing leads, but the one we just received seems ironclad. This morning, our agents in Hawaii were apprised of a heart attack death on the north shore of Kauai, which happened last night at approximately 2130 hours. The wife of the deceased identified Stevin McDonald as the person who last spoke to the couple before the husband died, and someone they'd had contact with at the St. Regis Princeville hotel. Our agents are en route to the hotel now and we are scrambling two tactical teams from Honolulu to intercept and assist. I have asked a tech team to set up comms in this room, so that all of you can watch as we attempt to apprehend Mr. McDonald. I don't think I need to remind any of you that this information does not leave this room. Doing so would put the lives of our agents and innocent people in jeopardy. We should be live in about fifteen minutes."

With that news, the room erupted in discussion. In the Chief's mind, he was selfishly relieved, thinking that Stevin was Hawaii's problem now, and that the city wasn't in any imminent danger. Then he began to wonder how in the world he got out of San Francisco and all the way to Hawaii. Everyone in the room had agents posted all over the West Coast looking for Stevin McDonald. His picture was on every news channel and at every airport, bus station, ferry dock, and Segway stand. Apparently, today's modern technology and advanced communications still has pores.

Across the room, DA Jolley cornered Agent Daily. "Agent Daily. My name is Holly Jolley. I'm the deputy district attorney. I'm wondering if you have a minute before this goes live," she inquired.

Special Agent Daily looked down. The last thing he wanted was to be cornered by some deputy DA who, quite obviously, was seeing the case slip from her State-of-California hands into the federal system. But despite the incredible lack of time, his polite character prevailed.

"Sure. Anytime," he said politely.

Holly was sharp, and she knew this case was all but gone from her department, but she still wanted to keep it close. She felt like one of the pieces of its great puzzle, so she quickly strategized a way to influence its outcome; her gut told her the hounds were seconds from cornering the fox.

"I just wanted to put a bug in your ear. All of the major resources for this effort are here in San Francisco. I think you should really make an effort to get him back here. For what it's worth, and from a prosecutor, the case is much stronger if you do," she reasoned delicately.

A puzzled look came over Agent Daily, like he'd heard what she said but couldn't quite figure out why or what her angle was. Besides, it was premature; they hadn't even found him yet. He agreed without fully understanding her reasoning, and then was called to the front again as the video feed from the aloha agents went live. When it came up on the screen, the room went dead silent as everyone watched. The two agents were pulling into the St. Regis valet. When the valet came to the driver's door, they could hear the agent state his name and show his badge and then discretely ask the valet not to talk to anyone, and to escort them directly to the property management office. Once there, they introduced themselves, and immediately asked management to review the guest list for Stevin McDonald.

"We don't show a Stevin McDonald here... let me check. No, no Stevin McDonald in the last 30 days," the manager reported, looking at the agents with a confused face. San Francisco watched as the agents batted around some ideas, and then finally, Agent Daily impatiently piped up on the line.

"Show them the picture!"

One of the agents reached in his jacket and pulled out a picture of Stevin, and he showed it to the manager.

"Have you seen this man?" he asked.

"No, I haven't," the manager quickly replied.

The agents were perplexed. Mrs. Spencer was certain it was him, and that he was staying at the St. Regis. Just then a voice came from the back. It was the valet.

"Can I see that?" he asked.

He held the picture up and stared at it intently for a few seconds. Little did he know that nearly 40 people were watching him on camera, and an entire nation was relying on his ability to recognize a face. He placed his hand over the hair of the man in the picture, with the forehead in the crotch of his thumb. The valet's white skin gave just the contrast needed for the light to go on... Finkle was Einhorn!

"Oh! That's Mr. Dunfey."

"When was the last time you saw him?" one of the agents demanded, grabbing him by the arm.

The valet was shocked. The casual vibe of the agents had turned to elevated panic.

"Um...I think he checked out today, around eight this morning. I saw Jerry loading their Jeep with luggage," he said, shaken.

"Their?" the agent drilled.

"He was with his wife or girlfriend, Mrs. Dunfey."

"I've got them!" the manager chimed in excitedly, clicking at his computer. "They were here for three days. Frank Dunfey, plus one. They *did* check out this morning."

Both agents turned to each other and simultaneously said "Airport," and then ran back to their car. Agent Daily was a step ahead of them. He was on the phone with his tech team at his office.

"I need you to find passenger Dunfey on any flights from Hawaii back to California today from eight a.m. on. Let me know when you find them. This is a top priority!" he squawked.

He turned to those in the room.

"We're close!"

Again the room erupted with talk, speculation, and anticipation, with some angry overtones. They hated this guy for what he had done to their city. They hated him more for relaxing in Hawaii for three days while they dug out of the rubble.

Agent Daily's phone rang right back. Being the good guy that he was, he put it on speakerphone and held it up to the room's microphone.

"We have a Francis Dunfey and Catherine Little flying first class on Hawaiian Airlines Flight HA34 through Honolulu. They just made their connection, and the plane is in the air—approximately four and a half hours from LAX," the voice said.

Agent Daily's gears were churning. He, along with everyone else, wondered why they would be flying to LAX, and what to do next. DA Jolley caught his eye. He looked at her. She was leaning back in her chair with her arms folded, a slight smile on her face. Without saying anything, her posture told him just what he needed to do. He pulled the mic at the podium close to his mouth, like John J. radioing Murdock.

"Attention, everyone. We are going to divert that flight to SFO and bring him back here for justice, *but* we need to be smart about it. First, every one of us needs to use our resources to figure out who Francis Dunfey and Catherine Little are. Someone needs to get the location of Alexes McDonald to insure she is not in cahoots with him. Whoever these people are, they might be in grave danger. While we're doing that, we need to move this meeting to SFO, but we're not going out the front door. I'll get tactical teams geared up at the airport. Chief Brenning, call ahead and let the force at the airport know that we're coming and are going to close the airport in about four hours. Mayor, you know this building. I need a back door, ASAP! Now let's move!"

The group snapped to attention and followed the Mayor through a service corridor and out onto a loading dock. SFPD had several black and whites waiting for anyone who couldn't get to their own cars in the front. DA Jolley again found herself in a backseat, this time next to Detective Howe.

"Looks like Uber needs a new car category...patrol car," she said, feeling a bit cramped behind the cage.

"Of all my time on the force, I don't think I've ever ridden in the back of one of these. Prior to joining, I sure did!" he said, laughing.

Holly smiled genuinely at the joke, even though she didn't really know the detective. A little comic relief was a nice respite from the situation, and she could sense that he was trying to impress her.

In about twenty minutes, the convoy arrived at SFO and set up a command center. Though they obviously told the pilots and informed the airport police, their plan was to keep it as quiet as possible, which meant that not even the plane's crew or the passengers were to know.

Two of those oblivious passengers were in first class, snuggling closely. Cate had her head on Stevin's shoulder, and the two shared a blanket. Stevin wondered how coming home would play out. He knew his past certainly wasn't just going to blow over, and he knew that it probably wasn't long before the police figured out that poor Francis Dunfey wasn't actually in Tallahassee. The thought of it all made him sick. He fought the reality that this dream he was living was going to end sooner or later, and a foreboding feeling told it him it would be sooner. He continued to sort Cate's hair with his finger, running it from her temple and over her ear. He loved the feel of it—heavy and thick, with a natural wave.

As he sat there looking at her, he began to think of a contingency plan. He thought about it in terms of *What if I'm gone? What can I do for Cate to try and ease her pain?* Then he started to think about

Alexes and her two girls, and how poorly he had treated them. He wished there was something he could do for them, too. Then the world crashed upon him as he wondered how to make amends for each and every person who he had hurt. He felt his sins engulf him, and he wished he could die to escape them.

Then something whispered to him...a fleeting idea of self-destruction. Maybe he should choose to go out on top. Maybe he should say the words and slip quietly away. It would be easier that way for Cate, and it would give a measure of justice to the many who he had murdered. He could just say the words here on the plane and fall asleep next to Cate. It would be so easy. He quickly resolved to do it, wanting to be free of his guilt.

"Silence..." he said with a crackly voice.

"Sometimes..." he said slowly, now expecting to feel some change in heart.

Just as he was about to complete the phrase, another voice whispered to him. It was different from the first, much warmer and more loving—a heavenly nudge of courage. His entire body welled up with goosebumps, and he immediately caught hold of a memory—a happy memory, something that had lodged itself deep within him from his childhood. He remembered again the words his uncle had told him, and the words he had casually shared with Francis in the solarium. This time, however, he heard distinctly in his mind the voice of his uncle saying, "Even the worst of sinners can be forgiven, if they change."

As he thought about it, he became emotional. He was the worst of sinners! *But can it be? How?* he wondered. He yearned to know, and for the first time since childhood, his life began to need meaning. There was something more; something more he had to do; something more he had to *learn*. His faith in himself and in his whispering mentor, though ever so fragile, began to take root, and though he knew there would be hell to pay for his deeds, finding redeeming truth would be worth every lash, every flame, and every horror on the journey.

Stevin sat still in his seat for a long time as he thought about his new odyssey. Then he realized that he needed to make right the wrongs he had done. As he contemplated what he might do, an idea came to him, but he knew he didn't have much time to pull it off. The pilot had just turned on the seatbelt sign and made the announcement that they were about 30 minutes from landing. The noise stirred Cate slightly, and Stevin took the opportunity to move her from his shoulder to the wall of the plane. As he did, he looked out the window and saw the blue of the Pacific, with little boats making little white wakes among ocean swells.

Once Cate was settled, he delicately slid her purse from under her feet and dug through its cavernous well until he located her checkbook. Then he tore out a deposit slip from the back and settled in his seat with his phone to punch out an e-mail to send as soon as he had service. The e-mail was to Jack at Morgan Stanley. The subject was "Gift to My Nieces".

Cate awoke right about the time he finished the e-mail and leaned over to kiss him. She embraced him with a long, strong hug—demonstrating with no words her love and trust. As she hugged him, the plane made a long turn north, revealing land below. Stevin's blood ran cold. As he sat hugging the love of his life, he caught sight of a bridge out the window. It wasn't just any bridge; it was unmistakably the San Mateo Bridge. His time was coming to an end much, much sooner than he had hoped. He closed his eyes and countered Cate's hug with the longing embrace of desperate man who was about to be ripped from her arms. His arms ached. His heart raced. His tears streamed onto Cate's bare neck. He could feel the landing gear go down and the plane slow. He had only a few minutes left before he would attempt to run.

"Cate," he said, still clutching her tightly. "I love you, and I'm sorry...more sorry than I can ever express, and more than you'll ever know."

Stevin unbuckled and stood in the aisle and looked at Cate. Her eyes were desperate, lost, and lonely.

"What is it? What is wrong?" she pleaded, as her own tears began to fall.

Stevin wanted to tell her everything, but he couldn't bear to crush her any more than he already had. He simply turned and walked down the aisle, toward the back of the plane, wondering what his next move would be. Then it hit him. He grabbed his phone. It had service now. He first sent a text to someone he had entered in his address book as "Mysterious Uber Guy". The text read *North end of SFO runway. 15 min. Hurry!* He got an almost instant reply, which said, *Bring a barf bag.* This seemed like an odd request, but he shook it off and pressed send on the e-mail to Jack.

CHAPTER 19

PICK A NUMBER

When Stevin got to the back of the plane, the flight crew was shocked to see a passenger standing in front of them when the plane was about to land.

Stevin motioned to one of them, while pulling the curtain shut.

"Come here!" he demanded.

The stewardess was hesitant.

"Get up!" he yelled.

The stewardess got up cautiously, expecting to be knifed or worse.

Stevin grabbed her by the arms, holding her tight, and whispered in her ear.

"I'm Stevin McDonald, one of the FBI's most wanted men. Call the co-pilot and tell him to come back here in ten seconds, or I'm going to kill everyone on this plane. Now do it!" he demanded.

Of course, he wasn't going to kill everyone on the plane—nor could he, really. In fact, his abrupt change of demeanor was entirely out of necessity; he didn't want to hurt anyone, but he didn't want to be taken into custody in front of Cate. Her confused and scared face was already sad enough; he wouldn't put her through the shock of more. He was determined to make a run for it, and he cast his die to chance.

As Stevin watched from behind the curtain, the stewardess quickly called the cockpit. In seconds, the co-pilot came running. When he got to the back and parted the curtain to look, Stevin caught him by the back of the neck and rammed him into the metal cabinets, knocking him out cold. Stevin pointed his finger at the remaining crew and said, "Not a sound!" He then commenced changing clothes—at least hat, shirt, tie, and jacket. He didn't have time for pants and shoes. When he was done, he approached the stewardess again.

"What's the code to the cockpit door?" he asked frantically.

The stewardess hesitated again.

"The code!" he demanded.

"One-two-three-four," she replied.

Stevin looked at her in awe; as if he was going to fall for that! "Do you want to die? Do you think I'm a fool?" he responded.

"I'm serious. One-two-three-four!" she said boldly.

Stevin turned to the rest of them and explained that this was merely a way to escape, and that he wasn't going to hurt anyone; then he moved back up the aisle, toward the cockpit. As he passed Cate, he looked down and the other way. He couldn't face seeing her again, and he hoped the coat and hat was enough for him to pass by undetected.

Just before Stevin got to the cockpit, the plane touched down, which jarred him a little and caused him to lose his footing slightly. Now, wobbling down the aisle, he was no match for the plane when the pilot hit the brakes. This sent Stevin smashing full speed into the cockpit door, like a mad bull against a bullfighter's metal cape. After he collected himself, he looked behind him to see if he was being followed. There was no one, but his eyes naturally gravitated to Cate in her seat. He didn't actually see her because he could only see the top of her head leaning against the wall. In his mind's eye, he imagined her staring out the window, crying, trying to piece together the last few days and the events that had unfolded. He closed his eyes in shame, turned, and opened them to see the eye of someone on the other side looking at him through the peephole. Stevin panicked. He needed to get in there before they barricaded the door or, worse, drew a gun.

He quickly keyed in the door code. When he heard the lock open, he burst in, knocking the peeping captain back and onto the controls, which startled the second co-pilot, who was trying to stop the plane. Once inside, Stevin slammed the door shut and barricaded it with a few loose bags. As the captain scrambled to his feet, Stevin tried to calm his and the co-pilot's nerves.

"Listen! Do what I say and no one gets hurt."

The captain stood in front of him, looking poised to pounce, which made Stevin a little uneasy.

"First, you're going to sit back in your seat," he said, pointing at the captain.

The plane was nearly stopped now on the runway. As the captain sat down, Stevin noticed a swarm of vehicles coming onto the runway. He needed to get out of the plane and somehow close to the road that bordered the airport to the north, in hopes of connecting with his ride. In the distance, he could see where he needed to go. He could see the 101 Freeway in the background, above the frontage road, which probably accessed the many commercial buildings and hangars that serviced the airport. With no other option, he decided to casually drive the plane there. It would sure beat running, and he could likely do so without getting caught.

"Throttle up a little," he said to the captain. "We're not stopping. Head to the end of the runway!"

The captain turned, put on his earphones, and throttled the plane forward into Calvary traffic. It was now a game of chicken with a clear 200-ton winner.

"Take off your headphones! No tower or cell calls!" Stevin said forcefully.

As the cars and trucks drew near, the captain turned to see what Stevin wanted to do.

"Keep going! They have steering wheels and brakes; they'll move," he said with a smirk.

Stevin was standing in the cockpit like a surfer riding a giant surfboard over a magic, lighted disco floor. He watched the ruckus below as much as he could before it passed beneath the plane. He could only imagine the confusion as 40 or so vehicles all tried to turn around at once.

"Full throttle, now!" Stevin commanded, wanting to put a little more turbulence in their U-turns.

The captain pushed the throttles and the plane sprung forward. The turbulence was much more effective than Stevin knew or expected. Directly behind the jets, several cars and a SWAT van were sent airborne, tumbling over the cars behind them and then into heaps on the tarmac. This caused the entire fleet of cars to delay, then move cautiously to the side of the plane, at a safe distance, giving Stevin a little running room.

The plane was nearing the end of the runway. Stevin could see a parking lot on the other side of the barbed-wire fence, and he figured that was where he needed to go.

"Park our front landing gear against that fence ahead," he said to the pilot. "And you! Open the escape hatch!" he said, turning to the co-pilot.

"Escape hatch?" the co-pilot said with forced surprise.

"Don't shit with me, Snoopy. You're a terrible liar. I know there is a hatch for you guys; now open it!"

The co-pilot knew he was made and stood to open the hatch, which was in essence a sliding window and a makeshift Rapunzel-style knotted rope, which they were to let down from the window and then climb to the ground.

The plane was now at the end of the runway, and the captain was doing his best to stop the plane right at the fence, which was difficult to do with no one on the ground watching the location of the front landing gear. He eased up to the fence. They could hear the underside of the plane scraping along the barbed wire, which was then quickly drowned out by the tide of sirens and screeching tires behind them. The end result was that the front of the plane hung neatly over the parking lot, guarded by a fence full of razor wire. Brilliant!

"You guys go first. If you make a noise about me, you die," Stevin bluffed, playing into everyone's fear that nobody really knew how he killed people. It's the unknown that grips people. If he'd had a knife or even a gun, the crew probably would have rallied the entire plane to dogpile him, but his wake of destruction left everyone bobbing in doubt and fear, and ensured their absolute compliance.

The captain went first and awkwardly descended the small rope. Once he was to the ground, the co-pilot went. Now alone in the cockpit, Stevin stuck his head out of the window and looked back over the fence to the runway. To his fright, all 80 or so eyes—and 40 or so guns—were aimed at him. He froze in fear, but then convinced himself that they had not figured it out yet. He climbed out on the rope, and, as he descended, motioned to the group, pointing to the body of the plane, as if to say, "The bastard is in there!" When he did, their attention and weapons shifted to the plane itself.

From his perch outside of the cockpit, Stevin then looked the other way, praying there was a black sedan idling in the nearby street. A pair of lights blinked. He looked up into the greying blue sky and whispered, "Thank you!" As he was about to climb down, he looked back into the cockpit and remembered that the driver had asked him to bring a sickness bag. He wondered if he should take the time to go back in and grab one. It seemed silly, under the circumstances, to even consider doing such a thing, so he settled on just taking a quick look under the window. As luck would have it, he spied one stowed in a small cubby. Stevin grabbed it, shoved it in his pant pocket, and climbed to the ground.

"You guys come with me, quickly!" he ordered the pilots.

The three made their way to the car. When they got there, Stevin looked back to see if they were being followed. Nobody could get over the barbed wire, but they did pull a van up next to the fence and he could see men climbing on top to look over. Just then he heard more sirens, this time coming up the frontage road on his side of the fence. He didn't think they knew he was incognito, but he could assume they were taking no chances. He hustled the group to the sedan and got in the backseat, instructing the captain and co-pilot to run back to the plane.

"Let's go!" he exclaimed.

"Did you bring the barf bag?" the driver asked.

"Yes! Let's go!" Stevin said, becoming very anxious.

"Keep the bag handy, please," the driver responded calmly.

Stevin's patience wore out. "Are you going to drive, or do I need to come up there and do it myself?" he demanded.

"Pick a number," the driver instructed.

"A number?"

"Look at the scale in front of you."

Stevin sat back in his seat. He could hardly read, he was so frantic. The sirens grew louder, and he could see the cars now.

The scale was simple. It numbered 1 through 10. Below the numbers were descriptive words, and below those were prices. Stevin struggled to make sense of it all. Under the number 1 were the words *smooth, comfortable, easy,* and a price of $250. This gradually increased in severity and price. By number 5 the words were *abrupt, speeding, aggressive,* with a price of $1,500. The scale culminated at 10 with the words *severe, crashing, injury,* and a price of $25,000. Stevin felt an incredible urge to get out and run instead of jerk around with this crazy driver and his whacko scale. He took a deep breath and composed himself. Up front, the driver could tell that Stevin was struggling.

"Under the circumstances, sir, why don't we start with 4 and see how we do?" the driver suggested.

Stevin took a moment to look at the man in front of him. The first thing that stuck out was that he was wearing a San Francisco Giants ball cap, which seemed odd for a professional driver, especially the mysterious type. Stevin kind of expected the typical black captain's hat and black suit and tie. Instead it was ball cap, hoodie, and the black driving gloves that Stevin remembered from their initial meeting. He could see that he was wearing jeans and driving mocs as well. He was an Asian man, maybe 5'6" tall and maybe 50 years old, chewing gum and sitting in the driver's seat as peacefully as if he were in the front pew at church. With few other options, Stevin took his suggestion.

"Okay...4. Just go already!"

"I'll need payment first," came the reply.

"How am I supposed to pay you a thousand right now?" Stevin asked.

The driver turned slightly, looked at Stevin, and shrugged his shoulders, still calm as a summer's night.

"Cash or trade, sir; cash or trade," the driver suggested.

"Well, take whatever the hell you want! Here's my watch and my wallet! Just go!" Stevin shrieked.

The man looked at the watch and wallet and determined that they would suffice...for now.

"That'll do," he said, and started the car.

By this time, the first police cars had rounded the corner from the frontage road and were seconds away.

"Go, go, go!" Stevin demanded.

"Where, to sir?" the driver asked, now having a bit of fun watching Stevin come unglued in the back.

Stevin was already beginning to learn that the quickest way to move the driver was to remain calm and follow his directions implicitly.

He composed himself and said simply, "North, please. The Marina District."

"I'll need an address...oh, just kidding!" the driver said, watching Stevin in the rearview mirror, and then he laughed heartily. "Now, just wait. Sometimes it's best to go slow."

As the police cars came into the lot, they blew right past the black sedan and headed toward the plane, about 100 yards away. As soon as they went by, the driver eased the car onto the road and slipped up San Bruno Avenue and onto the 101.

Up on the freeway, they clipped along at about 80 MPH, weaving discreetly through traffic. It was aggressive driving, but not out of the ordinary in the Bay Area, where new-money techies proved exotics on a daily basis. Stevin turned back to see if they were being followed. At first there was nothing, but soon he saw lights... then *more* lights.

"Shit! Shit! Those asshole pilots told them where I was!" he blurted, then turned to the driver. "You gotta go faster!"

He turned back. The giant arrowhead of police cars cored its way up the freeway. Before long, all civilian cars had pulled over, and it was just them, about a half-mile of empty road, and the police, the FBI, Frank Bullitt, Harry Callahan, and anyone else with a badge or a gun.

"We're running at a 4 right now, sir. If you would like to increase the number, please review the chart on the back of the seat in front of you," the driver repeated.

Stevin was about to yell "Ten," but then remembered that the driver wasn't going to do anything until he got paid, and Stevin was far from having anything close to $25,000 on him.

"Do you take credit cards, by chance?" Stevin asked sheepishly.

"Sorry. They are too easy to trace," came the reply.

Then, as calmly as he could, and as much as it killed him to think about how he might do it without getting caught, Stevin suggested that they exit the freeway and find a bank. With $3,000 from an ATM, he could boost the ride to a 6.

"You want to pull over and stop?" the driver said, surprised.

"Yes. I'd like to move our ride to a 6, but will need some cash to do so," Stevin explained.

"You did notice the helicopters above us, right?" the driver inquired. "Pulling over for an ATM might be a little tricky."

"Just exit here and drop me off at an ATM. If it gets too hot, you can leave. If you can manage to get me again, then get me," Stevin suggested, thinking that he might not even need the driver if he could find a way to disappear.

The driver slid off the freeway at Cesar Chavez and stopped at the light at the bottom of the hill. Stevin went bananas! "Why are you stopping? Do you not see a horde of police right behind us?" he shrieked.

The driver tapped his thumbs on the steering wheel and coolly replied, "We don't run red lights at number 4."

"You are driving one of the FBI's most-wanted men in your car! I don't think you want to get caught with me!

"Very good point," the driver reasoned. "But they can't catch me. We'll go to number 6 on loan."

"Whatever! Just go!"

The driver stomped on the gas and the engine roared like a great dragon that had been awakened from a deep sleep. The car darted onto the shoulder, through the traffic in the intersection, and up Potrero. Stevin was smashed in the backseat like he was riding one of those disturbing carnival rides that spins you until you're stuck to the wall before they drop the floor out from underneath you. The driver rammed through traffic, making abrupt turns and slamming on his brakes to avoid collisions with slow-moving Toyotas. Were it not for his seatbelt, Stevin would have been rolling like a rock in a tumbler, and he started to understand why he was told to bring a barf bag.

Suddenly, the car skidded to a stop. Stevin looked out and they were parked under some trees in a bus stop loading zone on 24th Street.

"ATM around the corner! Go!" the driver shouted.

Stevin ripped off the hat, jacket, and tie, and stumbled out of the door and onto the sidewalk. He struggled to get his footing as he watched the car roar up the street and then vanish.

Stevin then turned to see a surge of police coming from basically every direction. He stood there, dazed. The first car whizzed past him while two others blocked the intersection. Soon the whole armada had funneled on to 24th. He watched in utter amazement as they drove past him, one after the other after the other. It was then he realized that he had discovered the headwaters of Shit Creek.

"Hey, buddy. Move back, please," came a voice. It was one of the officers blocking the intersection.

Stevin stared at him in complete disbelief, but then quickly mustered a thumbs-up and spun around to walk up the street toward the ATM. The ATM was at the back of the building as an inset in the side wall. His hands shook terribly from nerves when he got the money. As the last bills cycled out, he wondered what he would do. Should he stand there and wait for the M.U.G. (Mysterious Uber Guy), walk up the block, or do something really bold like pop into L's across the street for a cup of joe? He thought about it briefly. His former self wouldn't have needed long to decide, but he was changed now, and struggled with how to shed the renegade angel of death in favor of the reformed saint of all that is wonderful—all while not getting caught. He recalled how movies always portrayed suspects walking up the street at a fast pace, often with their jacket collars flipped up to somewhat conceal their faces. With that, he decided to go completely contrary to the expected and walked back toward the intersection. He grabbed the phone from his pocket and pretended to have a lively conversation with a friend about how the Niners were going to go all the way this year. To his happy surprise, the police at the corner had been swept up with the others, so all was pretty quiet there. This was not the case in other parts of the Mission District, however. Stevin could hear the great echo of sirens far down the street. As he got back up to 24th and looked west, he could make out police cars frantically crisscrossing the street in both directions as far as he could see. The whole scene as reported from above would later be compared to a giant game of Pac-Man. Stevin could only imagine the hell the driver was going through trying to double back without getting cornered.

Stevin crossed the street and then stopped abruptly. Ahead of him, down Bryant, a lone, familiar cruiser was coming in his direction. Something about it, or the situation, looked familiar. He felt naked without his fireman's gear or a wheelchair, or some other manner of charade tackle. He quickly turned west and started to do just what he had decided not to do...walk fast and flip up his collar.

In the patrol car, there was both anxiety and dispute.

"I swear that's him!" Cesmat said.

"Man, even if that *is* him and we *do* catch him, the Chief is going to kill us for being so far off our beat. Not to mention him telling us distinctly to stay off this case," Bradley countered.

Cesmat thought about it and then let out a sigh of indifference.

"I don't really care what the Chief thinks. Plus, I think all bets are off after the Bridge terror. I don't think he'd care if a Chihuahua dragged him through the front door of headquarters wearing a fire hydrant costume. We've seen this guy face-to-face. No one else has. Are you with me? Or do you want to drop me off and take the car back north? I'm telling you, if we get this guy, we're heroes. If we don't, we'll just come up with some excuse why we're down here."

Bradley wasn't thrilled about the idea, but he went along. They sped up and turned left on 24th. Ahead, they could see a man who seemed out of place, walking briskly with his jacket collar flipped up. The man turned back to look as he darted left at Florida Street, and their suspicion was confirmed. They knew it was him.

Stevin began running. He didn't know what else to do. Chances were the car following him was going to drive him straight into the other frantic police cars. He wondered where his driver was, but he knew he probably shouldn't count on being picked up again.

Stevin continued up the street. He could hear the surge of an engine behind him, then he went left again at 25th Street and figured the only thing to do was to try and get back to the bus stop where he had been dropped off. He was at a full sprint now, with the police right behind him and certainly on their radio calling the others to converge.

When he got back to the corner by the ATM, to his immense frustration, there was no black car and no driver. He looked up and down 24th—nothing. Behind him, the patrol car skidded to a stop. It had come down to this: a footrace, and and Stevin was about out of gas. He darted across the street and into a market with fruit boxes out front. Cesmat and Bradley were right behind him—well, at least Bradley was. Cesmat was "pacing himself."

When Stevin ran into the building, Bradley yelled back to Cesmat to go around back.

"Okay," Cesmat said to himself, trying to keep up.

Just when Cesmat got to the corner of the building, he heard Bradley again from inside.

"He's on the roof!"

Cesmat stopped, caught his breath for a moment, and then hustled to the front of the building. He could hear some commotion up top, and then Bradley yelling again.

"He's coming to the front!"

Cesmat backed up so he could see over the awnings. He felt like a kid waiting for his ball to roll off the roof, not knowing exactly where it might come down. Then it came—a barreling bundle of exhaustion. Stevin flopped over the parapet onto the awning, and then slid off directly into Cesmat's arms, and eventually into his lap when the two tumbled to the ground. While Cesmat wasn't a runner, few knew that he was a high-school wrestler. Once on the ground, Stevin had little chance of escape, and within a few seconds Cesmat had him pinned and the struggle was over.

When Bradley came down, the two worked to cuff Stevin and check his pockets for weapons. When they finally lifted him up, the first thing Stevin saw was the M.U.G. driving by calmly. He couldn't see the driver through the tinted windows, but there was really nothing to say or to gesture. Once past, the car sped up, turned, and was gone. Behind him, though, came the surge of the rest of the force. For the last ten minutes, they had completely torched the Mission District trying to catch the black sedan; now, they all came to a screeching halt, filling two blocks of 24th Street with a parade of flashing lights. In front of them, with Stevin in hand, were Cesmat and Bradley, San Francisco's newly christened heroes.

"Well, partner, you were right," Bradley conceded, soaking in the awe of so many law-enforcement officials and agents staring at them. "But I still think we had better come up with an excuse."

"No excuses, brother. Just tell anyone who asks that it was destiny."

CHAPTER 20

GUILTY

San Francisco was ecstatic at the news of Stevin's capture, but no one was more thrilled than DA Jolley. Thanks to Cesmat and Bradley being first to have physical custody of Stevin, she would have a strong case to make as to why the feds should let the State prosecute him. Her first call upon hearing the news was to U.S. Attorney Mark Miller's office.

"Yes. Hi. U.S. Attorney Mark Miller, please. This is District Attorney Holly Jolley. I'm calling in regard to SFPD's recent apprehension of Stevin McDonald," she stated, putting extra emphasis on 'SFPD.'

"One moment, please," came the response. After a minute or so, the voice came back, "I'll put you right through."

After several rings, Attorney Miller answered. "So...you're calling to take my case, are you?" Miller joked, expecting some banter with an old flame.

"Mark, listen. I know you think you can pull rank here, but we have him and no one wants his blood more than the people in my district. You got to let me take this one," Holly said, not taking the bait.

"The terrorist asshole wiped out your city, and then killed someone in Hawaii. Terrorist...California...Hawaii...hmm. This one seems to have 'federal' written all over it. Hell, I'm surprised you even had the guts to call!" he mused, having a little fun with Holly before he gave in.

"Mark, where is Stevin McDonald now?" Holly asked.

"San Francisco County Jail, I suppose. Well, unless you still have your guest room downstairs," Mark responded, grimacing silently.

"Would you be serious?!?"

"I like getting you all riled up. It's *sexy!*"

"Oh, my hell. You are *killing* me! Can you be serious for one damn minute? We apprehended him. We have him in custody. Therefore, we have primary jurisdiction. I'm going to take you to the mat on this one, Mark. I'm *serious!*" Holly said forcefully, not realizing that she had just stepped into a snare.

"Oh, you remember! The yoga mat in front of the fireplace...the Dean Martin mix...the tall glasses of Bordeaux!"

"*Mark!*" Holly screamed in desperation. "You shouldn't joke about such things as convicting a murderer and breaking my heart...and especially not in the same conversation!"

"Oh, fine. You win. But I reserve the right to kick him out of the guest room and bring over a bottle of wine. Go ahead and take it, but be careful. You're going to have the world watching you, and it's not going to be easy. He obviously did it, but you're going to have a tough road proving it with very little evidence and very few witnesses," Mark cautioned, then continued. "And Holly, in all seriousness, watch yourself. No one really knows what he is up to."

"I'll be fine. I can't wait to nail him to the wall!" Holly said excitedly.

"Holly?" Mark asked.

"Yes?"

"You may want to rephrase that."

"Mark?" Holly asked.

"Yes?"

"You're hopeless!"

Mark could be heard laughing into the phone. "Love you too, babe! Let's talk soon."

Holly had won.

Up the street, the police had parked Stevin in the county jail. Stevin was no stranger to jail or prison or the court system, and he knew his indictment was going to be a cakewalk. The DA would surely bury him with charges, then he'd be arraigned standing next to his defense attorney, who would try and convince him to plead guilty. No attorney in their right mind would want to defend him; to do so would be career (and potentially personal) suicide. A guilty verdict would make it easy on everyone.

Deep down, Stevin struggled with the motivation to fight. He felt like he could put up a decent defense, because his method of murder was basically untraceable. Sure, like he'd told the Chief earlier, they had no murder weapon, no fingerprints (or so he hoped), and really no witnesses. But despite this possible reasonable doubt, he knew he'd done it, and that troubled him. After much soul-searching and analysis, he decided to just let the cards fall where they would. It would do his conscience no good to bend the truth, dodge, and duck while on his pilgrimage to find peace.

What really troubled Stevin, though, was the thought of going back to prison. Prison was a dire place, where unsuspecting people found a whole new set of rules, regulations, biases, prejudices, alliances, and violence. Prison just isn't what most people think, and Stevin had sworn he would avoid it again at all costs. He never wanted to be like the many who cycle back their whole lives, oblivious to the social design that prison should deter crime. The fact was that many career criminals considered prison basically part of the job.

When he was in last, he'd resided in a section that was moderately easy, with workouts, work programs, and the like. This time, he feared, would likely be very much different, with Death Row being a real possibility. Whatever his lot, he was prepared to serve and to try and make any amends possible.

He looked around his holding cell as he sat pondering his fate. It was a lone cell in the county jail with no contact with others. In fact, he had little contact with anybody. This was likely because no one knew how he was able to kill people without touching them or using a weapon. He was designated 'high risk'; thus, he wore a jumpsuit and his feet remained shackled. Law enforcement handled him as they might handle an evil supervillain with powers beyond those of this world. Time slowed. There was nothing to do but think and wonder. Outside of his cell, there were random noises: other cells opening and closing, people talking, alarms, bootsteps. Stevin couldn't see anyone or make out anything that was being said. He speculated that his court appearance would be lively, and that the entire world would be against him. His first appearance was in four hours, and he still needed to talk to his attorney if for nothing more than just the formality.

He thought back on the events that had led him here. There were very high highs and very low lows. He focused on the highs, like being at home eating ice cream with Alexes, seeing Taylor for the first time, and his wonderful trip with Cate to Kauai. He smiled when he thought of getting his new Mercedes sideways, and the look of the other drivers when he had to slam on the brakes. He laughed loudly, echoing in the jail, when he thought of his "dick" trick that took out the old lady's mean neighbor, and then his heart warmed at the thought of her finding the dog. He cried remembering Cate's lost and lonely expression on the plane. It was during this crying that the men came in.

"Prisoner! On the floor!" a voice yelled from out of sight.

"What?" Stevin asked, confused, while trying to see who was yelling at him.

"Get on the floor, face down! Hands behind you! *Now!*" the voice commanded.

Stevin moved the floor and laid down with his hands behind him.

"Clear!"

The cell door opened, and four men came in dressed in riot gear. They handcuffed Stevin, put a black hood over his head, and stood him up. "You'll be meeting with your attorney now. You will not stand once seated. You will not remove the hood in the hall," one of the men commanded.

They walked Stevin down a long hall, through several locked doors, and into an interview room. Once Stevin was seated in a chair, the four men took positions along the wall on either side of the door. Five minutes later, his attorney entered.

"Mr. McDonald, I am your assigned defense attorney, Mary Rodriquez. I am here to represent you at your arraignment in a few hours. Would you like to use my services?" she asked.

Stevin pondered for a moment. He had never considered whether or not he would use an attorney; he had always assumed that he would. He thought about the defense he might build vis-a-vis each of his victims, but his creativity and innocence ran out at the bridge. He didn't see any way around taking that one in the teeth. Even if there was no video and no witnesses and no evidence, the destruction was grand enough that they were going to skewer him.

"Yes, I would," he replied

"Okay, fine. Let's get started. First, I need to know if you've considered how you might plead. Like the rest of those incarcerated here, I know that you are innocent. Unfortunately, we are going to have to prove that. The District Attorney, Holly Jolley, will personally prosecute the case. The prosecution is not offering a plea bargain at this time and will likely seek the death penalty, so we have a lot of work to do," Mary explained.

Stevin sat quietly. The dire reality of his situation was sinking in. Just a few days ago, he was lying on a beach with the beautiful Cate; now he was staring down the long barrel of life on Death Row.

"Mr. McDonald? Have you thought of how you might plead?" Mary pushed for some sort of response. "Mr. McDonald?"

Stevin sighed. He felt like the fight had gone out of him. As much as he didn't want to plead guilty, knowing that the entire world wanted to tie this up in a tidy box, he knew it would be a lot easier on himself. He had just contemplated suicide; could this be worse? Certainly he could find some grain of hope and light in prison to live out his days. Who knows? Maybe he could even have some fun. But then again, if a guilty plea is life on Death Row and it doesn't really get worse than that, what's to lose by trying to fight it? Are they going to sentence him to two lifetimes in prison? At some point, one realizes that there are not two roads, but one.

"Ms. Rodriguez. I am no stranger to this process, which I'm sure you are well aware of. And, contrary to your statement, I do not believe that I am innocent, nor are the others within these walls. I could go on and on about how the system is broken, how social programs to rehabilitate us fail, how many of us actually prefer to be here because the world outside moves so fast—so fast!—and we just can't keep up. No. I will not fight my conscience. I will plead guilty, and to sweeten the deal, I will actually serve it out. On second thought, your services will not be needed. Thank you."

The otherwise statuesque guard at the door stirred, and Ms. Rodriguez leaned forward in her chair.

"But, Mr. McDonald, we should at least try, don't you think? What if their evidence is tainted? What if the jury finds reasonable doubt? Remember, you are innocent until proven guilty," Mary said, dumbfounded.

"Good day, my lady," Stevin said in his best British accent. With nothing to lose, Stevin realized it was time to let go a little and have some fun. He determined right then and there to do just that at every opportunity. "All right then, lads...shall we?" Sir Stevin said, standing.

The guards rushed in and surrounded him while Ms. Rodriguez left, then escorted him back down the long hall to his cell. Once in his cell, his hands were uncuffed and the hood was removed. Stevin was having fun with his new falsetto, so he continued.

"I'm fresh out of crumpets, but I do have a spot of tea. Would you boys fancy a cup?"

"Clear!" one of the guards yelled.

The door to his cell rolled shut. As the guards turned to walk away, Stevin heard the faintest little chuckle from one of them from behind his dark face shield. This made Stevin smile, and he wanted more. He felt good making others feel good. Could he be on to something here? What if his new life's pursuit, despite his bleak surroundings and dead-end road, was to make amends by promoting happiness?

This was a foreign idea to Stevin, however. As most of us are and most of us do, we go through life worrying about what we will wear, what we will eat, what we look like, how we feel, how we're going to pay the bills, and the like. For Stevin—and most within the U.S. correctional system—these trivial worries basically vanish. There are the occasional 'I hope I don't get raped or shanked today' concerns, but for the most part, food, clothes, hair, and finances are settled.

What if, under these dire circumstances, one could take the focus off himself and put that focus on others? Think how much more wonderful it could be for those on the outside who are able to do it, despite being bombarded by the pressures of life, like if a woman in line at Starbucks could muster a kind gesture of 'I'm buying your coffee today!' to the person in front of her while her phone is ringing for the fifth time and her baby just launched a bucket full of Cheerios onto the floor.

This was pure revelation for Stevin. A simple goal for someone who would likely never have one decent worldly possession again in his life...well, except for the model car, but that's in Chapter 23.

A few hours later, Stevin's security detail showed up again. This time there were six of them, and this time they were all going on a little walkabout to the courthouse. Unfortunately, though, there would be no beef jerky or pick-a-random-flavor Mountain Dew on this trip. Transporting high-risk inmates was a dangerous undertaking that required senior law enforcement with specific training. Typically, this is when the bad guy's henchmen blow a hole in the prison wall or rappel onto the roof with blowtorches. Not in this case, however. The walk from the jail to the courthouse was accomplished over an approximate 100-foot catwalk between the two buildings. How convenient! Like a having a Green Burrito and a Carl's Jr. in one stop or, if you're in Shenzhen, China, visiting a doctor who is both dentist and gynecologist. Wonderful!

The walk for Stevin was not only uneventful, but ominously familiar. While he was walking, Stevin remembered his new goal to gain small victories over his captors. He thought to himself how he might do it on such a short walk, and while not being able to talk. He decided to hum. When he first started, he was met by knee-jerk opposition from the officers.

"Quiet! No talking," one of them said.

Stevin looked at him, and then mouthed *I'm not talking* in silence, and then smiled at him. Then he continued humming. By the second line of the hymn, all present recognized it as "Amazing Grace." The guards likely would not have let him continue with any other hymn, and likely would not have felt as much compassion as they did hearing any other hymn. Under the circumstances, and despite him being a true-blue terrorist, these six burly men couldn't help but be touched. It was another small victory for a man with nothing.

At the courthouse, Stevin was brought before Judge S. Mark King for his arraignment. The judge started reading the charges, and, quite honestly, the first three or four were bad enough for a life sentence, so Stevin didn't pay much attention after that. The reality was that the system is broken, at least in California, and even if they did sentence him to Death Row, they would probably never actually execute him. There are too many bureaucrats who can't agree on the issue, so Death Row was basically just life in prison; it all came down to living arrangements and amenities. Stevin knew what to expect in the general prison area, and he had heard stories of Death Row which were not exciting. Nonetheless, today was simply time to plead.

When the judge finished reading the exhausting list of charges, including consideration of the death penalty, he turned to DA Jolley and asked, "DA Jolley, did I miss anything?"

"No, your honor. I think you got it all," she responded, turning to look at Stevin. She couldn't help but wonder why he was standing there without any representation.

"Mr. McDonald. You have heard a long list of very severe charges brought against you. Do you understand the consequences of these charges?" Judge King asked.

"Yes," Stevin replied confidently, feeling his conscience was a much worse captor than any prison could be.

"How do you plead, Mr. McDonald?"

"Your honor, I am prepared to plead guilty, with one consideration, and that is that you take the death penalty off the table," Stevin responded.

Judge King glanced at Holly, who was sitting wide-eyed and dazed. While he could guess at the cause of her confusion, what he didn't quite realize was that the DA had this case mentally choreographed from start to finish—including brilliant testimony from her favorite German doctor. A guilty plea threw a big, stinky pile of manure on the stage of her play, and the audacious request of no death penalty simply stupefied her. Such a possibility surely couldn't be in the realm of our universe.

"Mr. McDonald," the judge said, turning back to Stevin and pausing, "I'm going to go a little off script here and say that I'm surprised you're still alive, and that no one has come in here and shot you in the back. Hell, I might have done it myself if I weren't sworn to uphold the law, and that law requires that I allow you due process, as much as it drives me mad! You brought this city to its knees and killed over a hundred people in the worst terrorist attack we've ever endured. Now you're standing here asking me to take the death penalty off the table? I don't think so, Mr. McDonald! The crowd outside might require my blood if I did that. A guilty plea would make it easy for all of us here, let alone that you would be waiving your right to a jury trial."

Stevin was fixated on the crowd comment from the judge and didn't hear much else. *There's a crowd outside?* he thought to himself.

"Your honor," Stevin finally responded. "Please hear me out. I will plead guilty after I explain why I should not be given the death penalty. Then between now and sentencing, you and DA Holly Jolley can consider my statements, and when I come back before you to be sentenced, I will accept your decision, whatever it may be."

"Okay, Mr. McDonald, enlighten us!" the Judge said, leaning back in his chair to listen.

"Thank you, your honor. First, as you know, I've spent time in prison—four years, to be exact. I served my time without incident and was a model citizen of San Quentin Resort and Spa. Second, we all know that California hasn't carried out the death penalty for over ten years, so why send me there at great expense to the State? Let's save a hundred thousand of the taxpayers' money per year for the next 50 years. Lastly, you should know that I've changed, because I'm here before you today. And not only that, but *you* are here before *me* today. In fact, the power that I hold, whose burden I bear alone and have not revealed to another living soul, enables me to take life; my own life, if I choose, and the lives of those around me. So the fact that we're all standing here today is proof that I have changed. And with that, I plead guilty, your honor." Stevin stood resolute and still in place.

The judge was a little taken aback, and wondered if Stevin had just threatened him and everyone present or if he was just a complete idiot. Not quite sure what to make of it, the judge entered the plea and set the date for sentencing in two months, eager to get Stevin out of his courtroom and back to his cell. But before Judge King retired to his chambers, he instructed the guards with a special request.

"Guards. On your way back to his jail cell, make a quick stop at a window and give Mr. McDonald a glimpse of his supporters. Maybe that will humble him a little! Court adjourned!"

While the judge had barred the press and other visitors from the courtroom for safety reasons, outside was a different story. Hundreds of people had assembled on Bryant Street, marching in support of swift and decisive judgement for Stevin.

Stevin didn't know what to expect at "the window." Maybe there were riots. Maybe there were just a couple of bums taking inventory of their carts. When they got there, he looked out in amazement.

Hundreds of people had gathered, and many seemed to be chanting or yelling. Some were holding flowers; some were holding signs. One sign read **TERRORISTS DESERVE DEATH!**; another **SHOW NO MERCY!**; and another **REMEMBER THE BRIDGES!** As Stevin watched unbeknownst to the mob, something in the back of the crowd caught his eye. It was another sign, and it was different from all the others. It read ***I Love You*** on a simple piece of paper held by two angelic hands. He strained to see who it was, and finally he did, just as the guards pulled him away, leaving the window out of sight. A rush of energy, emotion, and regret overwhelmed him. He tried desperately to claw his way back, but two guards put their batons in his back and threatened to put them heavily on his head. All he had the power to do was to shout her name again and again.

"Alexes! Alexes! *Alexes!*"

Certainly the judge didn't expect this miracle at the window when he'd ordered the stop. Perhaps it was chance. Perhaps it was meant to be. Perhaps it was a tender mercy from on high. Whatever the case, Stevin would never be the same again.

CHAPTER 21

HELLO, OLD FOE

Because of Stevin's high-risk status, he spent his pre-prison days in his lonely jail cell sans visitor access. During that lonely time, he contemplated the incredible question of just how in the world Alexes could do that—still love a man who'd walked out on her, committed a laundry list of heinous crimes, cheated on her, and worst of all, be in the shitty position of never being able to go back home. He finally came to the conclusion that Alexes was just foolish, like a young schoolgirl willing to love anyone who would love her back; but then he realized that maybe she already got the $1,000,000 he'd transferred to her account. Thinking of this scenario caused Stevin to hoot loudly in laughter. He hoped that the transfer would go, and stick, prior to the police finding Francis' remains and freezing her accounts.

Then there was Cate, the other beneficiary of $1,000,000. Stevin was quite certain that no amount of money was going to make up for what he'd done. His only consolation was that he knew deep down that his feelings were genuine, though his actions and façade may not have been on the up-and-up. Stevin didn't expect to ever see Cate again, and his attention was ironically now refocused on Alexes.

The prospect of Alexes felt like going home after a long trip. There is something powerful about love, how it overcomes and conquers everything. Alexes' small gesture outside the courthouse warmed Stevin's heart. It was a different feeling than, say, a young woman sitting on your lap, revealing her sheer lace panties. It was real, genuine, unconditional, and heavenly, all rolled up into something only really possible from someone who you've been in the trenches with and sacrificed for. For Stevin, seeing Alexes that day was a beacon, a trail duck, an attaboy telling him he was on the right path—and this made him genuinely happy.

Stevin thought about the first time he'd met Alexes. Meeting women is never easy for ex-cons, and successfully doing so is usually only possible either by straight-up lying or aggressively networking. In Stevin's case, he convinced a friend on the inside to introduce him to his sister on the outside. Never hurts to ask, right? Stevin was due to get out five months before Chris. In the excitement of the idea, Chris must have figured that not much could happen in five months, and that Alexes would probably kick Stevin to the curb anyway. The day Stevin got out was the last day he saw Chris and the first day he saw Alexes. Chris was murdered in prison just weeks later.

Both Stevin and Alexes were crushed, and Chris's death became the tragic mortar that bound them as stones in a fortress. That was, until Stevin walked frustrated out of their house two years later, leaving the fortress in emotional rubble. Now, after seeing Alexes in the crowd, perhaps it was time to rebuild those ramparts and towers. For Stevin, it was like he wanted a new car, but in reality, he loved his old car, and all he needed was to give it a little love—a little shine.

After two months of grinding through endless love theories and enduring most of the time alone, Stevin actually looked forward to something different when it was time to go back to see Judge King for sentencing. The courthouse was again void of onlookers, his captors still fearing his unknown power. After all were seated and ready to begin, they ended up waiting almost 30 minutes for Judge King. When he finally came in, all could tell he was anxious, presumably about the sentence he was going to render. Once he got settled, he began the proceedings.

"This court is now in session," he said, looking down at his paperwork. "We are here today for the sentencing of Stevin McDonald, who has pleaded guilty to all charges brought against him with a request that he not be given the death penalty due to his good nature of keeping us all alive."

The few people in the courtroom didn't quite know how to take that last comment—whether to laugh or run. The judge continued.

"Mr. McDonald, the law requires that I give you an opportunity to allocate, or speak, prior to me imposing the sentence. Do you have any further words for the court at this time?" the judge asked, hoping Stevin would be silent. Indeed he was, but only for a moment.

Stevin stood up from his seat and said nothing for an awkward minute or so. There was no expression on his face; he just stared at Judge King, making him very uneasy. Then Stevin did something he'd never had the courage to previously do: sing in front of others. He fell back on the hymn that had touched the guards in the hall a few months earlier. It again felt right, and seemed fitting. Stevin was not a singer by any means, and it was only because of Alexes' love for the song that he even knew the tune; but, oh, what one can accomplish when the spirit quickens a humble man's conviction! He closed his eyes, bowed his head, and didn't hold back, singing with every ounce of energy as if the entire world were listening.

Amazing grace, how sweet the sound
That saved a wretch like me.
I once was lost, but now I'm found;
Was blind but now I see.
'Twas grace that taught my heart to fear,
And grace my fears relieved;
How precious did that grace appear
The hour I first believed.
When we've been there ten thousand years,
Bright shining as the sun,
We've no less days to sing God's praise
Then when we first begun.
Amazing grace, how sweet the sound
That saved a wretch like me.
I once was lost, but now I'm found;
Was blind, but now I see.

When he finished, he sat down with a smile on his lips and tears on his cheeks. He was a man who had made his peace, and he felt like he'd done all he could to appeal—not to the law or to loopholes—but to the grace and mercy of his fellow man. Perhaps they would pity him. Perhaps they would save him.

Judge King was floored by the performance. He had never had anyone sing in his courtroom before. Several times he moved to stop it, if for no other reason than it was out of the ordinary; but each time he did, something held him back. Now the judge faced the great decision before him: appease the crowds outside and banish Stevin to Death Row, or respond to the soul-sent request of what appeared to be, and what felt to be, a changed man with a sincere request.

"Mr. McDonald, you truly are a unique case. I feel inclined to grant your request from the last time we met. However, that being said, I'm afraid, based on the extent of mayhem and death you caused, that I should not. Common sense, decency, and moral obligation must be satisfied—and above all, justice. I fear the hundreds of people you've either killed or injured would haunt my conscience for the rest of my life. The law clearly gives me the right to sentence you to death, but does it force me to confine you to Death Row to rot out your days. You made a strange but compelling argument the last time you were here. If we had a firing squad out back, I think it would make it much easier for me. To send you—or anyone, for that matter—to Death Row seems frivolous until such time as Death Row actually does involve administered death. Therefore, I hereby sentence you to life in prison with no possibility of parole. Perhaps using the most hated man in the nation in this way might incite some change to the system."

With that, the Judge rapped his gavel, stood, and exited the courtroom in haste, leaving everyone absolutely dumbfounded—most of all Stevin. The judge, apparently, did not want to run any risk of being at odds with Stevin, even though he had just granted him his wish. Truth be told, the judge actually *did* fear for his life, as did everyone around Stevin. Now that Stevin was in custody, and the only explanation anyone could give for the many deaths that had taken place was heart attacks, the rumors, superstitions, and speculation of Stevin's infamy shrouded him with a sort of social reverence and caution, even if he was in a jumpsuit and shackles.

Before the judge could get away, Stevin stood and exclaimed, "Thank you, judge!"

Now guilty, sentenced, and victorious in avoiding Death Row, Stevin was taken back to jail while awaiting transfer to prison. He had served his prior term in San Quentin, and he had the eerie feeling that that's where he would be going back. If for nothing else, should the entire world appeal Judge King's ruling and win, it would be an easy stroll over to Death Row. Stevin started to think back to his time there, and how going back might be different. Undoubtedly, he would run into people he would recognize, some who'd hated him and some who'd tolerated him. Truly, his only friends there had been Chris and a man named Higginbotham, so he wasn't necessarily looking forward to seeing anyone except Higgy, if he was still there and still alive. He was, however, eager to find Chris's killer and perhaps introduce him to three special words, hoping the guy spoke English without an accent.

As he sat there thinking about how his three words worked for some and not others, he wondered if he could engineer three words in different languages that would have the same effect. It was an interesting thought. He pictured himself walking around with a little black book of phrases, all in different languages—and then, if people didn't speak English, asking them what language they spoke. He laughed at the preposterous thought of saying something like, 'Hey. What language do you speak, so I can have you read something and die?' But the more he thought about it, the more he wondered if it would be possible. He knew a little

Spanish. With all the time in the world on his hands, he decided to see if it might work. This was, of course, quite contrary to his resolve to do good, but there was this last bit of business he needed to handle for Chris if he was in fact headed back to Big Q; and he really had nothing better to do.

The next morning was transfer time, and again the same routine except this time they wouldn't be walking. The guards came in, shackled him, and loaded him on a bus. Stevin was shocked when the bus hit the street. There weren't people just on the street by the jail, there were people, several deep, from the jailhouse all the way to the Golden Gate—thousands of them. It was like a Fourth of July parade with just a lone smoke-belching prison bus as the grandmaster, bands, horses, and floats all rolled into one. The people of San Francisco were absolutely frothy in rage, and they were leaving no doubt to the world that they wanted the maximum penalty for the man who'd crushed their city and taken so many of their loved ones away. Their assembly served both as opposition to Stevin and in protest of Judge King. Stevin watched out the window as the bus lumbered down the streets. This time the signs of death didn't bother him as much, or the water bottles blasting against the barred windows, and he spent as much effort as he could looking out for one sign in particular—a light of hope in the darkness of his condemnation; however, his effort was in vain. To ease the pain, he told himself repeatedly that she was there, and that he just wasn't able to see her.

Once the bus got to the Golden Gate, the reality of his destination sucked any last bit of hope from Stevin. The authorities questioned whether or not they should use any bridges, with Stevin's history of bridge terror, but driving from San Francisco to San Jose to Stockton to Petaluma and then down to San Quentin was completely asinine, and still required a few small bridges. (It's really difficult to get anywhere in the Bay Area without a bridge, if you think about it.) Somebody threw out the idea of a boat, but that was scrapped for security reasons.

Stevin stared out the window as they crossed. It reminded him a little of being on the Bixby Creek Bridge. He remembered how beautiful it was that morning, and how much his car absolutely reeked from decomposing flesh. Then he thought of Francis' flight into the trees. He shook his head and snickered at just how crazy the last few months had been. Knowing that it would be his last taste of the outside, he soaked in as much of the bus ride as he could.

Across the Golden Gate Bridge, the landscape changes drastically. You leave the density and congestion of the city, and then immediately zoom through grassy foothills, tunnels, and small towns. Highway 101 cuts along the western edge of San Pablo Bay until Novato, then it turns inland for nearly 250 miles before spilling onto the coast in Eureka. Along the way, you pass through Leggett, where you can make a left and drive all the way back to Santa Barbara and LAX.

As the bus picked up speed across the bridge, so did Stevin's pulse. He wondered if he could eat his words in court and escape now, before he was confined again in his old loathsome home. He had no pen and paper, and there were six guards on the bus and a driver. The only thing he could think of was to breathe on the window and write it with his finger in the fog. He figured he might get one or two of them, maybe. But getting a couple wasn't going to help him much. The others would probably just shoot first and ask questions later. He decided to keep his powder dry and wait for a better opportunity, which meant that he was now headed back for certain.

During the few minutes left on the drive before intake, he focused on preparing his mind and body for the rest of his life. As he sat there, he had the nagging need to say goodbye. But to whom? With no other option, he began to speak to the guards, hoping they would hear him out.

"I was born to a common family in a common town. My mother worked as a school administrator. My..."

"Quiet! No talking!" one of the guards demanded.

Stevin was silent for a moment, and then continued, "My father was a car dealer and sold Porsches at one of the first dealerships in the U.S.."

"Quiet, I said! There is no talking on the bus!" the guard insisted.

Stevin didn't know why, but he just kept talking. "I wonder what they think..."

As soon as Stevin started again, the guard stood, unsheathed his baton, and hammered Stevin at the base of his neck, nearly shattering his collar bone.

"Shut up!" the guard said, standing over him.

"I just..." As Stevin began to speak again, the guard began whaling, repeatedly hitting him with full force, until finally the others pulled him off. Stevin had unexpectedly struck a vein, an artery, and a nerve. He sat crouched against the bus, praying it was over and that the others weren't lining up for their turn. In the end, he took a couple of shots to the head, and there was a good chance that his arm was broken. Logically, he decided a goodbye was not the best of ideas and that his luck of mildly breaking the rules had run out. Then the first guard started talking to the others.

"That piece of shit right there killed my mother! She was on the bridge. It's all I can do to not kill him right here and now. He deserves to be on Death Row, and I can hardly bear the thought of anything but him being dead!"

"Come on, Robert. We're pulling up now. We'll be done with him in a minute, and then the others inside will take care of him," one of the other guards said, trying to console Robert.

Stevin began to understand that when you kill someone, you gain numerous enemies, and they aren't always obvious or perceivable. Once this realization sank in, he began to multiply its reality by the hundreds of people he had killed or injured. His atonement was going to be much more difficult and long-lasting than he had anticipated. In fact, he realized that fully making amends for what he had done was probably not going to be possible. This was humbling—very humbling.

Up until this point, things had basically gone his way; he'd found ways out, dodged capture, loved the ladies, beaten the system in court. All of this came skidding to an abrupt halt in the bus, and he seemed to be moving in the opposite direction. He wondered if other guards at the prison were affected, and, worse yet, if other inmates were. The last time he was there, he watched a child rapist come in. Although the man didn't rape any of the inmates' children, crimes like these weren't tolerated on the inside. Stevin watched him die the next day when a group of men ambushed him in the yard and beat the life out of him. If Stevin's crimes were viewed as such, this was going to be a very short visit. He didn't make a peep the rest of the ride, with the guard staring at him the entire time, baton in hand.

The bus lumbered north and then exited the freeway in Larkspur. The coexistence of Larkspur and San Quentin is a strange dichotomy. Larkspur is a quintessential village on the Bay, with small shopping centers, ferry docks, and cottages. As you move west through the city toward the foothills, you find a vast mix of foliage, from palms and agave to oaks and redwoods. Contrastingly, San Quentin point is a flat and mostly arid plot to the east, just south of Interstate 580 before it rises to the Richmond Bridge. Although San Quentin's Main Street is small and runs along the water, it's not your typical Mayberry Main Street, and certainly not somewhere to go looking for an ice-cream shop. Actually, to be honest, the first half-mile from Interstate 580 is quite nice, with the ability to have a house literally on the water. But once you get to the prison gate, it turns ominous.

The road arced and skirted along the Bay. The bus was getting close. It slowed, then turned right onto Main Street, San Quentin, CA. They were at the West Gate.

Stevin looked out across the bay at the pleasure boats cruising the waters backed by the green rolling hills of southern Marin County. He took a long look, like one might take a long drink after crossing a desert. He wished the windows were down, so he could breathe the salt air. That's one thing they can't take away in prison: at least when you have yard time at San Quentin, you can always breathe the salt air. Granted, it's not always fresh air or fresh water, but at least it's better than down near San Mateo and Palo Alto, where it gets to be stagnant and foul. That's at least one thing San Quentin has over Palo Alto.

Stevin then looked ahead through the front windows. The guard shack was rather low-security and rather low-key. What made it forbidding was the great tall guard tower on the hill behind it. Stevin remembered it well. Because the prison was so old and had expanded so much over the years, this tower wasn't used anymore, but it represented a hard time in a hard place—and served as a landmark that signaled the end of the road.

Stevin broke his silence as he focused on the tower and whispered, "Hello, old foe!", then soaked in the last few seconds of the bay, the boats, and the hills.

CHAPTER 22

RECEPTION

If you've ever been to prison, you know that your first stop is the Reception Center, which is a polite name for Hell's Lottery. Reception Centers process incoming inmates with the end goal of assigning them to one of California's 34 state prisons. While in Reception, a prisoner's records (criminal, health, medical, dental, etc.) are reviewed, and a committee then decides where to best house the inmate. While this can take up to three months in some instances, Stevin's case was basically cut-and-dried; his family was close, he was close, he had been to San Quentin before, and San Quentin has the state's only Death Row. Even though Stevin hadn't been sentenced to Death Row, the powers that be weren't going to let him stray far away in case one of the many appeals that were already being drafted were successful. Along with all of the other factors, San Quentin was going to be Stevin's one-stop shop: reception to new address to eventual death, whether by age, injection, other inmates, or the guards.

The interesting part about Reception for Stevin in particular was that inmates are allowed to receive mail as well as writing supplies in order to respond to their mail. When Stevin arrived, he had ten letters waiting, complete with writing materials, from a mix of news organizations across the country—each wanting to know his story, or, in some bold cases, his secret to death. He didn't know this, but there were many more letters for him. Reception only allows ten, so the rest were put in storage until such time as he was assigned a new home.

In their letters to him, some attempted to make responding easy by providing a questionnaire to fill out, while others just asked him to write anything, only wanting to have some claim to him. Infamy does make celebrity, but little did they know that by sending him these writing supplies, they armed the nuke for a lifetime! Stevin had as much paper as he could ever want, but what he didn't have was any desire to respond. And he certainly wasn't going to tell anyone his secret.

Running a prison is no easy task, as you can imagine. Beyond housing society's rapists, killers, junkies, and dealers and the risks that come along with that, there is the challenge of reconciling security with everyday tasks such as eating, showering, free time, transport, and visitation. Then you mix all of that up with overcrowding and budget cuts, and you've got yourself one hell of a juggling act!

And we haven't even mentioned segregation. Nowhere in the nation is segregation more apparent, tolerated, supported, and requested than in prison. In fact, incoming inmates are asked point blank which race they identify with. Their answer becomes a large part of where they go and where they will be housed. Even if one doesn't see the world this way on the outside, they quickly learn that power in numbers means survival, and that prisons operate this way, ironically, because the inmates demand it. Blacks, whites, and Latinos are the three basic tribes, and once you join a tribe, there are expectations—expectations like fighting. If your race fights, you fight, even if it's not your issue and even if you don't want to. If you don't fight with your race, your race fights you, which could make your stay very short.

Stevin knew the drill, and knew what it would mean. He didn't like, however, how whites at San Quentin were assumed to be Aryan Brotherhood, since the gang traces its origins there back to 1967. Having to choose a gang meant survival, but it required an entirely new mentality about life, government, and self. This is especially true for first-timers, who come in without any concept of this reality. For Stevin, being part of a race in prison could very well be the most challenging aspect of serving time, like having to stay at the table and eat the vegetables that make you gag.

After a few weeks in Reception, Stevin had already been called to two fights. One was easy because it was against a rival gang of Latinos regarding drug dealings; the other was much more difficult because it involved retribution against a young Caucasian male for not fighting when called.

Were Stevin in his twenties again, much of this would be easier to adopt. Now in his mid-forties, he struggled with the demands brought on by the young and the eager, and he wished he could just sit it out once in a while. This was especially apparent as he watched his gang literally crush the face of the young man for not fighting. Stevin tried to go easy while at the same time appearing to participate. When they left him in the yard as the guards broke it up, the man was nearly choking to death on blood, and would probably be blind for the rest of his life. Stevin feared that his rising empathy was going to cause him to be the one choking on his blood someday. That being said, everyone there knew him, or knew of him. This luckily garnered some initial respect among everyone on the inside, including those from other gangs and races. His prison smarts, infamy, and mysterious method of death worked to protect him from much of the horrid realities of being new and classified him as someone of great worth by all, regardless of affiliation.

However, Stevin's motives were not for gang promotion and conquest, but to find Chris's killer, which was likely going to be very difficult and require a lot of effort. Snitching is a cardinal sin in prison, and that is just what Stevin was going to need.

Additionally, as a safety net, he still wanted to weaponize his phrase in Spanish, which would give him full coverage across 99% of the prison population. He had some ideas about what might work in Spanish, but it was going to be incredibly hard to test. He wouldn't be able to 'fishline' a Latino by flicking a note down the hall on a string, because Latinos were housed in different cell blocks. Hell, even getting close to another gang member, let alone striking up a conversation with one, was nearly impossible without getting attacked. Even if you were able to corner someone and have them read it, the risk of it not working was formidable. Nothing would be worse than having it not work and then potentially having to fight for your life. Doing this more than once was not advisable.

This day in Reception started like most of the others—the same routines, the same conflict, the same rage against anything and everything. Prison made him feel like a dog stuck in a barrel with 20 kids poking him with sticks. Every day, the kids would show up, and every day there was just nothing to do about it except growl and bite back. Blacks, Latinos, guards, and opposing whites all had sticks. It was just a hot mess of stick-banging, and it's no wonder that people go crazy here.

In the afternoon, during yard time, Stevin noticed something different. There was an eerie feeling of tolerance. Other inmates seemed to have more patience, and didn't necessarily want to slit your throat for looking at them awkwardly. Maybe it was because there were a lot of visitors to the prison. Maybe it was because it was Christmas. Like Belleau Wood, when all was calm and all was bright. Of course, while in reception, one isn't allowed visitors, but things trickle down from those in charge in the main cells, including the general feelings felt today. If someone hadn't said something, Stevin wouldn't have realized that the day was anything different than the 37 days before it.

As he sat in the yard breathing the salty air, he was approached by a lieutenant of the whites' gang leader named Benak. Benak sat next to him at a picnic table, which was put under white control with considerable effort and violence and had remained so for the last eight months.

"J.J. wants to know if you're truly dedicated to our cause," Benak said, speaking of the whites' leader.

This was the moment that Stevin dreaded and sensed was coming. His answer to the question was going to dictate whether he lived, or potentially died in the next few minutes. From the corner of his eyes he could see other members of the gang monitoring the lieutenant, ready to brawl at his sign. Stevin knew what he had to do, even though he didn't like it. Doing so was going to plot his course for the rest of his life, and it was a decision he loathed making. It would save his life, but it would obligate him to be someone he had no desire to be. In fact, it would obligate him to be exactly who he did not want to be: his old self.

He was grateful, however, for his previous time in prison, which had allowed him to sense the significance of the situation—

something many don't understand until they wake up in the infirmary. Certainly being allegiant to the whites was not as bad as, say, being in the Donner Party, and there were some benefits, like having others watch out for you in general population.

"Have I not already shown my dedication?" Stevin responded, trying to avoid what was coming next.

"J.J. needs you to do something for him. He wants to know if you'll do it."

Stevin paused for a moment and then looked with a solemn face at Benak and nodded yes. He didn't know what it was, but he could guess it involved nefarious violence.

"I'll let him know. Meet here again tomorrow," Benek said, and then got up and walked away.

That night, Stevin lay awake in his cell, not so much worried about what Benak might say but wondering how he might insulate himself from prison politics without getting hurt or killed. He needed to become untouchable, and the only way to do that, he feared, was to work his magic.

Stevin thought about the repercussions of killing people in prison. If a lot of people started dying of heart attacks, the authorities would know it was him, and would probably have the ammo they needed to move him to Death Row. Then he wondered: *What if not a lot of people died, but just a few? There are three snakes here. What if I simultaneously cut the heads off of all three?* He laughed at the idea, but then thought it through, rationalizing that killing three of the most notorious inmates in San Quentin would be a public service. Doing so, he thought, would either turn the entire prison against him, or would elevate him to untouchable status, where no one would dare cross him. He wasn't sure about the authorities, though succumbing to prison politics in order to survive was far worse than life on Death Row. On Death Row, at least you know where you stand.

The idea of killing again resurrected conflict in Stevin's mind, even if he was toying with the idea of a message *en Español.* To him, the other prisoners, the guards, and the authorities were all insignificant, and far less poignant than his own conscience. But the solution to this paradox was of paramount importance, so on his list of things to do were now: 1) find Chris's killer; 2) figure out how to be a happy killer; and 3) figure out how to kill in Spanish. All were going to take some time, which was something he did not really have, as it turned out. The longer it took, the more the whites would require of him. Until he liberated himself through murder, he was going to have to be one of their rank and file, and he really wanted to solve the Spanish mystery before leaving Reception, which he figured was only a few days away.

The next morning, in his cell, Stevin scribbled feverishly any and all Spanish words he could think of that began with the letter S, or had any part remotely sounding like S. His list was meager to say the least. Apparently, his command of *Español* was not as healthy as he thought. Wait! *Español* is another S-word! He looked down at the paper at the few words that were there, and started to realize he was probably going to need a lot of help. Four meager words stared back at him in silent defiance: *cinco, seis, siete,* and *Español.*

"Shit. I've got to get serious here! Think! *Think!*" Stevin whispered loudly, hitting the pencil against his head.

"Okay. 'Silence' in Spanish is probably something like *silencia,* so let's assume that is good." He looked down at his feet. Shoes. *Shoes.* "How do you say 'shoes'? *Zapatos!* That's a good one! Okay. I need a couple more." He continued by randomly rattling off any Spanish word he could think of—*burro, cerveza, tequila, chicas, la migra, cholo, padre, madre, Estados Unidos, el Jefe, los amigos, andale, amigo, vato, cabron.* "Okay. This is going nowhere fast. Actually, *Estados Unidos* might work, or at least parts of it," he realized.

The whites had the yard first today, and it was time to go. This was fortuitous, because the Latinos were to follow later on in the morning. Stevin scrambled to piece the words together the best he could and to write them down before leaving. He came up with '*Silencia siete seis*', which made absolutely no sense but seemed to have the same alliteration as 'silence sometimes speaks'. As he wrote it down, he caught himself speaking the words. Although the phrase was likely not going to work, and his accent would hopefully safeguard him, saying the words was something he would have to avoid in the future.

Out in the yard, he made his way to the picnic table and sat quietly alone. He only had about 45 minutes, there and he needed to ensure that his piece of paper would be conspicuous, but not so conspicuous that a guard might walk by on patrol and trash it. He casually looked around and then set the paper on the ground near the table leg, so that if someone were sitting on the bench with their elbows on their knees, they might see it by their feet.

Once the paper was on the ground, he stayed for a while to see how it would react to wind. It lay steady, like a good trap. With confidence now that it would stay, he stood up and moved across the yard to watch a basketball game that was getting heated. As he watched, he wondered if someone would see the small paper. He wondered *more* if it would work. The idea of killing across language barriers was a broad, new, and exciting possibility, which a lifetime in prison would obviously squash. But perhaps it would be of use here, in his new little world.

Stevin watched as the game went on. There was a bloody nose here, a shove there. Albeit rambunctious, the game was in good fun, with players all playing for the whites. Were it whites verses another team, it would basically be: 1) tip off; 2) brawl to the death, with a score of 0-0 and many injured or dead. Much like church ball, you know...the only brawl that begins with prayer!

Stevin watched in good fun, but something wasn't right. Not with the game, but with his plan. He began to worry and then stress, because his time in the yard was nearly up. Then it hit him. He couldn't leave a paper! He couldn't leave *any* tangible evidence. As he hurried back, trying to be discreet, he wondered what he might do. Really, the only thing to do was to write it in the dirt and hope that if it *did* work, the scuffle would erase the evidence. He sat at the bench, quietly took the paper, and then shredded it. Looking around, it didn't seem like anyone noticed him, so he wrote the words in the dirt. Just as he finished, Benek came and sat on the table behind him. Stevin froze, expecting a bludgeoning blow or a knife to the back. He had forgotten that he was supposed to meet him here again today. He felt lucky that he was inadvertently sitting there when Benak showed up.

"When they move you to the main quarters, J.J. needs you to take care of someone," Benak said, staring out across the compound.

Stevin played it cool, not wanting him to see the words on the ground or have any remote knowledge of what he was up to.

"Who is it?" Stevin inquired.

"The name is Higginbotham. Make it happen in the first 48 hours, or hour 49 is not going to be pleasant for you."

Stevin's face lit up. What he wanted to say was, "Yes! Higgy is still here!", but he caught himself before he blurted it out. What saddened Stevin was to know that his friend was in dire trouble, so much so that there was a hit on his life. Luckily, this new regime had no idea of Higgy and Stevin's relationship, and Stevin was probably the only one in the world who could save his friend.

"Okay. Consider it done," Stevin replied calmly.

Benak got up and walked away, looking back once with an evil smile, as if to say "I hope you fail, old man."

The whistle blew. Yard time was over. Stevin walked away from the picnic table and his dusty, sprung trap. He figured in an hour and a half or so, he'd know if it had worked. There was always a commotion when someone was hurt or when someone died; he would just have to listen for it.

In the meantime, he had someone else to consider: Benak. His little gesture rubbed Stevin wrong, and despite the general calm in the air and spirit of the season, Stevin's crosshairs had just lowered on the lieutenant. The good news was that Stevin could easily fishline Benek from his cell. The bad news was that he had to fabricate a note that could not only be read but could also be retrieved without the other person tying it back on the string. Stevin thought about how he might do this, and the only thing he could come up with was a double string. But then he thought he would just toss his entire small spiral-bound notebook. He could tie the string extra-tight on the wire loops and write something like *Read Before Untying* on the front. Most people are programmed to follow instructions without asking questions, especially ones like this. Now, if Stevin were sliding a VCR or a leaf blower next door, the instructions probably wouldn't come out until it was time to set the clock or figure out how to attach the extension cord

After roll call, several random strip-searches, and a bit of a scuffle, the whites were deposited back in their cells, which meant the Latinos were headed out to the yard. Time for Stevin to go fishing. Fishing was usually done at night, when there was less surveillance in the halls, but Stevin couldn't wait. He'd had enough. The risk was having his phrase of death out of reach and in the open. If a guard came along and intercepted it, he might kill a guard, or if another prisoner fished it out of the hall with his own fishline, Stevin could end up killing the wrong prisoner. Benak's cell was close and Stevin was pretty good at fishing, or, as many called it, "sending a kite." Stevin pressed his face against the cell door and did the best he could to see if any guards were near, then he called out to Benak.

"Benak. I'm sending you something. Fish for it," he called.

Benak answered, a little surprised, "You dumbass. Don't send it now! The guards are going to get it."

Stevin went with the assumptive close: "Coming your way!"

Stevin slid the small notebook under the gap in the cell door and into the hall, then waited anxiously for Benak to get ahold of it. Seconds seemed like hours; then, finally the fish began to take line. Now even more anxiety struck Stevin, as he strained to listen over the noise of the prison for the signature choking and gasping. There was nothing. He waited a moment and then called out again, in a strong whisper.

"Benak!"

Nothing. He called again.

"Benak! You're out, f'er!"

Stevin could do nothing but reel in his bait, which slid smoothly across the floor and up under his door. He opened the notebook to find, surprisingly, that Benak had written in it. It was a simple message in return, and one that told Stevin that Benak was dead. The note read simply *Fuk u,* with the *u* so widely scribbled on the page, it was clear that it was probably all Benak could do to actually get it written with his dying breath.

Stevin quickly tore out the small page, shredded it into twenty pieces, and then flushed it all down the toilet. After the flush, and as the toilet quieted in the growing silence, he took note of his feelings. He had been on a quest to do good, and now he had just killed again. Oddly, he felt nothing—not good or bad. Okay, actually he felt proud that he could pull off such a feat and rid himself of a growing enemy; but the reality was, Benak's death was likely going to put a world of suspicion on Stevin, which is not a good thing in prison. Perception is reality on the outside, and anything can be reality within. Those inside were going to be looking at him, along with those outside once the autopsy report came in.

The silence continued—no sirens, no commotion—until Benak didn't emerge from his cell at dinner time. Then the place lit up like Times Square.

One white down; all Latinos apparently still breathing.

CHAPTER 23

OLD AND NEW FRIENDS

The Spanish word for assassin is *asesino,* and being one was proving to be a challenge. Stevin had spent the last six days carefully writing Spanish phrases in the dirt by the table, each time with a tweak here or there. While being skunked so far, he knew someone was reading them, because occasionally they would write back. Generally, they wrote words he didn't understand but assumed to be either discourse on ancient religious texts or, more likely, just vile swearing and death threats. There was really no middle ground in prison; one was either an ally or a mortal enemy, which is why any hope for finding *Feliz Navidad* in the dirt was clearly out of the question.

These six days were also a time of intense observation on the guards' behalf. With Benak's death and Stevin's prior fame, they were laser-focused on Stevin as a suspect. Every day brought surprise inspections, pat-downs, and searches. Though many other prisoners used their colon as a sort of internal purse to hide knives and cell phones and other contraband from surprise searches, Stevin could never bring himself to such loathsome prison ingenuity.

If he was going to be here, he was going to survive with any measure of decency he could muster, which is why he started bantering with the guards each time they put the gloves on for the body cavity searches. He would hearken back to his time in jail and try and make someone's day a little brighter—like a few days ago, when he'd erupted with a lively rendition of "Here Comes Santa Claus" just as the guard's finger went in. The guard with the glove was unimpressed and very frustrated, but his observing assistants couldn't help but crack up, which eventually led the guard with the glove to smile. Truly, if there were something or someone who could break down prison walls and the dreary task of penetrating a rectum with one's finger, it was Santa!

Unlike the guards, the other prisoners generally left Stevin alone. The swelling mystery of his infamy grew stronger with the death of Benak, and most wanted nothing to do with him—especially those who'd heard Benak's last correspondence with Stevin in the cell block. This gave Stevin greater opportunity to practice his weaponized Spanish and readjust to life and boredom in prison.

On the seventh day, in the morning, Stevin sat in his cell staring at his last iteration of Spanish possibilities. He was out of ideas, and more importantly, out of words. He was also out of time. He had been informed that he would be staying at San Quentin, and that today was the day he would move out of Reception and into general population. There were benefits of being in general population, like visitation, but it was also a much more dangerous place, especially since he would be expected to carry out a hit on his buddy within the first 48 hours.

The guards assembled, the buzzer rang, and it was yard time again.

"Well, *silencia estados zapatos,*" Stevin said in his worst Spanish, somewhat flirting with death while being entirely suspicious of its lethality. “Let’s hope you’ve got what it takes! *Olé!*”

Again Stevin made his way to the picnic table. There, again, he found Spanish that he didn’t understand. By the amount of exclamation points and capitals the guy used, it was clear this exchange was getting heated. Stevin sat on the bench and laughed as he looked around the yard to see who was watching him. He was going to miss this little exchange. It was like a having a pen pal from far abroad, even though the guy was sometimes only several yards away. Stevin didn’t know him, and he didn’t know Stevin—and making it even more intriguing was the lack of translating ability. Well, if nothing else, Stevin figured that if his *amigo* didn’t die, the writing did make him a little crazy.

At the end of yard time, Stevin penned his last attempt and walked away, not looking back. It was a Hail Mary pass, and he wouldn’t know if it was caught for another hour or so.

Back in his cell, Stevin organized what few things he had and waited. He was anxious about his move, as most people are about a move. After nearly two months in Reception, he was just starting to get some rhythm. Now that rhythm was going to be interrupted in a big way.

As he sat thinking of ways to either get around having to kill Higgy or to somehow protect him, his peace was interrupted by sirens and commotion. At first, he didn’t think anything of it—just another poor soul getting knifed, or a riot breaking out, or someone choking on a donut. But then he remembered the Alamo! Could it be? He jumped to his feet and listened at the door. The ambulance sirens drew closer and the prison siren blew, notifying all prisoners to return to their cells. Then he heard footsteps in the hall, strong footsteps of heavy boots. He leaped onto his bed just as the guards arrived in full riot gear.

"Well, this looks familiar," Stevin mumbled to himself.

"Prisoner. On the floor with hands behind your back," one of the guards commanded.

Stevin was puzzled, but not really so much. The fact that they were in riot gear was a clear indication that Stevin *hablo Espanol!* He didn't say a word as he climbed off his bed and onto the floor. Once cuffed and with his head covered, the guards led him out of the cell block under substantial fanfare and hollering from other prisoners, and into a van.

Stevin thought this was very strange. This was not how it went down the last time he was here. The van drove no more than a half-mile. He felt like they were still within the prison compound when it stopped, but he knew they were outside of the cells, perhaps near a service or administration building. Once there, Stevin was taken out of the van and led through a series of doors and into a small room where they unbagged him, unhandcuffed him, and left.

As Stevin sat there, he could tell he was in some sort of makeshift interrogation room. Although the room was small, it felt enormous to Stevin after spending so much time in a roughly 6'x12' cell with only a bed, a toilet, and a sink.

He looked around. There was really nothing there except the small table in front of him and himself, sitting on a chair. On one of the walls, though, was the quintessential one-way glass. He thought about getting up and trying to punch it like Superman would, just to let them know that he knew they were there. But they obviously weren't trying to hide. They were just watching.

Stevin decided to stay put, and instead of singing or pulling some other stunt, play it cool. This was clearly out of the ordinary and special, and something told him to be still.

After what seemed like an hour, the door handle turned slowly, the door opened, and in came two gentlemen in suits, each carrying a chair. They settled across from Stevin and then, after a bit of awkward silence, one of them spoke.

"Mr. McDonald. We've been watching you," the man said.

"And you are?" Stevin interrupted.

The man smirked, impressed by Stevin's confidence.

"We're from a special branch of a special agency. We'd like to talk to you about..." The man hesitated to find the right words, but never fidgeted or shifted in his chair; just looked at Stevin with a poker face. "...working for us," he finished.

Stevin looked at them like they were crazy, and finally replied sarcastically, "Are you guys with the laundry department here? Because I'd really prefer that over the kitchen."

Without saying another word, the man in the suit reached in his jacket pocket and pulled out a toy replica of a Mercedes-AMG GT in black, just like the one Stevin had left parked at LAX, and set it on the table.

Stevin became very serious very fast, realizing that something life-changing was happening. He didn't know what exactly, but the fact that they had a car like his made him very uneasy and extremely intrigued regarding what line of 'work' they had in mind.

"I'm listening," Stevin said seriously, staring at the toy car.

"As I said, Mr. McDonald, we are here from a special branch of a special agency that operates across the globe in a role similar to the CIA, but with, let's say...*extraordinary* resources and very private operations and executions. It has come to our attention that you possess a unique ability to, shall we say...*influence* the lives of others, which influence you have demonstrated even today. Now I will say, we haven't quite put our finger on your skill, though we are trying; but we have traced your influence to a certain apartment of a certain writer in a certain city to the south of us. Regardless, I'll get to the point."

"Kind of like S.H.I.E.L.D.?" Stevin interrupted again, trying to wrap his curiosity in some humor.

"No. Mr. McDonald. No Iron Man or Hulk on the team, but we would like to know if you prefer the red or the blue pill," the man said with a smirk, playing into Stevin's comic relief.

Stevin smiled and nodded in approval. He liked these guys.

The man continued, "We're here to offer you a deal, Mr. McDonald—or more specifically, a career in our organization, whose mission it is to defend our great country and protect its interests abroad. You would serve as a resource, using your special talent to further the goals of the organization."

"Assuming that I do have such a 'special talent,' as you put it, it sounds like you're asking me to kill people," Stevin responded, trying not to admit anything, one way or the other.

"Kill is a very harsh word, so perhaps we could agree upon 'influence the lives of others' as a professional alternative," the man suggested.

Stevin sat and thought for a minute, and then struggled with no less than a thousand questions. "I'm in prison for life. Am I to work from my cell?" he asked. His fingers were crossed and his lip was bitten, hoping, praying the answer was no. It didn't matter so much what they wanted him to do, as long as they could arrange his release.

"We would orchestrate your release and set up a new identity and a new life for you in a city east of here. Of course, this is all contingent on your agreeing to join the organization and put your special talent to work."

The offer was incredible, the possibilities endless; but there was one massive problem, and Stevin had no idea how to rectify it. He sat in silence running through every possible solution. The men watched him intently and then sensed his confliction.

The other man spoke now, breaking the silence. "As for your wife... and any others," the man said with emphasis, letting Stevin know that they were well aware of his trip to the Garden Isle. "She, or rather, they, will not be able to come with you. We'll give you the opportunity to say goodbye to those you wish to, but the position requires that you have no official ties for the rest of your life. To have such would compromise you and the organization."

"So kill people and get a divorce, or rot in prison?" Stevin said a bit rhetorically. This was a very difficult decision, and one that was quite possibly contrary to his resolution to do better and do good; he couldn't sort it out quickly in his head. But maybe this was meant to be. Maybe this was a second lease on life sent from the Almighty. Maybe this would allow him more opportunities to bring joy into the lives of others—when he wasn't killing them, of course.

Isn't it funny how we can rationalize things when we really want them? Besides, Alexes deserved better. When that thought crossed his mind, so did the solution to the problem.

"Okay. But you have to kill me here. I mean, I need to die in prison, so that my wife can move on," Stevin requested.

"Mr. McDonald, this is why we like you. You're a quick thinker and are able to make tough decisions in a way that produces the best outcome. Your thinking is right in line with our thinking. So, Stevin, are you ready to join us?" the first man asked.

"I have just one more question. Is the President aware of your organization?"

The man said nothing, but simply shot back a look that told Stevin he was clearly out of bounds.

"Okay," Stevin said hesitantly, but then his tone changed abruptly to excitement. "I'm in! And I'm taking this car with me," he said, grabbing the Benz.

"Excellent. It's going to take us several months to get it set up."

"Several *months? Several* months? What does that mean, like, one and a half?" Stevin asked impatiently.

"If you want to die in prison, it's going to take some time to make it look real. We also need to arrange things. Be patient and know that we are watching."

With that, the men stood to leave. When they reached the door, the first turned and cautioned, "Remember, Mr. McDonald. This meeting never happened. You can tell no one. We will contact you. Be strong. Survive. Remember: survive."

After the men left, the riot crew came back in and escorted Stevin back to the cell block, but it was not his old cell. This time, they essentially moved him in with the general population. He was now an official lifelong tenant at San Quentin State Prison.

The good news was that they did not confiscate his toy Mercedes, and it appeared that the items he'd organized in his old cell had already made the move. He got back just before dinner, and it wasn't long before it was time to eat.

Stevin didn't know what to expect in the mess hall. Mess halls can be dangerous places for anyone, including guards and servers. Stevin felt a little out of place, having just been moved by the riot guards, but those uneasy feelings dissipated once he got there. The mess hall was very familiar because he had been in this particular one many, many times before. He got in line and kept as quiet and as inconspicuous as possible.

About the time Stevin made his way through the line and to the crackers, he started to think about where he might sit. Sitting in the mess hall for the first time was like being a freshman all over again, but this time there were not only fierce upperclassmen waiting to beat you down, but also land mines on the seats. Although he saw a lot of familiar faces, nobody was enough of an acquaintance to approach and request safe passage from. Then, suddenly, someone approached him from behind and pushed something forcefully into his back.

"Make a move and I'll kiss you!" the deep voice threatened.

Stevin was horrified at first, and then confused with a sort of 'WTF?' perplexity—but then, finally, he realized who it was.

"Higgy. You had better put that down before I pants you, yell 'free hot dog', and watch fifty guys line up!" Stevin joked.

He turned to find his friend almost unrecognizable except for his unforgettable, cheery smile. Beaten, battered, and war-torn, Higginbotham had clearly endured much torment the last few years. Nonetheless, he was a dear friend and ally, and it was good to see him.

"Higgy, be cool. People are watching. And there is something I need to tell you," Stevin said, coolly turning to finish getting his food.

"Let's sit down and talk," Stevin said, talking with his back to his friend.

After the two finished the line, they sat with a group of men who were somewhat tolerant of Higginbotham. Stevin and Higgy spoke quietly but quickly; there was much to catch up on and much to say.

"I heard about the Bridge," Higgy said.

"Yeah. Let's talk about that later. Listen, I need to tell you about something in Reception. J.J. wants me to kill you. I told his minion, Benak, that I would out of self-preservation; but you need to know, buddy, that I never intended to harm you. I've just got to figure out how to protect us from them. They gave me 48 hours," Stevin explained.

Higginbotham sat quietly in his chair, saddened that Stevin had been recruited for such a task, and knowing the consequences of him not carrying it out.

"Listen, they don't know about our history—you, me, and Chris. But I've got an idea of how to make this all go away," Stevin continued.

"Stevin, I appreciate you trying to protect me, but you know what that means for you. They will come for you too if you don't. They have been trying to kill me ever since you got out. They got Chris."

"They got Chris? *Who* got Chris?" Stevin interrupted. Here Stevin thought it would take months or years to track Chris's killer; now he was on the verge of figuring it out inside of 15 minutes.

"J.J. did it. Tommy, the old leader for the whites, had J.J. kill him for not supporting the white cause. J.J. has been after me ever since, as you can tell," Higgy said, pointing to his battered face.

"Which one is J.J.?" Stevin asked, feeling the rage build within him. He had taken out one of J.J.'s lieutenants, and now it was time to cut down the general.

"Do *not* look around. He or one of his men is most likely watching us. If they asked you to kill me, they are probably scrambling to figure out how we connected so quickly, and they will probably just go ahead and assume we're in cahoots. You'll know J.J. by his size."

"He's a really big guy?" Stevin asked.

"Not big and fat, but tall. He's probably one of the tallest and skinniest guys here. Think Shawn Bradley meets Adolf Hitler. You can't miss him. He has a fuse as long as his pencil dick and is often causing trouble. But with that trouble, he gains many followers, and he has zero tolerance for guys like me who want nothing to do with him."

Just then, there was some commotion across the hall. Higgy didn't bother to turn and look. He already knew what it was. "There he is now."

Stevin shifted slightly to see past his friend. Several men had abruptly stood up and were now looking for new seats. A tall, very white man with a collage of tattoos stood over them. He said nothing—just shot lasers out of his eyes, and cleared the table for himself and several of his thugs. J.J. apparently loved random table-switching. It kept everyone on edge.

Before he sat, J.J. looked up and directly at Stevin. Stevin was a little surprised to be singled out by the stare from across the room; he thought he was concealed by Higgy. J.J. shook his head and then tapped his wrist as if to say "Clock is ticking."

Maybe it was Stevin's age, maybe it was that his confidence was bolstered by the men in suits, maybe it was that he had locked eyes with his buddy's killer and he tilted; whatever it was, it blocked any and all fear and rationality in Stevin. Stevin leaned out a little more and then flipped J.J. off with a majestic and regal bird. When Higgy saw Stevin's hand, he spun around to see that his worst fear was true. Stevin was in fact flipping off the leader of the whites. The good news was that J.J. was smiling, almost laughing.

"Well, looks like my 48 hours are up," Stevin said calmly.

"Are you out of your mind?!?" Higgy bellowed. "Do you know what's going to happen to you...to *me*?"

"Don't worry, old friend. I've got this. He'll come for me first, then he won't bother you ever again."

CHAPTER 24

ALL SHADES OF MEN

Stevin had almost no time. There is a brief window of opportunity to jump other prisoners in their own cells each time they return, and that is exactly when most beatdowns and deaths happen outside of the yard and mess hall. Stevin knew J.J. was probably right behind him as they returned from dinner. He heard menacing footsteps coming down the walkway toward him. He braced himself and began to hurriedly write his three-word weapon in a notebook, but before he could finish, a pair of guards arrived.

"McDonald. You have a visitor. On your feet. Hands behind your back."

Stevin was so surprised he had trouble following directions, which resulted in one of the guards knocking him around a little to get him in line.

Stevin could not for the life of him figure out who it might be. It could be a newsperson wanting an interview. There was no way it could be Cate. Even the thought of Alexes visiting was far-fetched. The last person to visit him in prison several years ago was his father, Doug, but he had passed away. Along with ice cream, Stevin loved surprises, but this one made him very uneasy.

When he arrived at the booth, the guards removed the cuff from his left hand and fastened it securely to a circular bolt in the table. This kept him locked down, but able to use the archaic phone on the wall. A minute later, Alexes came and sat across from him.

Stevin's heart raced, and tears welled up in his eyes. He could hardly even pick up the phone, he was so shaken. When he heard her voice for the first time in many months, it was like an angel was calling to him in the Outer Darkness, piercing and pure. He wept profusely, and then finally composed himself enough to speak.

"I'm so sorry. I'm so, *so* sorry. I wish I could take it all back," he sobbed. "You deserve so much better."

"I know, love. But, that's behind us now," Alexes responded compassionately.

"I saw you at the courthouse, in the street. I saw your sign. I couldn't believe it. It meant so much to me. How?" Stevin said, struggling. "How can you be sitting here now? You should be cursing my name."

"I made a commitment to you two and a half years ago that I intend to keep. Remember? For better, for worse, for richer, for poorer, in sickness and health?"

"Oh, Alexes. I love you, but you *can't*. You just can't stick with me. I'm never getting out. I'm dead to you now. Besides, I'm a killer and a cheater. You need to move on as best you can," Stevin reasoned across the static in the line. Then he remembered the money.

"Wait!" he said, perking up unexpectedly with bright eyes. "Did you get the money?"

Alexes leaned in quickly and put her finger to her lips to motion for him to be quiet, then grinned from ear to ear and nodded her head.

"Yes!" Stevin exclaimed. "That would explain your pretty new purse!"

Alexes nodded again with a wink while petting her purse.

"Oh, Alexes! I need to tell you something. I know who killed Chris, and he's going to try and kill me tonight!" Stevin said, oddly excited by the prospect. He could see that Alexes was instantly horrified, so he explained.

"It's okay! It's okay! He can't get me." Stevin hesitated, looking around. "But I can get him, and I will."

The two looked at each other through the glass with a mutual understanding. No words were said. They just sat unified, warming their hands and hearts by the fire of revenge.

A robotic voice came on the phone, "One minute remaining."

Stevin looked at Alexes longingly. They both sensed this would likely be the last time they would ever see each other. But, strangely, they both were at peace with this realization—both feeling like somehow their relationship had morphed from husband and wife to that of brother and sister. It was Chris who brought them together, and it was Chris who would keep them bound beyond the confinement of jail and the slow erosion of life apart.

"Ten seconds remaining."

"I love you, Stevin. I forgive you," Alexes said, putting her hand on the glass.

"I love you, Alexes, with all my heart," Stevin said, putting his hand opposite hers.

"Now, go get that murderer!" Alexes said with a stern look just before the line clicked off.

As she stood to leave, Stevin gave her a thumbs-up. Alexes smiled, gave him the "I love you" hand sign in sign language, and walked out of his life forever.

Back in his cell, Stevin hoped for the best but prepared for the worst. The first order of business was to finish writing his little note for J.J. No sooner had he finished it and sat down on his bed than J.J. and his crew appeared at the still-open door. They didn't seem to be in too great of a hurry, which was strange, and probably meant that some guard somewhere had just happened to delay lockup a bit. Gee, what a coincidence! Probably a guard who had been affected by the Bridge.

"McDonald! Time to die!" J.J. announced, storming into the cell with two others in tow.

Stevin knew he had to get J.J. to read his notebook, so he baited him. Instead of standing to defend himself, he lunged for his notebook like it was his mother's open urn and J.J. was the west wind.

J.J. hesitated, thrown off by Stevin's strange move. Then it dawned on him that the notebook might contain the secret to Stevin's mysterious power. Robbing him of such a thing was far more seductive than beating him down. J.J. spread his arms to stop the attack.

"Give me the book!" J.J. demanded.

As J.J. paused, his henchmen drew back, not knowing quite what to do or when the cell door might close.

Stevin was half sitting and half lying down on his bed. He held the notebook tightly to his chest and painted a horrified look on his face to make sure J.J. took the bait.

J.J. stepped up and pretended to throw a punch, which caused Stevin to flinch and release the notebook...all, of course, calculated by Stevin. As much as he wanted to just beat in J.J.'s face, Stevin stayed calm and stuck to the plan. He stayed on the bed and pretended to be horrified.

"What the hell is this?" J.J. said, taking a step back. He expected something more profound, and something that at least made some sense.

Stevin could feel himself moving into checkmate. All J.J. had to do was read it. Stevin's pulse began to race. He was moments away from watching J.J. choke out on the floor.

"What does it say?" Stevin asked.

"You know damn well what it says! You just wrote it," J.J. countered.

Stevin hadn't planned on arguing about it. Usually, when asked, people would look down and read it. This time was going to be a little more of a challenge. One thing Stevin did know was that the paper was not leaving his cell, and now that J.J. had read it but not said it, he could not leave either.

"It says 'Silence Often Speaks'," Stevin said.

"You dumb bastard! It says 'Silence *Sometimes* Speaks.' What...?" J.J. corrected and then paused, unable to speak. His eyes grew wide in horror. The notebook dropped to the floor as he fought for his fleeting breath.

Stevin shook off the scared façade and sprang to his feet.

"Who's the dumb bastard now? I forgot to tell you, no dumb bastards allowed here! You're out, f'er!"

With that, Stevin turned and pushed off the back wall, took two steps on the rebound, and then launched a classic WWF two-footed flying kick into J.J's chest just before he collapsed. The force sent J.J. careening out of the cell and into the other thugs like a bowling ball picking up a spare. As the three men tumbled to the ground, the cell door shut with a forceful thud.

"You bitches are mine now!" Stevin said eerily to the two bewildered men scrambling to their feet outside of his cell. He thought he would add a little flare to the scene, so he threw in some wild eyes and a toothy snarl to really make the point.

With the door closed, their immortal leader dead at their feet, and no idea what had just happened, the other two bolted. Stevin couldn't help but chuckle at himself. He had no clue why he'd decided to act crazily, and he ended up cracking himself up when he thought about it. But there wasn't time to gloat; the guards were certainly on their way, and Stevin had to again dispose of the evidence. There would certainly be more ensuing inspections and searches.

When the guards arrived, they looked at him with a sort of 'What did you do?' gesture. They were cautious in their movement, never taking their eyes off Stevin, who was lying coolly on his bed.

Finally, he responded to their glares.

"What?"

The men stepped away without answering. Stevin could hear them run once they were clear of his cell.

Well, that was weird, Stevin said to himself. He felt empowered lying there. The whites were sure to revere and fear him, and now even the guards were on their toes.

What he didn't know, though, was that there was movement, or rather progress, on the outside that was moving toward his demise. The wheels had been put in motion. Even with no evidence after rampant searching, the perception within and without was that Stevin had killed Benak and Johnny Apricio, Stevin's Latino pen pal. Stevin's reputation was growing and growing, in a bad way. He was painted as a threat to society, a threat to prisoners, guards, drivers, AARP members, LGBT defenders, mothers, Latinos, and bicyclists. When you kill over a hundred people, apparently you piss off a very large collection of the general public—people who overcome their differences and unite to vanquish a common enemy. Such was the case in the courts, where partisan denizens forgot all about winning and themselves, and were working together to overturn Stevin's conviction and fast-track him to lethal injection. Stevin's recent work inside prison not only made people uneasy; it made him a huge risk while still alive. The feeling within and without was that he needed to die, and die as soon as possible.

Within minutes, several guards returned in riot gear. Stevin could hear them coming down the hall, along with loud calls and chatter from the other prisoners. Once they arrived, four of them stood in front of Stevin's cell with shields against the iron bars, while two others gathered J.J.'s body and disappeared.

"Prisoner, on the floor, with hands behind your back!" one of them yelled.

Stevin was actually excited to comply. This was roughly the same drill he'd gone through when he'd met the men in suits. After being bagged and bound, he was once again led out of the cell house and into the van. Then, after a short drive, they stopped and got out. Stevin was sure he was there to meet the men again. This time, however, when they took the bag off of his head, he found himself in San Quentin's Adjustment Center. This was not good. Not good at all.

The Adjustment Center was a bad place, the place Stevin had convinced Judge King to take off the table. Life was hard here—solitary and confined. This was a place where people went crazy, where society lets you rot until they get around to killing you. Stevin objected strongly.

"Hey! I can't be here! The judge sentenced me to life, not Death Row! You can't put me here!" he pleaded. As he spoke, the demeanor of the guards deteriorated rapidly, and the batons came out. Stevin continued, becoming frustrated and physical, trying to escape their grasp.

"*You cannot do this!* I want to talk to the men in suits. They know me. They are going to get me out!"

As he continued to push the point and struggle, already sounding crazy with mention of the "men in suits," the guards unleashed their fury, beating him relentlessly until he stopped talking and stopped moving. Then the solid steel door shut and remained so for what seemed like a lifetime.

It wasn't until someone called out to him hours later that he got up off the floor and tried to inspect his face in the dull reflection of the steel sink.

"Who's the new guy?" the voice called.

Stevin remained silent. He wasn't in the mood for socializing with strangers through steel doors.

"Who is it?" the man called again.

"Speaks!" Stevin replied impatiently.

"Speaks is yo name?" came the voice again.

Stevin stayed quiet.

"What color is yo hand, Speaks?"

That question intrigued Stevin, so he decided to answer.

"Silence Sometimes."

There was a long pause, then the voice came back.

"Dat don't make no sense, Speaks. Are you messin' with me, Speaks? You don't want to mess with me, Speaks. You don't want to know. My hand is black, and my hand handles shit in here and out there. My hand drives all cars up in dis bitch! You hear me, Speaks? You hear what I'm sayin', Speaks?"

Stevin rolled his eyes, tiring of prison and prison mentality. It was quite clear to him now that the voice talking to him, the driver of all black cars (or groups of black inmates), was the leader of the blacks. Stevin hated how he kept saying "Speaks," but Stevin was trolling...and trolling takes a lot of patience and persistence.

"What's your first name, Speaks?" the voice asked, growing angry.

Stevin couldn't help but laugh a little. He knew that his answer was going to incite a lively reaction.

"Silence Sometimes," Stevin responded smugly.

"*Bitch!* Don't be like dat, Speaks!" the man responded, and then violently crashed against his cell door. "Don't be telling me dat yo hand and yo first name is Silence Sometimes Speaks!"

Stevin closed his eyes and shook his head slowly in the ensuing silence. Certainly silence does sometimes speak. This was the first time Stevin was able to kill without writing the phrase down and having someone read it, or even seeing the person. It was surprisingly easier than he'd thought. Somewhere out beyond Stevin's cell door was a dead man, coaxed that way by a sly and lazy killer armed only with words.

With J.J. and Marcus, the leader of the blacks, down, Stevin's last notch was the leader of the Latinos. Stevin sat in his cell and thought about his circumstances. He thought back to jail, to Alexes, to his effort to change, and then tried to reconcile his resurgence as a killer. Perhaps here in prison his killing was justified. Surely many of these men deserved it. As he reasoned along these lines, he laughed, thinking that probably no one deserved it more than him!

With the ease and serendipitous way he was able to take down Marcus, Stevin hoped that crossing paths with and cutting down the leader of the Latinos would come as easily. Then again, the whole idea had somewhat lost its luster with the possibility of getting out and joining the men in suits. *I wonder when they will come, and how they will orchestrate my death?* he thought to himself.

Hopefully soon. I've only been in AC for less than 24 hours, and I'm already going crazy!

Days passed. Time slowed. The routine of life in AC truly was maddening. There was an hour each day to use the yard, which in AC was a small steel cage where one could stretch out and exercise; there were no basketball hoops or picnic tables, and no fellow inmates to banter or fight with. The other 23 hours of the day were spent in the lonely and claustrophobic cell. Day in and day out. Routine, routine, exhausting routine.

In such a place, with so much time, one can't help but seethe at the eerie feeling of one's mind systematically draining out of one's ears. Then, after a while, the drain becomes imperceptible. Stevin had been there so long, with very little input from the outside, that even his meeting with the men in suits seemed a dream, and he began to question whether or not his hopes of escape were in fact true or just fancies of an eroding mind.

Every once in a while, though, he would catch glimpses of reality, like the time the other day when he'd heard a faint comment from a guard about Christmas. Stevin knew that it had been at least a year since he had come to San Quentin, around Christmastime, but he couldn't really reckon much more. It could easily have been two years or eight years, because tracking time in prison was about as easy as getting out, especially when you have no letters, no visits, and no stimulus from the outside.

One day, that all changed. It seemed the winds that had been stirred up early in his incarceration had culminated in change. Appeal after appeal and enduring public outcry had finally prevailed; Stevin's life was weighed and found grossly wanting. After a long hiatus, the California death penalty and San Quentin's first death by lethal injection might actually take place on their new and fancy teal-colored injection table, and Stevin was moved to the front of the line.

He didn't think much of it when they first told him. There was no thought for appeal or for a last-ditch effort to request clemency from the President. With no family and the promise of the men in suits a bygone delight, it seemed the right thing to do was to just see it out. He had gotten Chris's killer, Benak, his Latino pen pal, and the leader of the blacks, all of whom he took the blame for despite no supporting evidence. His work was done. He proved his formula was potent across all shades of men and over various media. He could move on to the next life now and hope for unimaginable amounts of mercy, knowing full well that the amount of good in his life was far less than the bad.

Because Stevin would soon be executed, and being a stern but compassionate man, Warden Money, who was new to the post and wanted to gain favor among the ranks, authorized a few of Stevin's belongings be brought out of storage and given back to him while in the AC. These were placed in his cell one day while he was in the yard.

When Stevin saw the small box on his bed, it made him very anxious. It was so foreign to see something like that in his cell. He approached it tentatively, speculating that it was a box full of stamps—prison currency—as a gift for his final days. When he finally opened it, he found his old notebook (the one he'd used to get J.J.), some unread letters from news organizations, a pen, the half pack of gum he'd had in his pocket when he was arrested, and, most importantly, most preciously, most wonderfully, a black toy model of a Mercedes-AMG GT. With eyes fixed, he took the small car in his hands and held it like a delicate newborn chick.

"The men were real!" he whispered to himself. His brain began to fire, like someone had just cranked up an old Model A that had been mothballed for decades. Pop, pop, pop: his motor sputtered and memories flooded in. Stevin was beginning to become Stevin again.

CHAPTER 25

A NEW LEASE

Dawn broke over the calm water of San Francisco Bay. It was a quiet new day, almost as if it were a holiday, with little activity on the surrounding roads and freeway, which added to this morning's peaceful brilliance. The only noise that could be heard was the occasional call of a gull or, if one fully concentrated, the sleepy wash of small waves on the shore. It had been nearly three months since the box had appeared in Stevin's cell, which was three months longer than Stevin had hoped before the men collected him. He was certain they would have figured something out prior to today, the day of his execution—hoping all this time that the box with the car was a sign of imminent extraction. Now, months later, his hope for such a new lease on life was essentially no more. Within hours, he would be dead.

"Prisoner! On your feet! Hands behind your back!" a voice from behind him commanded.

Stevin spun around, surprised. There was the riot crew again, only this time they'd managed to get there without him hearing their bootsteps. Stevin was sluggish to comply, not wanting to go. He put the little car down on his bed and laid down slowly on the floor. Once he was handcuffed, the guards stood him up, but this time they did not bag his head.

"Excellent. Now I can remember this walk in the eternities," Stevin quipped sarcastically.

The guards marched him down the cell block through a series of locks and keys, and then out into the general yard. Stevin was in awe at its vastness and emptiness, and at the glory of the clear heavens above. It had been a long, long time since he'd had such a sensation, and a long time since he had been here. He felt like chimps must feel when they first behold the outside world after a lifetime of being harassed and caged.

After uncuffing him, the guard left him alone, all alone in the big yard. Stevin knew why. It was for much the same reason he'd received the box in his cell. He stood there soaking it all in for a moment, and then saw his favorite picnic table across the yard and started walking to it. Then he started jogging. After a few feet, it felt so good that he started sprinting, running clean past the table and making an arcing turn to the basketball court. He remembered his freshman year on the basketball team in high school—the Patriots—and how the coach would drill them into the ground running sprints. Back and forth from the baseline to the free throw line and back, then to half-court and back they would go. Stevin remembered always wanting to be first, and today he would be! The snipers on the towers looked down in reluctant joy as Stevin ran the sprints. Something made them want to be there too, just running. Running was invigorating. There was so much openness and freedom, and it had the amazing ability to make him feel like a kid again. The world would be a much happier place if everyone did more running!

After a few back-and-forths, Stevin blew past the foul line and arced back to the picnic table, where he took a seat and breathed heavily. He could feel his heart racing and had trouble sitting still, so he got up and started to walk—walking across the yard and into the outfield of the baseball diamond. Standing there, he wished others were around so they could knock a few fly balls to him.

In addition to sunlight, it had been a long time since he'd had basic human interaction. The whole situation was overwhelming. He almost wished he could be back in his cell, because it would mean his time wasn't upon him. He could hear rumblings to the east in the main parking lot. He knew what that was—the protesters—but he wasn't sure if they were there protesting the death penalty or vehemently supporting it in order to be done with him.

Overwhelmed, he lay down on his back in the lush green grass of the outfield. Actually, it was dirt of the hardest nature, but can't a dying man dream? He started to sing to the best of his recollection a song he remembered that Johnny Cash had sung at Folsom Prison:

The old town looks the same
As I get down from the train
La, la, la, la, my mama and my papa
Down the road, here comes Mary
Hair of gold and lips like cherries
I long to touch the green, green grass of home

Yes, they'll come to see me
Arms stretched and smiling sweetly
It's great to touch the green, green grass of home

Then I wake up and look around me
Four gray walls that surround me
I guess I was only dreaming
There's a guard and la, la, la, la
Then we'll walk at daybreak

As Stevin remembered the words "walk at daybreak," he realized just how fitting the song was, and began to choke up. He couldn't remember much more. There was something about being buried underneath an old oak tree. Fighting the tears and the difficulty speaking, he lay there and repeatedly sang the last line with his eyes closed and hands outstretched, smoothing the dry dirt:

Again I'll touch the green, green grass of home
Again I'll touch the green, green grass of home
Again I'll touch the green, green grass of home
Again, I'll touch the green, green grass of home

"Mr. McDonald. Stand up, please. Please place your hands behind your back."

Stevin sighed, wiping the tears from his eyes with his dusty hands and soaking in the last bit of sky and air and sun imparted to him by the world. To his dismay, the guards had done it again.

"Do you guys train as ninjas? You know, ninjas don't have mustaches," Stevin joked as he stood putting his hands behind his back. "And what's with the 'Mr. McDonald' stuff? Since when are we civil around here?"

None of the guards answered the question, but they did have one for him.

"Mr. McDonald. We're going to the mess hall now. Any last requests?" one of them asked.

Stevin thought for a minute, but really didn't need to.

"Ben & Jerry's New York Super Fudge Chunk...two of them!" Stevin responded.

One of the guards tilted his head and radioed in the order. That was probably something they were going to have to run to the store for.

In the mess hall, he was again left mostly alone, except for a few servers. They had managed to drum up a steak and potatoes and some corn on the cob. Stevin wasn't sure why a dead man with a history like his was getting the royal treatment, at least by prison standards. He wasn't sure who to thank or how to thank them, but he was grateful for it.

After he finished his steak, two pints of ice cream were set in front of him, which immediately reminded him of several Gaffigan jokes, and he smiled and handed back the lids. Stevin looked at the small containers and then at the server who placed them there, as if the server had just set down two bars of pure gold.

As he took the first bite, his mind raced back to Francis's house, where he'd last had this flavor—the stale smell of an old person's home, the feel of the sun in the solarium, the race of wind in his hair when driving the car. As he sat there with his eyes closed, thinking, he fought off with much effort the memory and smell of the blasted towel in the bathroom and *all* that had come with it. In the end, though, nothing was going to deter him from enjoying the ice cream, which he did, licking both containers clean.

When he finished, he looked around, expecting the guards to be there ready to move onto the next event, but now even the servers were gone.

After a few minutes of Stevin not knowing what to do, a man walked out of the kitchen and stood behind the service line. He was an old man dressed in a suit, but he was also wearing a bulletproof vest. Stevin swiveled on the bench to face him from about 30 feet away.

"Hello, Stevin. I'm Warden Money," the man said. "Please stay seated. There is a man with crosshairs on you, so please don't make any sudden moves."

"I'm so full, I don't think I could do anything but lie down and take a nap," Stevin replied warmly.

Warden Money smiled, knowing exactly how Stevin felt.

"I guess you're the one I should thank for all of this. I really do appreciate it, though I don't think I deserved it," Stevin continued.

"Son, every man deserves the decency of a good meal and some time to contemplate things before he dies, no matter what he might have done. I wanted you to know that the good Lord is mindful of you, and that he inspired me to do this for you. Besides, I'm not a judge. I'm a warden. I run the prison and try not to judge the people. Hell, we've all done things we shouldn't have."

As the Warden spoke, he had Stevin at "son," and Stevin couldn't help but tear up again. He was especially touched by the Warden's kindness, truly feeling that he was not deserving of the treatment.

"Warden, why are you here with me now? It seems too risky for someone like you to be here with someone like me. You can't be doing this for everyone," Stevin asked, cutting through it.

"To tell you the truth, son, it's not every day that I have to take someone's life, especially when that person is the one responsible for my wife's death."

The Warden paused for a while, and Stevin stayed dead silent. Then the Warden continued with focused effort. "My wife was in the city one day. She was walking to get some lunch, and a young man approached her. Shortly thereafter, she died of a heart attack. I couldn't believe it was related to the others, since we're old. But that was until you took many, many more lives on the bridges."

The warden paused again. "I've wrestled with this since I came here. There were so many times I wanted to march down to your cell with a shotgun and shoot you so many times that we could just flush you down the toilet. But I knew that wasn't right. After many months of struggle and anger, something happened to me that changed my life, and that is why I'm here today. I woke up one morning a few weeks ago, and the anger and hate had left me. I realized that the struggle and anger was killing me, and I had to let it go. Now, I don't know if you're a believing man, but I want you to know that the Lord healed my soul and brought peace to my life. And even more, he gave me a little glimpse of what He faces each and every day as He looks down on all of us. I look at you and people like you differently now. I still do my job, but like I said, I'm a warden, and not a judge. Son, I'm here to tell you that I forgive you, and I wanted you to know that, at least from one of your victims, before you go to meet the Lord. May He have mercy on you and me alike."

When he finished speaking, the Warden turned slowly and walked out of the room. Stevin didn't move. He couldn't move. He was absolutely dumbfounded, and not so much with what the Warden said or the coincidence with his wife, but with what he'd done and how he was able to do it. Stevin felt incredibly lucky. His life could have been much, much worse here in prison, given his unfortunate impact on the Warden. Sitting there thinking about it caused Stevin to finally accept that he was dying today. Until this point, the idea was there, but the weight of it hadn't hit him until the Warden had talked of forgiveness.

"Mr. McDonald. It's time," a soft voice said from the door. This time, the ninja guards allowed him to come to them as opposed to teleporting themselves right behind him.

As Stevin walked to them, he joked, "Well, I guess Zuckerberg is going to be beat me in the most-time-in-one-outfit contest."

Stevin knew this was the end. He stood and walked to the door, where he met just three guards in regular uniforms. They walked until they came to a door that led to a new white building, built as an afterthought along the back wall of the cell block. Don't worry, though! Any good agent knows that most buyers will focus more on the "white water" Bay views and paint color than on the building permits.

Inside, Stevin was placed in a holding cell. There next to him, was a small space for a religious person, in case Stevin wanted his last rites read, which he declined. He felt like he had nothing more to say and that, quite honestly, the Warden's talk had fulfilled any spiritual need he had.

The rest of the building was a series of rooms that allowed the workers to prep the prisoner for the procedure. After 15 minutes in the holding cell, Stevin moved to what they called the Prep

Room. As he sat there, he stared at the next door he would walk through, knowing that on the other side he would get his first glimpse of the injection table. He felt his heart start to race. He wanted to cry out and reason with those in the room that the men in suits had promised him a position in their organization, but cold fear stole his words and any confidence he'd had in such a reality. He could do nothing but stare at the door, "as a sheep before her shearers is dumb."

At last it was time when the door opened; there, in ominous splendor, was the injection table, adorned with teal-colored pads and large, heavy black straps. Stevin was surprised to see so many windows in the room. There was a large area for the press, which was, not surprisingly, absolutely jam-packed. There were also two other separate viewing rooms, one for victims and one for family. Stevin noticed that one of the rooms was completely empty and the other was filled with people who had no cameras—just hatred on their faces. He closed his eyes, not wanting to see any of them, or be the animal in the cage they came to see. He wondered if he could come up with a miraculous way to kill them all and be rid of them. He envisioned having a banner and leading the group in reciting the words like a choir leader would, but alas, it was all in vain.

"Mr. McDonald. Please lie on the table," one of the guards requested.

Stevin climbed up on the table. The pads were ice-cold and hard. As they strapped him in, he stared at the artificial lights on the ceiling and noticed how ugly and fake they were compared to the brilliant sky he had observed on the baseball diamond.

Once he was restrained, the doctors came in wheeling the tools and drugs they would need to kill him. A phone rang. He couldn't hear much. There was some talking and then someone clearly saying, "Yes. We will proceed." Then, the pinch of the needle. Then people began to leave the room.

Stevin raged against the restraints. There was nothing he could do. He absolutely couldn't move. He focused his eyes as best he could toward his feet as a doctor approached him.

I'm out, f'er, he thought to himself in surrendering fear.

"Mr. McDonald. I am Dr. Lomel; I will administer the injection," the doctor said. Then, leaning down to Stevin's ear, he continued with a whisper, "Remember: survive!"

Stevin's eyes grew wide and his body grew perfectly calm. That phrase meant something wonderful. Somehow, he knew it would be okay. They were here.

A man spoke to him for some time, but none of it registered with Stevin. He was still focused on what the doctor had said. After the man had finished speaking, he said, "The time is now 2:46. Please proceed, Doctor."

As Stevin lay there on the cold table in front of the angry world, he braced himself, focusing solely on staying awake. The only thing he had left was the fight to stay awake. He wondered if his life would flash before him like in the movies, but there was nothing—just the warm liquid in his arm.

The sounds in the room grew softer. The table wasn't as hard anymore; in fact, he could barely feel it, or anything at all. Then there were the lights. Someone had somehow turned them up. He watched them grow brighter. With great brilliance and alluring beauty, they warmed him until there was no table or pads or straps or observers; just glorious light. And then, Stevin was gone.

What happened in the time between Stevin's passing and his awakening is not germane to this story; however, it is germane to the epic of mankind. The important thing to note now is that in fact, Stevin did awaken.

As the drugs wore off, Stevin's senses came back to him. He opened his eyes slowly, still very drowsy. He was still restrained, but not as tightly as before, and he was able to tilt his head slightly to try and figure out where he was. From his gurney, he saw small round windows and a large leather chair. He thought he was dreaming, somewhere between life and death, and then he succumbed again to the sedation.

An hour later, he woke once more. This time, someone was speaking to him.

"Stevin. How you feelin', buddy?" the voice said.

Stevin opened his eyes to see the men in suits.

"Oh, shit!" Stevin whispered with a very dry mouth and a smile, closing his eyes again. "You guys really know how to fake a death. You even had me believing it!"

The two men grinned, and one of them patted him on the shoulder.

"Where are we?" Stevin asked.

"Well, we're in a Gulfstream jet, probably over Oklahoma somewhere."

Stevin beamed.

"I can get used to this," he said, letting the roar of the jet engines anchor him to the reality of being alive.